The Time Hunters

By

Carl Ashmore

ISBN: 095685950X
ISBN-13: 978-0956859501
Addlebury Press

For Alice and Will and Lisa.
My world.

ACKNOWLEDGMENTS

Kath Middleton.

I would also like to thank the following people for the unwavering online support for 'The Time Hunters.'

In the USA: Libby, Marty, Stephen, Hannah, Abby, Heidi, Austin, Wyatt, Dakota, Petrona, Grayson, Johnna, Keegan, Kolson, K England, Alina, Eric and John.

In the UK: Gingerlily, Vanessa Jackson, Dawn Hills, Claire Thacker, Sue Pearson, Emma Sly, Lynn, Kay Fisher, Tracey, Heidi, Willie and Max.

Cover Design: Andrew Gaia:
andrewgaia13@gmail.com

I can be contacted at carlashmore@mailcity.com

In memory of Bernard Ashmore.

CHAPTERS

Chapter 1

A Blast from the Past

January 15th 1900. London.

Bernard Preston shut the door to number 17 Cromwell Gardens and scurried down the steps onto the bustling street, acting as casually as he could. He had never knowingly committed a crime before, and certainly not theft.

Reaching the pavement, he stared out over the Thames. Mist clung tightly to the water. He turned right and began to walk, the Houses of Parliament rising majestically before him. Ordinarily, he knew the sight of it, coated in snow like icing on a cake, would have taken his breath away. But not today. Today, he just felt anxious. He knew he had to get out of here, and fast.

Preston levelled his bowler hat and quickened his pace; the package in his overcoat pocket felt unnaturally heavy, a reminder of the crime he had just committed. Still, he didn't feel a trace of guilt. He had the Theseus Disc. That was all that mattered.

Walking briskly now, he turned his collar to the wind and watched a hansom cab rattle by. As it passed, it revealed an enormous man with cropped flaxen-hair, on the opposite side of the road. At first glance, the man appeared to be dressed in a manner befitting a Victorian gentleman, but since when did Victorian gentlemen wear thick black sunglasses?

The man's lips curved into a mocking smile.

Preston's spine froze. 'Oh, please, no,' he begged to no one. He watched with dismay as a second man, slightly shorter, joined the first, and together they walked parallel to him, their expressions cold, impassive, like shop mannequins.

He knew he was in trouble now. If only he had brought his pagidizor. But then what use would it be? This wasn't a registered trip.

No one knew he was here.

Taking a moment to contemplate his next move, he gulped a lungful of icy air. And then ran.

Struggling to keep his footing on the slippery ground, he sidestepped a bewildered pedestrian, and then another, his mind fixed on one thing: Ethel. If only he could reach her he could escape in an instant.

Looking back, he saw four of them now, powering towards him like juggernauts. Turning a corner, he found himself in a long, narrow alleyway. It appeared deserted, but he knew it wasn't.

Ethel was there - invisible maybe, but definitely there.

Tiring now, legs like girders, he reached the alley's midpoint and glanced back. To his astonishment, the four men had stopped at the alley's mouth. He skidded to a halt, puffing madly. Had they really given up? Before he had time to dwell on this, however, he heard the following words.

'Hello again, Bernard.'

Preston spun round to see a tall, sallow-faced man emerge from the shadows, a wide brimmed top hat covering his raven black hair, pitching his face into darkness.

Preston couldn't believe his eyes. Words caught in his throat. 'Y-you?' he stammered. 'It can't be.'

'Oh, I assure you it can,' the man said coldly. 'Now, if you would be so kind as to give me the Theseus Disc. For some reason, the Omega Effect has stopped me procuring it at every point. It can be such an annoying occurrence, don't you think?'

Preston couldn't find a reply.

'Cat got your tongue, eh? Good. I always thought you a supremely dull conversationalist. Very well, Bernard, allow me to put it another way: pass over the Theseus Disc or you will answer to my Associate, Mr Kruger, and his trusty service dagger. Believe me, I wouldn't recommend that option.'

Preston turned deathly pale. 'Otto Kruger?' He glanced round to see the flaxen-haired man striding towards them, his huge right hand curled around a long knife that glistened in the misty light.

With a roar of desperation, Preston rushed the man, knocking him off-balance, and continued his charge.

Nearing the wall that marked the alley's end now, he pulled a small device from his pocket and pressed a button marked with the letter 'T'. As if from nowhere, a small, mint green, three-wheel car materialised just ahead of him: Ethel.

He threw open the driver's door when a loud bang echoed off the walls. At once, he felt like he'd been punched in the back. Pain seared his body. He collapsed on to the driver's seat, his trembling hands reaching for the dashboard, where he typed six numbers onto a keypad. Within seconds, a blinding silvery light filled the car, and with an ear-splitting *crack*, it vanished.

*

The stars glittered above Bowen Hall in an inky black sky. The lawns, the forest, the lake were as still as a tomb. Yes, everything seemed in place for a perfectly normal summer's night. Everything was just as it should be.

But then something peculiar happened. An unnatural wind swept the grounds; the temperature plummeted. Just then, an explosion of light erupted above the front lawn - crackling, twisting, brilliant. Whipping the air, it spiralled like a dazzling whirlwind. Then, with a shattering BOOM, it had gone.

Bernard Preston's Reliant Robin stood where the light had been.

The driver's door creaked open and Preston stumbled out. He was fading now, his body shutting down. He knew he had only minutes to live. He had to make them count. After all, he had made it to Bowen Hall, the home of his dearest friend - the one person who could right these terrible wrongs.

Hunched over, numb with pain, Preston limped forward, his gaze fixed on the Hall, never looking back at the bloody trail behind. Resolutely, he staggered on, further and further, before slowly mounting the high stone steps to the front door, where he rapped twice before his legs gave way and he crumpled to the ground. Using the last of his strength, he pulled the package from his pocket.

At least this would be in safe hands.

The door opened. A tall, willowy figure stood there wearing a crimson dressing gown and novelty slippers in the shape of two loaves of bread. Percy Halifax stared into the distance, a bemused smile on his face as though the victim of an impressive practical joke. He heard a rasping voice from below. 'P – Percy…'

Horror-struck, Percy Halifax dropped down and cradled Preston in his arms. His eyes widened as a scarlet puddle leaked all around. 'Bernard, what the -'

'Y-you must listen to me. He's alive. It was n-no accident.' Preston's eyelids flickered. 'F-find the Fleece … S-see Aubrey…'

'Bernard, stay with me. Just - '

Preston clawed for air. 'Take this,' he slurred, pressing the package into Percy Halifax's hand. 'And P - Percy...' As his voiced trailed to silence, he whispered 'Find … Suman …' His body grew still.

With these dying words ringing in his head, Percy Halifax closed his friend's eyes and held up the package. Shakily, he unwrapped it carefully to reveal a gleaming orange disc; a number of strange markings were etched around a central hole, the size of a coin. The disc blurred as his eyes misted over.

Percy Halifax felt hollow. One of his oldest friends was dead. Shot in the back. But who could kill a man like Bernard Preston? A good man. The finest of men. And as his gaze fell on an unusually large black bird circling overhead, a crushing sense of purpose swept over him. He could do something about it. He could try and prevent Bernard from dying. He knew it was a long shot, the Omega Effect, as a rule tended to prevent it, but he could try. It had worked before.

For the next hour, Preston's words visited him again and again. 'Find the Fleece' - 'He's alive' – 'See Aubrey.' And then there was the mysterious disc. What could it all possibly mean?

Percy Halifax demanded answers. And he was determined to get them. However, no matter how much he discovered about Preston's final hours (and in time that would be a great deal) something still puzzled him: who or what was Suman?

Chapter 2

Becky, Brothers and Budgies

Becky Mellor lay in bed, her eyes wide open and fixed on the ceiling. She had woken up in a bad mood and just knew today was going to be one of those days. For one thing, she'd discovered a spot the size of a gerbil on her forehead.

But then her eyes were drawn to the gap in her curtains and her heart fluttered. Sitting on the ledge, as still as a statue, was a small bird with a mint green chest and a yellow head marked with black stripes.

The budgerigar's head slanted left and, for the briefest of moments, Becky had the strangest feeling it was watching her. Then, to her surprise, the budgie tapped three times on the glass.

Becky couldn't believe it.

The budgie did it again.

A tiny smile arched on Becky's mouth. She was about to go and open the window when the door crashed open and her younger brother raced in, his hands flapping like a seal. The budgerigar flew off at once.

'C'mon, Becks!' Joe yelled impatiently. 'Mum says we'll be late if you don't get a move on.' He grabbed her duvet, hurled it to the floor and dashed out of the room.

Becky growled loudly. She loved Joe, she really did, but there were times she wanted to beat him with a garden spade to within an inch of his miserable life. Furthermore, she was definitely awake now and the full horror of today struck her. For the next six weeks she had to stay with an uncle she'd never actually met.

Her fingers reached to her neck. As she clasped her lucky pendant, she couldn't help but think today would be the worst in her thirteen years of breathing. Who was this Uncle Percy anyway? From what little she did know, he sounded like a total loon - a batty hermit who spent his days inventing silly gadgets that probably didn't work. It didn't matter how upbeat her mum tried to be, the reality was that for six long weeks she wouldn't be able to see her friends, go on Facebook, sleep when she wanted to, or do anything that resembled her normal routine, which she happened to enjoy very much. No, this would without question be the dullest summer of her life.

She was determined to hate every minute of it.

*

Becky brushed the knots from her wavy black hair, cleaned her teeth and smeared half a tube of concealer over the offending spot. After changing into a t-shirt and jeans, she slouched downstairs into the small but tidy kitchen.

Joe was sitting at the table. Glancing up at Becky, utter joy spread across his face. 'Look at that zit, mum. It's like a third eye.'

'Shut up,' Becky snapped at him, as she sat down.

'Seriously,' Joe replied, 'it could be a horn.'

Becky's fists clenched. 'I won't tell you again, digweed.'

'Oh, pack it in, you two,' Mrs Mellor said firmly, pushing a bowl of cornflakes in front of Becky. 'And I really could do without any trouble from you today, young lady. It's going to be hard enough as it is.'

'Tell monkey boy to keep his gob shut then.'

Joe's grin widened. 'I'd rather be a monkey than a rhino.'

Becky plunged her finger into the bowl and flicked it at Joe. A soggy cornflake landed on his nose.

'Oi!' Joe barked, wiping it off.

'Becky!' Mrs Mellor snapped. 'We'll have none of that, thank you very much.' She shook her head and joined them at the table. 'I really don't know what's got into the two of you lately? Why does everything have to turn into a pitched battle?'

'It's her,' Joe said.

'It's him,' Becky said at exactly the same time.

Mrs Mellor turned to Becky, whose gaze was fixed miserably on the table. She hesitated for a moment, and her voice grew soft. 'Can I assume you're still not keen on going to stay with Uncle Percy?'

Becky looked up and noticed her mother's blue eyes seemed dimmer than usual. 'I can't wait. I think it's brilliant that I'm being abandoned by my mum for the summer and palmed off on a barmy old nutter that I don't know. What's not to like about that?'

'Uncle Percy is not, as you so delicately put it, a 'nutter'. He's a little eccentric perhaps, but also very warm, exceptionally kind and lots of fun. Your dad thought the world of him, and I know you will too. His home, Bowen Hall, is a wonderful place. I'm surprised you don't remember it.' Mrs Mellor looked at Becky, hoping for a change of heart. She didn't get it. 'You'll be able to ride, swim - '

'If it's so great,' Becky said sharply, 'why aren't you coming?'

'Because I need to work,' Mrs Mellor replied. 'Because if I don't work, how will we keep a roof over our heads?'

Becky sighed. 'I know you have to work, but that doesn't mean we have to be sent away. I can look after the house while you're not here … I can even look after him.' She waggled her finger at Joe. 'I'm old enough.'

Joe looked distinctly put out. 'I don't need looking after.'

'You're thirteen, Becky,' Mrs Mellor said simply. 'Joe's eleven. You both need looking after. I mean, if your dad was alive then …' her voice faltered, 'but he isn't, so that's that.'

Becky felt guilty. It had been six years since her dad had drowned in a boat accident off the Welsh coast, and she knew this coming Thursday would have marked their wedding anniversary. Her voice softened. 'It's just we've never met this Uncle Percy.'

'You have met him,' Mrs Mellor said, composing herself. 'We'd see him all the time when you were little. He thought the world of you - of both of you. I'm really surprised you don't remember it.'

'Then why haven't we seen him since dad died?'

Mrs Mellor shifted uneasily on her seat. 'Well, some time ago, he and your father had an argument and they didn't speak for a while. Your father died before they had a chance to settle their differences.'

'What was it about?' Becky asked, suddenly intrigued.

'I honestly don't know. Your father wouldn't talk about it, but I know he deeply regretted it. Anyway, I was delighted when Uncle Percy phoned to invite you for the summer.'

'Why didn't he invite you?'

'He did, silly,' Mrs Mellor said, smiling, 'but I have to work. Besides, you're always harping on about wanting more independence. This is the perfect opportunity. And it's not like I won't be seeing you. I'll visit every weekend and some evenings. Trust me, you'll have an amazing time...'

Becky wasn't convinced, but decided against pressing the matter further. It was only for six weeks, and six weeks was a relatively short space of time.

Wasn't it?

*

It was a stifling July day as the sun pounded the terraced houses of Lyndon Crescent. The glint from the house windows opposite made Becky squint as she and Joe loaded two heavy suitcases into the boot of their mum's tiny car.

'This is going to be awesome,' Joe said excitedly. 'We haven't been on holiday in years, and this is loads better than that boring caravan park in Llandudno.'

Becky was about to spit a reply when she heard a soft, melodic twitter from the tree to her left. She turned round to see the budgerigar sitting on a branch. Her expression softened.

Joe noticed. 'What's the matter with - '

'Shhh!' Becky cut in. Her voice fell to a whisper. 'Look...' Slowly, so as not to frighten the bird, she inched towards the tree. The budgie's head bobbed up and down eagerly.

'Hello,' Becky said softly, moving her hand up to the budgie's chest. It chirped happily. She began to tickle its tummy.

Without warning, the budgie gave a spine-chilling squeal and, claws extended, wings thrashing, swooped at Becky's throat.

Becky screamed. She held up her arm, blocking the assault, when suddenly the budgie swerved right and flew away, hovering just above them.

Joe froze with shock.

The budgie's dull black eyes locked on Becky again, unnatural, eerie, and it attacked again, talons aimed at her neck.

Joe snapped out of his daze. Looking round, he saw a gnome set in a thick patch of Azaleas. He scooped it up. 'Get away from her,' he yelled, swinging the gnome with all his might. The budgie ducked the blow.

Trying to run to the house, Becky stumbled, landing face down on the ground. The budgie saw this and hurtled towards her, screeching wildly.

This time, Joe leapt in front of his sister. Timing his swing to perfection, the gnome connected with the bird with an oddly dull clank, and it was pitched into the air. Joe watched, relieved, as it gave up the fight and soared off into the distance.

Confused, Becky got to her feet, panting heavily. 'Has it gone?'

Joe nodded. 'Yep.'

Becky's voice trembled as she spoke, 'Since when do budgies act like that?'

'No idea,' Joe replied, bewildered.

Just then, Mrs Mellor appeared at the door jangling her car keys and grinning.

'Are we ready to go then?' Mrs Mellor's smile soon faded when she saw Becky's disheveled hair and frightened expression. 'You two haven't been fighting again, have you?'

'No,' Becky replied, colour returning to her cheeks. 'But Joe did use a garden gnome to save me from a demented budgie. Thanks, bro.'

'Anytime, sis,' Joe replied.

Mrs Mellor didn't know what to say to that.

Chapter 3

Uncle Percy

They all went inside and Becky proceeded to tell her mum everything. Immediately, Mrs Mellor phoned the Greater Manchester Police to warn them a psychotic budgerigar was on the loose, only to be accused of having one too many gin and tonics and that if she phoned again she would be charged with wasting police time.

Becky went to her bedroom to calm down and fix her hair. For a fleeting moment, she was sorely tempted to use the incident as an excuse to get out of (or at least delay) going to Uncle Percy's. However, she couldn't bring herself to do it. Joe hadn't hesitated in leaping to her defence and he had been so looking forward to the trip. Much as she would never admit it, she really didn't want to disappoint him.

Thirty minutes later, they had all climbed into the car and Mrs Mellor was rifling through the cluttered glove compartment. 'This should do the trick,' she said, a tattered CD held triumphantly in her hand.

Becky groaned. This was the moment she dreaded - sing-along-a-parent time, and her mum had the musical talents of a dishcloth. She closed her eyes, wishing she could do the same with her ears.

Manchester Piccadilly station bustled with people as Becky trailed Joe into the gleaming white concourse. She had pushed the budgie incident from her mind and had resumed her grumpy stance at being sent away for the summer. Spotting a trolley, she and Joe piled their cases onto it and watched as their mum paid for two tickets. Then they walked to platform fourteen.

The small platform hummed with activity as commuters rushed from the standing train and scampered up the steps to make their next connection.

'You've got your mobile phones,' Mrs Mellor said, voice quivering. 'I'm only a phone-call or a text away. It really isn't that far and if you're genuinely unhappy I'll come and get you at once.' She bent over to embrace Becky.

Becky knew the hug she returned was half-hearted - she couldn't help it. Still, as she felt her mum's trembling body she felt a twinge of guilt and said, 'We'll be all right, mum. Don't worry about us.' She forced the best smile she could. 'I'm sure it'll be brilliant.'

'That's the spirit.' Mrs Mellor sniffed loudly. 'I know it will be. You just look after each other and have a wonderful time.'

Becky and Joe scaled the train's steps, lugging their suitcases behind them. They moved into the nearest carriage, wedged their cases into an already heaving luggage compartment, and moved down the aisle to a vacant table. Mrs Mellor, tears flowing freely now, trailed them to the closest window.

The train shuddered and Becky's heart sank further. Throwing her mother a final wave, she felt the train edge out of the station.

'So what d'you reckon he's like?' Joe asked excitedly.

'Who?'

'Mr Potato Head. Uncle Percy, of course.'

Becky shot him a dismissive look. 'Well, if you want my honest opinion, he sounds like a right numpty.'

'Why?'

'Well, firstly, he claims to be an inventor. I mean it's not the coolest job in the world, is it? Secondly, from what I can gather, he's a recluse and we've got to put up with that for six boring weeks … and, unlike you, I actually have a life.'

'I think he sounds great,' Joe said truthfully. 'Mum says he's well funny and dad liked him, so I don't see why we won't. She says he's got a massive house.'

'Yeah,' Becky said with a snort, 'and it wouldn't surprise me if we were there to clean that massive house, to cook for him, wash his clothes. And if that is the case, then you're in charge of washing his pants.' She gave a doleful sigh. 'We'll be a couple of house-slaves, you mark my words!' And with that, Becky made it perfectly clear that was the end of the discussion.

The train rattled through the Cheshire plains, passing mile upon mile of patchwork fields, thick woodland, and stopping at, it seemed to Becky, every boring village in the North West of England. After a very long hour in which she said nothing to Joe bar the odd grunt, she watched as a rusty sign heralded the final stop: Addlebury.

As the train juddered to a halt, Becky stood up to see she and Joe were the last passengers in the carriage. With a huff, she grabbed her shoulder bag and marched to the luggage compartment to collect her case.

'Come on. Let's get it over with, then.' Becky waited as the doors opened and a gust of warm air brushed her face. Hesitantly, she took her first step onto the platform. Looking round, she saw it was deserted. 'See… the old codger couldn't even be bothered to meet us. I say we get back on the train and -' But before she could finish, a man appeared in silhouette at the end of the platform, his dusky shadow lengthening before them. He strode into the light, a glowing smile on his tanned face.

Uncle Percy was not as old as Becky had expected - maybe fifty years of age - with broad shoulders, shoulder-length grey hair, and warm hazel eyes. 'Welcome, Becky. Welcome, Joe. How wonderful to see you both again.'

Joe threw him a wide smile.

Becky didn't.

'I'm your Uncle Percy,' he continued, oblivious to her lack of enthusiasm. 'But you can call me whatever you'd like. I've always been partial to the name Colonel Igidor Puffbury if you'd prefer that.'

Even Becky's lips curled into a smile at that point, although in truth it was chiefly due to her uncle's peculiar dress-sense. He wore a cream linen jacket with a striking crimson rose in the lapel, a gold tie with the letter 'G' embroidered on it, Bermuda shorts and a violet waistcoat. He was also holding the largest pair of driving goggles she'd ever seen.

'Hello, Uncle Percy,' Joe said enthusiastically.

'The pleasure is mine, Joe.' Uncle Percy gave Joe's hand a sturdy shake.

Becky offered a considerably more muted, 'Hiya.'

'And hello to you, Becky.' Uncle Percy bowed deeply. 'My, my, you have grown into a dazzling young woman.'

Becky considered belching just to see his reaction.

'Please, allow me to lighten your load.' Uncle Percy leant over and took their cases. 'I trust you had a pleasant journey?'

'It was fine,' Joe said. 'I like your flower.'

'Thank you. It's a Stephanie Rose. It's unique to Bowen Hall, that's where I live. Anyway, shall we get going. I know a few people who are most eager to meet the two of you.'

'Who?' Becky asked warily. There had been no mention of anyone else.

'Just my friends,' Uncle Percy replied simply. 'Maria is particularly excited. I've told her so many stories about you both, she feels like she knows you already.' Spinning sharply on his back foot, he marched towards the exit. 'Follow me …'

Becky arched her eyebrows with suspicion. How could he know anything about them?

'Who's Maria?' Joe said, struggling to keep up with his uncle's lengthy strides.

'I suppose you'd call her the housekeeper,' Uncle Percy replied. 'That's certainly what she calls herself.'

'You have staff?' Becky asked.

'Gosh, no,' Uncle Percy replied. 'Well, I don't consider them staff, anyhow. They're my friends. I'm sure Maria would disagree, however. I think she rather likes the idea of being an employee. She even insists on wearing a uniform, which rather puzzles me.'

'Are you, like, dead rich?' Joe asked bluntly.

Uncle Percy chuckled. 'To be perfectly honest with you, I really don't know. I think some of the patents do rather well, but I leave those things to other people. Most of the profits go to various charities. I have no interest in money, whatsoever. No, as long as we can maintain the integrity of the Hall, that's all that concerns me.'

Becky stifled a laugh. She didn't believe a word of it. She followed Uncle Percy to the car park where she froze to the spot. Standing there, glinting in the brilliant sunlight, was an ancient silver car the likes of which she had never seen before, except in history books or very old films.

'Wow!' Joe exclaimed.

Becky's eyes widened with horror. It's Chitty Chitty Bang Bang! she thought.

'Do you like her?' Uncle Percy asked.

'That's yours?' Joe asked.

'Indeed, she is,' Uncle Percy replied. 'It's a Rolls Royce Silver Ghost. There are only two with the original chassis still in existence, and I'm fortunate enough to possess one of them. Of course, I've made some minor modifications to make it a tad more suited to modern driving, but essentially it's the same car.'

'It's ace.' Joe turned to Becky. 'Isn't it, Becks?'

'Yeah,' Becky lied, thankful her friends couldn't see her.

Uncle Percy swung open the passenger doors and gestured for them to climb aboard. Joe leapt in. Becky followed, glancing from side to side to check no one was watching.

Uncle Percy mounted the side step and settled onto the claret leather seat. 'Now, seatbelts on, please,' he said. 'We don't want any accidents, do we?'

Becky couldn't help but think that a minor accident resulting in her being sent straight home was a perfect solution to a very big problem.

Fixing his goggles, Uncle Percy turned the ignition key and the engine purred into life. He swung the car down a leafy side street and in a matter of seconds they were surrounded by countryside.

'Uncle Percy, mum says you're an inventor,' Joe said.

'I am, indeed, Joe.'

'So what was the last thing you invented?'

'Erm, let me see … The Gumchumper, I think.'

'What's a Gumchumper?'

'Well, have you ever noticed how much discarded chewing gum litters the streets of every town? The Gumchumper is a device to remove even the most stubborn gum off the pavements, leaving the surface as good as new. It's like a lightweight vacuum cleaner but considerably more powerful. I've sent them to a number of town councils, free of charge, of course. I do hope they use them.'

The Gumchumper? Becky found herself thinking. What a dweeb!

They stopped at a set of traffic lights, when they heard the deafening blast of a car horn. A black convertible car pulled alongside them. Two young men wearing baseball caps and tracksuit tops were smirking at Uncle Percy. The driver, who had very short mousy-brown hair and a flat, pimply face nudged his friend and sniggered.

Becky suddenly felt very exposed.

'Oh, dear,' Uncle Percy said quietly. He flashed the young men a courteous smile and said in a loud, steady voice, 'Good morning, gentlemen.'

The driver responded with a rude hand gesture.

Uncle Percy exhaled heavily. 'I do loathe bad manners.'

The driver sounded the horn again.

Uncle Percy tutted disapprovingly. 'Becky, Joe, are your seatbelts securely fastened?'

'Y-yes,' Becky and Joe stammered, as the traffic lights flashed amber.

Immediately, the spotty driver revved his engine and a cloud of fumes billowed from his exhaust.

'Brace yourselves, please!' Uncle Percy shouted over the din of screeching tyres. 'Things are going to get rather stirring.' He reached for the gear stick, flipped open its cap to reveal a scarlet button and pressed it. At once, the Silver Ghost made a deep rumbling sound, like an aeroplane readying for takeoff. 'I'd prefer you didn't mention this to your mother ...'

The amber light flashed green.

VVRRROOOOM! The black car's tyres spun furiously and it sped off. At the same time, Uncle Percy placed his foot calmly on the accelerator. There was no screeching noise - no cloud of smoke - but, with a soft swish, the Silver Ghost soared away at an astonishing speed.

Becky had never experienced anything like it. Her stomach performed somersaults. She arched round to look at the black car, now a tiny dot on the horizon.

Smiling contentedly, Uncle Percy steered the Silver Ghost with ease and after two miles slowed to a regular speed. Lifting his goggles, he said, 'Did you enjoy that?'

Becky and Joe were speechless.

'That was one of the little modifications I mentioned: an ultra-booster. I know it was reckless, and by and large I do respect the national speed limits, but I also deplore rudeness and those gentlemen were rather loutish. Wouldn't you agree?'

'Y-yes,' Becky spluttered, still confused as to what had just happened.

'Are you all right, Joe?' Uncle Percy asked.

Joe paused for a moment, his mind still playing catch-up. Then his face exploded with delight. 'THAT WAS GREAT!'

'I'm glad you enjoyed it. Now, Bowen Hall's not far now, and I believe Maria has prepared a magnificent lunch.'

But Becky couldn't begin to think about food now. Her thoughts were fixed on one thing, and one thing only. If Uncle Percy could turn an antique car into the fastest she'd ever seen, then what else was he capable of doing?

Maybe he wasn't such a dweeb, after all.

Maybe …

Chapter 4

Bowen Hall

They drove for a further five minutes and then curved right into a narrow road, flanked by giant trees and very thick hedges.

'We're here,' Uncle Percy announced.

Becky twisted her head, eager for the first glimpse of her summer home. She saw nothing but an impenetrable wall of greenery.

'Where is it?' Joe asked impatiently.

'Just beyond that perimeter fence.' Uncle Percy nodded at the hedgerows.

'I can't see a thing,' Joe said, sounding rather disappointed.

'That's the point. Security is of the essence at the Hall, so I've installed a number of measures to ensure the average rambler can't just wander in.'

They passed a succession of wooden signs that read 'PRIVATE PROPERTY – KEEP OUT OR DIE!' - 'TRESSPASSERS WILL BE BLOWN UP!' - 'INTRUDERS WILL BE FED TO VERY BIG DOGS!' and 'BEWARE OF THE LIONS!'

Becky did a double take. 'You have lions?'

Uncle Percy laughed. 'Good heavens, no. Don't take those signs literally. I just thought they were funny and they certainly get the point across. We never have any unwelcome visitors.'

Becky nodded. Somehow, she wasn't surprised.

The Silver Ghost turned left and Becky saw a wrought-iron gate set back from the road. Bringing the car to a halt, Uncle Percy removed his goggles and climbed out. He approached a piece of foliage at the side of the gate and inserted his hand until it disappeared, swallowed by leaves.

Becky watched, intrigued, as the foliage slid to the left and an electronic keypad appeared.

Uncle Percy bent over and stared into it. The pad made a soft whirring sound and a fine ray of brilliant white light beamed from its center, gliding over his left eye. 'Percy Mathias Halifax,' he said. Then he did a very strange thing. He plucked a strand of hair from his head, inserted it into a tiny slot on the panel. A second later, a shrill beep rang out, a light bulb flashed green and the gate slowly opened.

Uncle Percy returned to the car to see two very puzzled expressions staring back at him. 'Oh, they're just some of the precautions I've installed: A retinal scanner, voice remodulator and a DNA verifier.'

'You can never be too careful,' Becky said, pretending she understood what he'd just said.

Facing forward as they entered the grounds, Becky saw a stretched driveway, lined with dozens of spruce trees. But where was Bowen Hall? She felt Joe's hand tighten around her arm. Glancing over, she saw his eyes were fixed on something in the distance. Following his gaze, she saw eight very small, coffee-coloured animals frolicking in a field. 'Are they dogs?'

'Oh, err, no, they're horses,' Uncle Percy replied, somewhat vaguely.

Becky looked again. She couldn't believe it! Horses? They were no taller than her knees. 'Are they babies?'

'Fully grown,' Uncle Percy said. 'The Eohippus is just very small. I didn't expect to see them, they're usually very shy, but I think they must be rather enjoying the sun. As a matter of fact, we have lots of rare animals at Bowen Hall.'

'Like what?' Becky said eagerly. She adored animals.

'Well, we have some hazel dormice - they're quite rare, and a family of Natterjack toads. We're very fortunate.'

'How about budgies?' Joe smirked at Becky, who scowled back at him.

'No budgies I'm afraid.'

'And how big are the grounds?' Becky asked, keen to steer the conversation away from budgies.

'A few thousand acres. There's a lovely lake, stables, a maze, a sizeable forest, that's where Will lives - '

'Who's Will?' Joe cut in.

'He's a good friend. A fine chap,' Uncle Percy said. 'He tends the grounds.'

'And he lives in the forest?' Joe asked, intrigued. 'Why doesn't he live at the Hall?'

'He's the outdoorsy type,' Uncle Percy said simply. 'Besides, he's got a wonderful tree house he made with his own hands. You'll like Will.'

'A tree-house?' Joe breathed.

'Yes. It's an amazing construction and very comfortable. I'm sure he'll let you sleep there one night, if you ask him nicely.'

Becky realised if she heard this a few hours ago she wouldn't have believed a word. Now, anything was possible. As they reached the end of the driveway, Becky and Joe let out a simultaneous gasp of astonishment.

Uncle Percy smiled. 'Home sweet home.'

Becky couldn't believe her eyes. Before her stood an enormous Jacobean mansion of red and orange brick with large windows that reflected the sunlight from countless panes of glass. A central clock tower overlooked a series of weather vanes, domes and spires. Passing a central fountain, the Silver Ghost stopped before a series of stone steps. Uncle Percy leapt from the car, opened the rear doors, and Becky and Joe stepped out.

Then, with a shattering bang, the front door burst open, and a short, elderly woman wearing a black and white uniform appeared. She had curly black hair, a round, pink face and a wide smile that showed off her misshapen teeth to full effect.

Becky thought she resembled a human skittle.

'It's the children – the children …' the woman screeched with an accent, rushing down the steps, her apron billowing before her. 'Jacob! It's the children.' A very thin old man with agreeable eyes, shuffled through the door, his right leg affected by a slight limp.

'My angels,' Maria gushed, just managing to stop herself before slamming into Becky. 'My little darlings… look at you both! You must be Miss Becky?' Maria cupped Becky's astonished face in her sausage-like fingers. 'Look at your pretty face and your lovely long hair. Isn't she beautiful, Jacob?'

Jacob joined them at the car. 'She is very beautiful,' he said in a soft voice that shared the same clipped accent as his wife.

Becky blushed and returned Maria's smile. 'Thank you. You're Maria, right?'

'Yes, indeed, Maria, that is me. And this is my husband, Jacob. We are so pleased to meet you finally.'

Jacob bowed. 'It is my great honour, Miss.'

'Nice to meet you, Jacob,' Becky said.

Maria turned slowly to Joe. Then she pounced, grabbing him with the force of a wrestler. 'And you must be Master Joe? You are such a good-looking boy, too. You will be a strong man, one day, as strong as a lion. I know these things.'

Joe's face reddened. 'Thanks.'

'The bags, Jacob. Get their bags!' Maria ordered in a way that suggested refusal would be punishable by death. 'These children must be fed. They are far too thin.'

Jacob nodded and grabbed the cases.

'No, let me take those, Jacob,' Uncle Percy said, moving to the rear of the car. 'They're heavy.'

Scowling, Maria blocked his path, arms folded. 'You will do no such thing. Jacob, take the luggage to their rooms at once.'

'No, Maria, really… I want - '

Maria shot him a ferocious glare. 'Do not dare! That is my husband's job. You try, and I jolly well kick your rump for you. You are the master - '

'I'm really not!' Uncle Percy muttered awkwardly.

'Jacob. Do as I say,' Maria yelled. 'NOW!'

Jacob bowed and limped off dutifully in the direction of the Hall. Satisfied, Maria turned to Uncle Percy and smiled sweetly. 'Now, sir, I have prepared -'

'How many times, Maria, must I ask you to call me Percy?'

'I will do no such thing, sir,' Maria replied. 'Now you will be shutting your mouth.' She grabbed Uncle Percy's head roughly and planted a wet kiss on his forehead. 'This is a happy, happy day. The children are here.'

Uncle Percy looked at Becky and shrugged. It was clear this was a battle he'd fought and lost many times before.

'Now, please,' Maria said to Becky and Joe. 'You must be following me, and I will be showing you to your rooms.' She led them up the steps, and through the open door.

It took a moment for Becky's eyes to adjust from the daylight, but when they did she found herself in a gigantic entrance hall with a patterned marble floor. There were eight closed doors and, on the left-hand wall, a stone fireplace with a coat of arms bearing the inscription 'Tempus omnia sed memorias privat' carved into the chimneypiece. A number of stone busts of very serious looking bearded men lined the walls. Portraits of all shapes and sizes filled every inch of wall space. However, the most impressive object stood in the center of the room - a life-sized bronze statue of a Roman centurion wielding a sword.

'Cool,' Joe said, his eyes glued to the sword.

'Very,' Becky replied, facing a grand staircase that divided into two curving flights and led to a balcony above.

'Come, come… I will show you to your rooms, my angels,' Maria said, guiding them up the left flight.

Becky followed Maria as she passed through an archway into a narrow corridor lined with doors, more portraits, and wall lights that shed a homely auburn glow.

Stopping at the end of the corridor, Maria took a heavy set of keys from her waistband. 'Miss Becky, this is your room.' She unlocked a thickset oak door and pushed it open. 'I hope you will be happy here, if not you will tell me at once. There are seventy two others from which to choose.'

'I'm sure it's fine, Maria,' Becky said, surprised to find she felt suddenly nervous. She took a hesitant step into the room.

'We have all been looking forward to you being here, Miss Becky…' Maria said softly. 'Your uncle, especially.' Before Becky had a chance to thank her, Maria had gone.

Becky stood there in a rapt silence. The room was enchanting. Scarlet and gold tapestries tumbled from the ceiling and a huge four-poster bed with silk hangings tied back with silver ribbon stood on the right hand wall. A mahogany dressing table with an ornate copper framed mirror rested beneath a window, a yellow cushioned stool tucked neatly between its legs.

Becky was about to unpack when the door burst open and Joe raced in.

'This place is amazing, isn't it?' Joe panted.

'Yes, it is,' Becky said softly.

'Do you still think Uncle Percy's a loon?'

'Absolutely,' Becky replied warmly. 'In the best possible way…'

Together, and for what felt like hours, Becky and Joe sat silently on the bed, neither of them daring to close their eyes for fear of waking up from the most delicious dream. A sharp knock at the door brought them back to reality. 'Err, come in,' Becky said.

The door opened to reveal Jacob, wearing a black double-breasted tailcoat. 'Would you care to take lunch in the morning room, Miss Becky, Master Joe?'

Following Jacob, Becky and Joe walked through the archway and down the right-hand staircase. At the bottom, they bore right through a side door into the morning room and saw Uncle Percy sitting at a wide bay window, reading a book entitled The Myths of Stonehenge: Fact and Fiction. He lowered the book and beckoned Becky and Joe to join him, smiling all the time. 'First things first, are your rooms to your liking? You must say if they're not, we do have plenty of others. You can even have mine if you'd like."

'They're terrific,' Joe said.

'Really great,' Becky said sincerely and, as her eyes met his, something quite unexpected happened. Somewhere in the deep recesses of her memory something stirred. She did recognise him. She couldn't pinpoint the time or place but she felt certain he represented something good, something significant. 'Uncle Percy, I hope you don't mind me asking, but how can we be related to you? I mean, you're like royalty, and we're just - well, we're ordinary -'

'Gosh, I'm not royalty. Between you and me, I'm not exactly a royalist. And you - you are far from ordinary.' A glint flickered in his eye. 'You see, I was your late grandfather's cousin. God rest his soul. And I did know your father very well. We were -' he fell silent for a second, '- we were close friends. No, if truth be told, you are my only true family. There's Maria, Jacob and Will, of course, but - '

'You don't have any other relatives?' Becky interrupted.

'I'm afraid not. My parents died many years ago,' Uncle Percy said. 'I've never been married and have no children.'

'What about brothers or sisters?' Becky asked.

'I had a younger brother, Myron.' Uncle Percy looked away. 'But sadly he passed away many years ago.'

'I'm sorry,' Becky said sympathetically.

'No matter,' Uncle Percy said. 'Fate is a peculiar bedfellow, and, sometimes, what is meant to be is not always what will be. Anyway -'

Before Uncle Percy could continue, the door opened and Maria and Jacob each pushing a trolley brimming with food: an enormous roast chicken, freshly baked crusty bread, an assortment of hot and cold pies, various cheeses, and a colossal strawberry trifle laden with fresh cream and chocolate.

'Thank you so much, Maria, Jacob,' Uncle Percy said as they made to leave. 'Please, won't you join us? There's plenty for everyone.'

'No, thank you, sir,' Maria said. 'We will eat in the kitchens, where we belong.'

'I've told you a thousand times you don't belong -' Uncle Percy said, but Maria and Jacob had left the room. He shook his head and sighed. 'It doesn't matter what I say. They just won't listen to me. Anyway, tuck in then.'

Becky and Joe needed no further encouragement and piled into the feast, filling their plates as high as they could.

'How long have Maria and Jacob lived here?' Becky asked.

'About eight years. The place really wouldn't be the same without them.'

'What about their family?' Becky said. 'Do they have children?'

'No. I don't believe they do,' Uncle Percy said as though keen to drop the subject. 'Anyway, tell me more about the two of you. Joe, how are you doing at school?'

But Joe had stopped listening, his gaze transfixed on something outside.

Becky looked out of the window and saw a man riding a horse at speed in a distant meadow. 'Who's that?'

Uncle Percy retrieved a pair of glasses from a silver case and fixed them to the tip of his nose. 'Oh, that's Will.'

'What's he doing?' Joe asked, captivated.

'Practicing his archery, I suppose. He's a remarkable bowman – never misses a shot.'

Then Becky took a sharp intake of breath. 'Is he – is he standing on the horse's back?'

'Probably. He likes a challenge,' Uncle Percy said casually. 'Would you like to meet him?'

'Yes, please,' Joe said without hesitation.

'Well, finish up your lunch then,' Uncle Percy said, looking at Joe. 'He's most keen to meet you...'

Chapter 5

The Discovery

A short while later, Becky followed Uncle Percy and Joe, a half-eaten apple in his mouth, through the kitchen door, across the terrace and on to the path that divided the rear lawns. Dawdling at the back, she enjoyed watching her uncle walk. Although a very graceful man, his walk had a definite air of the ridiculous about it. His back seemed stiff as though his spine had been replaced with a cricket bat, yet his legs seemed unusually bendy as if they contained very few bones at all.

'What's that building?' Becky said, pointing to a windowless outbuilding to the side of the Hall.

'That's the one place that's out of bounds,' Uncle Percy said in an uncharacteristically serious manner. 'That's my laboratory and I must insist you don't make any attempts to explore it or you'll blow us all to bits and probably take the North West of England out, too. Is that okay?'

'Err, sure,' Becky replied hesitantly.

After negotiating a cluster of trees, they entered the field to see Will sitting astride a magnificent ebony horse, a bow in his hand and a leather quiver slung over his broad shoulders. Steering the horse by its mane, he trotted over then dismounted. About thirty, he was tall, powerfully built, with chestnut brown hair that fell down his back.

Becky's jaw dropped. He was gorgeous.

'A fine day to you all,' Will said in a soft, mellifluous tone. 'I am Will Shakelock.' He faced Joe and extended his hand. 'Hello.'

Becky noticed he wore a large gold signet ring on his index finger with a white pouncing lion engraved on the bezel.

'Hi,' Joe replied, shaking Will's hand.

'And you must be Miss Becky?'

Becky's hand shot up and covered the spot on her forehead. 'Yes,' she squeaked in a trill voice that didn't appear to come from her at all.

Joe gazed at the ten straw targets on the field. Each had an arrow embedded dead center. 'You're ace with the bow and arrow.'

'I thank you,' Will replied. 'Where I hail from we're taught archery at an early age.'

'Are you?' Joe said enviously. 'We're just taught rubbish, like maths.'

Uncle Percy frowned and opened his mouth to challenge when Joe continued, 'Where are you from?'

'Nottingham.'

'I - I've got a Facebook friend in Nottingham,' Becky blustered. 'Anna Perkins. Do you know her?' Before the words left her mouth she knew how foolish she must have sounded.

'I do not, miss,' Will said kindly.

Becky decided to keep her mouth shut from now on.

'I've been watching a TV series about Nottingham,' Joe said, ignoring his sister. 'The Tales of Robin Hood. Have you seen it?'

'No, Will replied, 'but it's a most celebrated tale.'

'It's pretty good,' Joe added. 'But Robin's not my favourite character.'

'And who may that be?'

'Little John.'

'Ah, John Little was a good man.'

'And Friar Tuck,' Joe said. 'He's well funny.'

'Indeed.' Will hesitated. 'And there's Will Scarlet, of course, a fine and noble character.'

Joe paused for a moment. 'Nah, I don't like him. He's a pansy.'

Will's expression turned from interest to disappointment. Suddenly, Uncle Percy gave a rather loud cough. A cough that for a fleeting moment, Becky thought was a laugh.

Joe didn't notice. 'Would you fire an arrow for me?'

'Indeed,' Will said. 'And what should the target be?'

'What about the apple?' Uncle Percy said, pointing. 'Have you finished with that, Joe?' Joe nodded and passed it over. 'Ready, Will?'

Will drew an arrow from his quiver. Then Uncle Percy pitched the apple into the air with all the strength he could muster.

In a flash, Will took aim and fired. The arrow sliced the air and with a dull thump, struck the apple through its core.

Joe panted with disbelief. 'Whoa!' He turned excitedly to Will. 'Would you teach me? Archery, I mean.'

'I would enjoy that.'

'Can we start now?'

Will smiled warmly. 'Unfortunately, for now I must feed Epona.' He stroked the horse's shaggy mane. 'Perhaps we could begin on the morrow?'

'Great,' Joe said. 'I'll try really hard.'

'Of that I am certain.'

'You must come for dinner, William,' Uncle Percy said. 'Maria is preparing something of a treat in honour of our guests. I think she's hoping you may join us.'

'Maria is far too formidable a lady to disappoint. Please inform her I accept. Farewell to you all.' Will offered a parting nod, and guided Epona into the forest.

As he strode away, Becky felt sure she heard him mutter something about flowers.

*

The weather remained glorious throughout Becky and Joe's first week. Uncle Percy ensured their every moment was filled with fun. Each morning, he would escort them to the lake, where they would swim in the shallow black water or take a rowing boat to the center and enjoy a light breakfast beneath the early morning sun. Will kept his promise and spent hours teaching Joe archery. He was a patient teacher and Joe an eager pupil. Will gave him an exact replica of his own bow, if slightly smaller, and Joe cherished it. Indeed, Will was impressed with Joe's natural ability as an archer and Joe was delighted with his tutor's encouragement.

Uncle Percy had decided that, whether she liked it or not, Becky should learn to ride and would take her every afternoon to the musty stone stables that bordered the lake. At first, Becky was hesitant, particularly when she saw the horse he had selected for her - a decrepit, grey horse with a white streak on its nose and bandy legs that he referred to as 'Charger'. In her opinion, the only way it could charge anywhere would be strapped to a short-range missile. Nevertheless, she felt satisfied Charger looked far too old, bored and generally worn out to cause her any serious damage. Each afternoon they would traverse the grounds and Uncle Percy would explain about the history of Bowen Hall.

'It was originally built in 1632 by an architect called William Pumpkin. And it remained with the Pumpkin family for over a hundred and fifty years until his great grandson, an idiot of a man named Jedidiah Pumpkin, lost it in a game of cards. Of course, Jedidiah was furious and insulted his opponent, insisting on a duel the following morning. Alas, Jedidiah was such a buffoon he shot himself in the head loading his dueling pistol. Anyway, his opponent was my distant ancestor, Herbert George Halifax, and it's been with our family ever since.'

Becky smiled as Uncle Percy recounted the tale. She enjoyed listening to him tell such richly detailed stories, particularly about history, and felt ashamed she once thought such dreadful things about him.

And when Mrs Mellor came to visit at the weekend, Uncle Percy arranged a black tie banquet in her honour and spent her entire stay showering her with luxuries at every possible opportunity. As the weekend drew to a close, Mrs Mellor found it almost impossible to leave. Delighted that

Becky and Joe were having such a lovely time, she promised to return the following weekend.

*

By Tuesday of the second week the weather had turned. A ferocious storm battered the Hall, shaking its very foundations and an angry wind wailed like a siren. It was two in the morning when Becky was jolted from a deep sleep by a forceful shove to her ribs.

'Get up!' Joe said, struggling to catch his breath.

Becky turned away, pulled her duvet close and mumbled, 'Bog off.'

Joe pushed her again. 'Will you get up!'

'What is it?' Becky growled, refusing to open her eyes.

'Come with me,' Joe said urgently. 'You must see this. It's unbelievable.'

'I'll see it in the morn -'

'It has to be now!' Joe bellowed. He switched on the bedside light. 'Come on. You'll never believe me. You have to see it for yourself.'

Becky forced her eyes open. Joe stood in front of her, sopping wet and shivering. 'Have you been swimming?'

'Not exactly,' Joe replied, wringing water from the cuffs of his dressing gown.

'So why are you wet?'

'You'll see. Now, come on.'

Becky yawned. 'It had better be good.'

'Oh, it is,' Joe breathed. 'It's very good...'

Two minutes later, Becky followed Joe out of her bedroom and up the corridor, a thick overcoat covering her pajamas. Although it was a warm, airless night there was something about the Hall at this hour that sent a sharp chill through her bones. By day, it was such a cheerful place, quite befitting the people who lived there, but at night it seemed to adopt a new personality entirely. Eerie. Mysterious. Disquieting. The walls groaned and creaked as if scolding them for being out of bed at this time of night; the portraits appeared to come to life, their empty, soulless eyes seemed to trail their every step.

By the time they had descended the stairs, Becky felt thoroughly miserable. She looked ahead at Joe and silently plotted her revenge, which involved his nose, four peanuts and a chopstick. Her heart sank further when she saw him tiptoe silently towards the front door. 'Where are you taking -'

'Shhh,' Joe said, inching the door open. 'Now, whatever you see, don't - make - a – sound. That means no screaming! Okay?'

Screaming, Becky thought. What exactly would she see? Following Joe on to the porch, an icy blast of rain spattered her face. Thanks a bunch, Joe, she thought. I'm going to get told off, sent back to Manchester, and catch pneumonia, all in one night.

'This way,' Joe said, and he dashed off.

Becky pulled her coat tightly around her neck and followed him to the side of the Hall. She watched horrified as he approached a familiar outbuilding. Joining him, she shot him an angry look. 'You haven't broken into Uncle Percy's laboratory, have you? He said it was out of bounds. If you have, I'll thump your face so hard it swells like a - '

'Quiet,' Joe barked. 'Listen…' He pressed a finger to his lips.

For once, Becky did as she was told. The rain was fading now and even through the moaning wind she could hear muffled voices. She grew intrigued.

'Look round the corner,' Joe whispered, pointing to the edge of the wall.

Becky hesitated. Slowly, suspiciously, she bent forward and peered round.

'Can you see? Are they still there?'

Becky didn't respond. She couldn't. Mesmerised by the astonishing sight before her, she didn't even hear his words.

Will was crouched on the waterlogged grass; beside him, a large sandy-coloured animal was in a heavy sleep, its chest moving up and down in a slow, consistent rhythm. Uncle Percy stood over them, soaked and exhausted. He held a pair of pliers jubilantly in his hand. The pliers contained a fat, yellowing tooth.

'Good girl,' Will breathed, softly patting the creature's back.

'Milly should be out for about half an hour,' Uncle Percy said with a smile. 'What do you say to a nice cup of tea, William? I believe we've earned it.'

Will laid the animal's head lightly on the grass. 'I deem we have.'

Becky's head spun like a top. She felt confused, bewildered, dazed. Not to see Uncle Percy up at this time of night - she half-expected this would be when he did his inventing. No, looking at the sleeping animal, she knew it shouldn't be alive at all. She'd seen one before at the

Natural History Museum in London. But that was only a life-like reconstruction and not the genuine article.

A Sabre-tooth tiger lay sedated on the lawn of Bowen Hall - a very large, very real Sabre-tooth tiger.

Chapter 6

A Question of Time

Becky felt numb. Questions surged through her mind. Then, as if to make matters worse, she heard a soft growl and felt a sharp tug at the hem of her pajama bottoms. Looking down, she saw a small brown cat gnawing on the fabric. Her eyeballs nearly popped from their sockets: a Sabre-tooth tiger cub. 'Get off,' she yelled instinctively, giving the cub a light kick. Uncle Percy's head jolted up. Becky dipped behind the wall, but she knew it was too late.

She'd been seen.

Colour drained from Uncle Percy's face. 'Oh, crikey,' he uttered. 'SABIAN! Come here… NOW!' The cub released Becky's robe and padded obediently over to him. Uncle Percy scooped him up and took a very deep breath before he spoke, 'You can come out now, Becky.'

Becky emerged, her eyes fixed resolutely on the ground. Hesitantly, Joe followed.

'And Joe too, I see,' Uncle Percy said flatly. 'Deary me.'

'It's his fault.' Becky nodded at Joe. 'He was spying on you.'

'I wasn't,' Joe said defensively. 'I - err - I woke up, went to the loo, heard a roar outside and then - '

'That's quite all right, Joe,' Uncle Percy said.

'That's a - a - Sabre tooth tiger,' Becky blustered.

Uncle Percy paused. 'Yes. Her name's Milly. She had a nasty abscess on a back molar. We had to remove it.' He gave a weak smile and held up the bloody tooth as if it made the explanation more palatable.

'But…it's a Sabre-tooth t-tiger?' Becky repeated.

'A Smilodon, to be precise, and this little tyke is her son, Sabian.'

'How - how have you got a Sabre-tooth -' Becky's words were interrupted by a deep rumbling sound beneath her feet.

'Oh, no…' Uncle Percy's body seemed to deflate like a balloon and he dropped the pliers on his foot. In that instant, the air filled with thick streams of light.

'What's g-going on?' Becky shouted, shielding her eyes.

A mighty crack echoed all around. And then silence. Slowly, Becky lowered her hand and gasped. A milk float had materialised on the lawn.

*

Becky froze like a statue and gawped at the milk float. A thickset middle-aged man in a racing green blazer and cravat was sitting in the front seat. His fine blond hair, slicked back with wax, made his large round head glisten like a Christmas bauble. 'Greetings, Percy, old boy. What's the matter with Milly?'

'Evening, Keith,' Uncle Percy replied awkwardly. 'Milly's fine, she's just sedated. We had to perform a minor tooth extraction.'

'I see,' the traveller replied. 'Well, you're quite right, of course. Best do it yourself, most vets wouldn't fancy a twelve-thousand year old tiger on their operating table.' He chuckled and his chins rippled wildly. 'Anyway, I found the Stonehenge manuscript you wanted.' He pulled a folded piece of ragged brown parchment from his pocket.

'Excellent.' Uncle Percy's eyes flicked from the traveller to Becky and Joe.

'You were right, Rodney Taylor had pinched it,' the traveller continued. 'He's a rum 'un that one. Oh, and you were right about something else. Bernard Preston had paid him a visit, and it was about the manuscript. So, whatever your theory about his murder is, well, you seem to be right on the money.'

Suddenly the traveller noticed Becky and Joe and his broad smile fell from his face. Turning back to Uncle Percy, he arched his eyebrows. 'Ooops, I didn't -'

Uncle Percy shook his head and placed Sabian on the grass. 'Not to worry, Keith. Thanks for this.' He seized the manuscript and slipped it into his coat pocket. 'Care for a nightcap?'

'No thanks, Perce. Things to do and all that.'

'Another time, then?'

'Absolutely. Anyway, must be off.' Offering a hasty wave, the traveller fumbled about frantically on the dashboard. 'Cheerio, Perce, Will. Ta ta everyone.' A few moments later, the milk float had vanished.

Uncle Percy unbuttoned his top collar and forced a weak smile. 'I do believe I have some explaining to do...'

'T-that was a milk float,' Becky said, staring at the empty space where the milk float had been.

'Yes it was.'

'But - but it disappeared.'

'Yes it did.'

'How?'

Uncle Percy exhaled heavily. 'Well, that's because it isn't strictly a milk float. It's a time machine.'

'A time machine?' Becky snorted.

'Indeed. And that gentleman was Keith Pickleton, a good friend of mine and a very experienced time traveller.'

'Don't be ridiculous,' Becky snorted. 'Time travel is not possible!'

Uncle Percy inclined his head towards the sleeping tiger. 'Well, I didn't get Milly at Asda.' He gave a half-hearted chuckle.

Becky's head reeled. 'But … h - how?'

'Well, how, would take some time to explain. But the process involves Einstein's general theory of relativity, time dilation, four-dimensional wormholes, temporal curvatures, and quantum mechanics. But you have no idea what I've just said, have you?'

'Uh,' Becky grunted.

'And you're a t-time traveller?' Joe gasped.

'I am,' Uncle Percy said. 'Now, I think we'd better get out of this rain and have a little chat, don't you?'

*

'Drink up, you'll feel better.' Uncle Percy placed two mugs before Becky and Joe. He pulled up a wooden chair and joined them at the kitchen table. 'Now, I'm sure you have lots of questions. So, please, fire away …'

Becky and Joe sat there, staring dumbstruck at the swirling liquid.

After a long pause, Joe spoke first, 'Why doesn't Milly eat you?'

Uncle Percy smiled. 'Well, she's really very tame and exceptionally loyal. And we do feed her well. Personally, I think she'd rather chew on a juicy steak than my scrawny ankle.'

Becky didn't smile. 'Did you invent time travel?'

'Good heavens, no. The credit for that belongs to a remarkable scientist named Henry Locket in 1946 when he created 'Old Betty' the world's first operational time machine. Anyway, he told some of his contemporaries about Betty and, before long, they were using his specifications to build their own machines. Over the next few years, even though Locket insisted their activities remain secret, word got out. By 1955 there were thirty two time travellers, world-wide.'

'And how many are there now?' Becky asked.

'Over two hundred.'

Becky couldn't believe her ears. 'Two hundred?'

'Oh, yes.' Uncle Percy smiled weakly. 'And it's quite the global affair.'

'How did you get involved?' Joe asked eagerly.

'Well, much later, Henry Locket was one of my tutors at Oxford. I had always been fascinated by the concept of time travel and, aided by some fellow classmates, conducted some experiments of my own. Anyway, I think Professor Locket appreciated our efforts and took us under his wing. And that's how I first became involved with the community.'

Becky took a moment to digest the information. 'So… what's the future like?'

Joe's eyes lit up. 'Do Man City ever win the Premiership?'

Uncle Percy gave a somewhat relieved laugh. 'I have no idea, to either question. You see, it is only possible to visit the past, and back again, of course, but not the future. The limitations of the technology dictate that a time machine can only ever return to the present, not travel to the future.'

'It's still pretty cool,' Joe said. 'I mean, you could keep going back to 1966 to watch England win the World Cup.'

'I knew someone that did precisely that,' Uncle Percy said, a slight edge to his voice.

'So have you met any famous people?' Joe asked.

Uncle Percy relaxed into his chair and tapped his long fingers on his chin. 'Let me see … I met William Shakespeare.'

Becky shuddered. That name had always filled her with dread ever since she read Macbeth at school.

'And what was he like?' Joe asked.

'As dull as his plays,' Uncle Percy replied, winking at Becky as though he could read her thoughts.

Becky grinned back at him. 'Have you met anyone else?'

'I was fortunate enough to meet Gandhi; he was a wonderful chap, great sense of humour. Martin Luther King - he was smashing, a bona-fide gent. Florence Nightingale - she was an extraordinary woman and a devilishly good poker player. Oh, and The Duke of Wellington, but I found him a bit too big for his boots.'

Becky almost laughed but stopped when she noticed Joe staring darkly at Uncle Percy. 'What's the matter with you?'

'Will's from the past, isn't he?'

An uncomfortable silence cloaked the kitchen. After a few seconds Uncle Percy spoke, 'Yes.'

Joe nodded solemnly. 'Who is he?'

A very slight smile formed on Uncle Percy's face. 'Well, I heard you mention a television programme about Robin Hood.'

Joe's face ignited. 'He's Robin Hood!'

'Err - not exactly,' Uncle Percy said. 'Robin Hood didn't exist. However, some of the Robin Hood legend is indeed based on fact - the so-called merry men, for example, did exist. They did steal from the rich and give to the poor. And, for a while at least, they all lived in the great trees of Sherwood. Their leader was - '

'- Will … Scarlet?' Joe breathed.

'I suppose so, yes,' Uncle Percy said.

Then another voice floated on the air. 'And methinks I should have remained in my own time.' Will stood at the kitchen door, silhouetted by the glassy moon behind.

Joe's jaw dropped. 'You're the real Will Scarlet?'

'I am the real Will Shakelock.'

Dumbstruck, Joe asked, 'So, why are you here, in our time, I mean?'

'Your uncle saved my life, and -' Will paused, about to say something else but changed his mind, '- and I owe him a great debt.'

'You owe me nothing, Will,' Uncle Percy said simply. 'You know that.'

'You saved his life?' Joe said, looking at his uncle with newfound admiration.

'Not really. He's exaggerating.'

'He did a very fine thing,' Will added sincerely.

'What?' Joe asked.

Will was about to reply when Uncle Percy cut in.

'It's a long story that happened a very long time ago,' Uncle Percy said. 'Besides, it's late and -'

'- And there is still one member of the household yet to meet,' Will said mysteriously. Becky and Joe swapped bewildered glances. Someone else lived at Bowen Hall?

Will whistled loudly. A sturdy, grey creature stomped into the kitchen and knocked over an umbrella stand. About five foot in length, it had a large fan-like plate on the back of its head. A horn protruded from its beak-like mouth and two larger horns from above its eyes.

At first, Becky thought it was a rhinoceros. She was wrong.

'Ah, of course,' Uncle Percy smiled. 'Becky. Joe. Meet Gump.'

After seconds of stunned silence, Becky managed to speak. 'I-It's a d-dinosaur?'

'Indeed, he is. A Triceratops,' Uncle Percy said. 'Only a baby, of course, an adult Triceratops would be as big as a lorry.' He tickled Gump under his chin. 'You can stroke him if you'd like. He does enjoy a good mollycoddling.'

Trembling, Becky and Joe crouched beside the Triceratops and patted him. Gump made a soft groan that sounded rather like a cow mooing.

'Anyway,' Will said. 'I shall retire to my lodgings and take our grey friend with me. I bid you sleep well, although I predict that easier said than it is done.' He smiled at Uncle Percy. 'I wish you luck, old friend.'

'Thank you and good night, William.'

'Night,' Becky and Joe said at the same time.

'Come, Gump.' Will held a carrot to the Triceratops' nostrils and moved towards the kitchen door. Gump followed.

Joe panted as Gump lumbered into the night. 'Wait 'til I tell Zimmo about this,' he said, voice trembling. 'He'll never believe me.'

Uncle Percy's expression grew stern. 'Now, both of you, I must ask that you do me a favour. And I'm deadly serious about this. What you see at Bowen Hall must remain our secret. Absolutely no one can know about what happens here… not your friends, your teachers, not even your mother. Do you understand?'

'But -?' Joe said.

'There can be no buts, Joe,' Uncle Percy said firmly. 'I must ask you to give me your most sincere assurance you won't tell a soul. If you did, everything here - every person, every animal - would be in danger. In fact, the whole world would be in danger.'

'What kind of dang -' Joe said.

'Just promise, dweebling!' Becky snapped. 'Of course, we do. Don't we, Joe?'

'Course,' Joe said sincerely. 'We won't tell a soul.'

'You give your me your word?'

Becky and Joe nodded.

Uncle Percy looked relieved. 'Excellent,' he smiled, stretching in his chair.

'May we …may we come with you on a journey?' Becky asked nervously.

Joe's face ignited like a firework. 'Pleeaaase.'

'I'm afraid not,' Uncle Percy replied simply.

'We'll be good, I swear,' Becky added.

'I'm sure you will, but travelling can be dangerous. I wouldn't want to put you in harms way.'

'Then take us somewhere you know is safe,' Becky said.

'Can we see a T Rex?' Joe said.

Uncle Percy chortled. 'I wouldn't say that corresponded with my definition of the word 'safe', young man.'

Joe shrugged. 'It would be cool though. Wouldn't it, Becks?'

Becky ignored him and looked again at Uncle Percy. 'Seriously, you wouldn't have to take us back far, either. Debbie Crabtree was run over by a granny on a mobility scooter in Primark last week. I'd give anything to see it.'

Uncle Percy looked quite shocked. 'Poor Debbie.'

Becky gave a flippant wave of her hand. 'Oh, don't worry about her. She's a bully and a right cow.'

Uncle Percy was about to reprimand her, when she appeared to notice this and continued. 'And she wasn't hurt. No, my point is, it doesn't have to be years. It's just the fact that we would've done it.'

Uncle Percy hesitated. 'I'm sorry. I really can't. I could never forgive myself if something happened to either of you.'

'Nothing will happen,' Becky said. 'And as mum always says, 'you can't lead a horse to water and not expect it to take a drink.'

'But I didn't lead you anywhere, did I? You stumbled upon across the whole thing because of Joe's bladder.'

'Either way,' Becky grinned. 'We know about time travel now and we won't stop badgering you until you take us on a trip. And we can be pretty annoying when we badger, can't we, Joe?'

'Dead annoying,' Joe smirked. 'We're great badgerers.'

'And we're here for another four weeks,' Becky said. 'That's a lot of badgering.'

'Badger, badger, badger,' Joe said.

Uncle Percy looked defeated. 'Then let me sleep on it. I promise you I'll give it some serious thought. Now, is that okay with the two of you?'

'I think so,' Becky said, casting him the sweetest smile she could. 'And you know it makes sense.'

'That's right,' Joe agreed.

Uncle Percy laughed. 'For now though, I think we should all get some rest. It's been a very long and most eventful night.' Raising himself from his chair, he scooped up the mugs and approached the kitchen sink.

Joe gave an almighty yawn, his eyelids wilting. He folded his arms on the table, lay down his head and closed his eyes. Becky waited a minute, watching as his breathing grew heavier, then rose quietly from her chair and joined Uncle Percy at the sink. 'Can I ask you a question?' she said softly.

'You can always ask,' Uncle Percy replied in a way that suggested he knew what her question would be. 'I can't guarantee you'll receive an answer.'

'Jacob and Maria are from the past, too, aren't they?'

Uncle Percy stopped what he was doing and stared darkly at the window. 'Yes.'

'Where are they from?'

'They're German.'

'From what period?'

'The Nineteen Thirties.'

Becky looked up at Uncle Percy's eyes. For once, they seemed sad and colourless. She nodded coolly and moved back to the table to wake up her brother. She didn't know why, but something told her she shouldn't ask about Jacob and Maria's past.

A short while later, Becky lay in bed, listening to the dying gasps of wind outside. Sleep was out of the question. In a matter of hours her understanding of life - past, present and future - had changed, and changed forever. She was living in a stately home with a time traveller, Will Scarlet, two Sabre-tooth tigers and a dinosaur. A house where milk floats appeared on the lawns in the dead of night.

A house of miracles.

Chapter 7

The Time Room

'We're going!' Joe bellowed. 'We're going!'

Becky's eyes shot open to see him burst through her door, eyes wide, ruby faced. Even half-asleep she knew the reason for his elation. Uncle Percy had agreed to take them on a journey through time. He'd actually agreed.

She, Becky Mellor, would be a time traveller.

Becky and Joe ate their breakfast as quickly as they could; in part, to get the day underway, but also, and more significantly, to get out of Maria's way.

Maria had been in a terrible mood all morning, banging pots and pans around the kitchen, chasing Gump with a mop for tramping dirt on her freshly scrubbed floor tiles, and screaming at Jacob for having a particularly loud cough.

'It's not right. It's not right,' she grumbled, ferociously scrubbing the breakfast dishes. 'Little ones should not be messing with such things. Stupid man - stupid, crazy, man!'

By the time she had finished washing up she had broken three glasses, a carafe and a rather old bone china teacup. And when Uncle Percy appeared at the door, Maria barged past him, yelled 'BAH!' in his face and stamped on his right foot before clumping off down the corridor, shouting, 'Dummkopf. Idiot!'

'Maria's in a peculiar mood today.' Uncle Percy winced, rubbing his foot.

'I don't think she likes us going back in time,' Becky said.

Uncle Percy sat down at the table. 'Really? I don't see why not.'

'That's not what you said last night,' Becky said.

'I've had time to think about it. I can't deny it is a marvelous scholastic experience, and who am I to stand in the way of your education?'

'That's the spirit,' Becky said.

'So where are we going?' Joe asked impatiently. 'And will we see a T- Rex?'

'I certainly hope not, Joe,' Uncle Percy said. 'No, today I'm taking you somewhere very special to me. Very special, indeed. In fact, with the exception of Bowen Hall, it's my favourite place in my favourite period in history.'

'So we're not going to see Debbie Crabtree get knocked over then?' Becky quipped.

'Where's the educational value in that?'

'There isn't any,' Becky replied. 'But I bet it's hilarious.'

Uncle Percy sighed. 'I think I can do a little better than Miss Crabtree's accident.'

'Go on then,' Becky said eagerly. 'Where?'

'You'll have to wait and see,' Uncle Percy said secretively. 'Anyway, I suppose we'd better get this show on the road. It's about time I showed you my laboratory?'

'The laboratory?' Becky said. 'I thought we weren't allowed in there.'

'Well, if truth be told, it's not a conventional laboratory. It is, however, where I keep my time machines.'

'Time machines?' Joe said. 'You've got more than one?'

'Oh, yes,' Uncle Percy replied casually. 'I have five…'

*

A cool breeze whipped Becky's hair as she trailed Uncle Percy along the path to the side of the Hall. She grew more nervous with each step, and found herself questioning whether this was a good idea. She didn't particularly enjoy flying, how on earth would she feel about travelling through time?

When they reached the laboratory, Uncle Percy pulled what looked like a tiny mobile phone from his pocket. Keying in a sequence of digits, he pointed it at a circular pad to the right of a thick steel door. A light shone green and a loud grinding sound as though a thousand metal bolts were rotating could be heard. Slowly, the door inched open. 'I call this The Time Room.'

Becky gasped loudly. She was staring at a cavernous room with high white walls lined with towering stacks of computers, their monitors displaying endless streams of numerical data. Above each screen were hundreds of soundless clocks, each reading different times. A metal spiral staircase led to a raised platform that overlooked the large, empty space in the middle of the room.

'This-is-ace,' Joe said, enthralled.

'Do you think so?' Uncle Percy said. 'The lower levels are much more impressive.'

Becky glanced at Joe. Lower levels?

Uncle Percy led them up the stairs. Stopping at a computer terminal, he spoke into a microphone, 'Percy Mathias Halifax. TT98.'

An automated voice spoke back: 'Embarkation procedure initiated. Today's password...'

'Sagacious Sprouts,' Uncle Percy replied.

The workstation burst into life. Immediately, the beaming face of a middle-aged woman with long, curly auburn hair and rather too much lipstick appeared on the monitor.

'Well, well, stranger,' the woman said brightly. 'I've not seen you for a few weeks.'

'Good morning, Annabel.' Uncle Percy flashed her a wide smile. 'Love the new look. My compliments to your stylist.'

'Thank you very much,' Annabel said, coiling a lock of hair between her fingers. 'You're positively the first TT to notice.'

'Well, the rest of them are too blind to see anything in the present.'

'How very true,' Annabel replied. 'Anyway, what can I do for you today?'

'I'd like to log a trip, please.'

'No problem,' Annabel typed something onto a keyboard. 'Is it just you or is Will going too?'

'No Will today. However, my niece and nephew will be joining me.'

'Becky and Joe?' Annabel said, sounding shocked.

Uncle Percy motioned for Becky and Joe to join him. 'Come, meet Annabel Mullins – heart, soul and if I may so bold as to say, the gorgeous face of the travelling community.'

Annabel's already blushed face went a deeper shade of pink. 'Oh, shut up, Halifax, you old dog. Hi, kids. I've been so longing to meet the two of you.'

'Hi, Annabel,' Joe said.

'Err, hello,' Becky said.

Annabel noted the look of surprise on Becky's face. 'Don't look so shocked, Becky. I knew you were staying at Bowen Hall for the summer – it's all your uncle's been talking about for months. In fact, he's been more excited about your visit than I've seen since he invented the Dungwamblefigger, or something equally ridiculous as that.'

'The Duncloxifier, my dear,' Uncle Percy corrected her. 'And I'll have you know that it's quite an innovative contraption if you're interested in Flimpostatic imuldification.'

'Yes, but who is?' Annabel replied with an impish grin. She looked at Becky and Joe. 'Anyway, I've only ever seen photographs of you but you're both much more lovely in person.'

'Thank you,' Becky said.

'Cheers,' Joe said.

'It's my pleasure,' Annabel said sincerely, before turning back to Uncle Percy and saying, 'So much for you saying you wouldn't be introducing them to time travel this summer, eh?'

Uncle Percy looked rather awkward. 'I'm afraid my plans changed when they discovered me performing some dental work on Milly last night, rapidly followed by Keith

Pickleton's arrival in his magical milk float. I'm afraid even I couldn't talk myself out of that one.'

Annabel laughed. 'I see. Well, Percy, where are you taking them today?'

'Timeline 14, sector 2, coordinates 10 - 10 - 79.'

'Not there again,' Annabel replied. 'I swear one day you'll go there and never come back.' She inputted the data and a buzzing sound rang out; what looked like a fat cube of jet-black marble fell into a slot beneath the monitor.

'Many thanks, Annabel. Please pass on my best to your husband and cheerio.'

Becky and Joe exchanged their farewells with Annabel, and Uncle Percy logged off the terminal and picked up the strange-looking block.

'What's that?' Joe asked.

'This, Joe, is Gerathnium. It's the power source that makes time travel possible. It's very rare. That's why we keep it stored at a central base, ready for distribution to travellers across the world.'

'A central base?' Becky said inquisitively.

'At GITT headquarters.'

'GITT?' Becky laughed.

'It is rather amusing, isn't it?' Uncle Percy chuckled. 'Henry Locket came up with the acronym. It stands for the Global Institute for Time Travel. It's a worldwide organisation for the regulation, sanctioning and coordination of all travelling activity. In actual fact, the Institute fulfills many functions.'

'Like what?' Joe said.

'Well, primarily, it ensures the safety and welfare of the travelling community. For instance, if a traveller gets stuck in time, for whatever reason, it can send someone to fetch them. It's a very big operation.'

'How come no one knows about it?' Becky asked.

'The Institute goes to great lengths to maintain its anonymity. You see, time travel is potentially the most destructive power that the world has ever known. That is why, today more than ever, it must remain secret. For that reason you can't mention this to anyone.'

'We understand,' Becky said.

'So who wants to go back in time?' Uncle Percy asked.

Becky and Joe eagerly nodded their agreement.

'Why have you got five time machines?' Joe asked.

'Each one is a different type of vehicle, for different types of trip. Today, I think we'll use Bertha. She's my favourite.' He clapped his hands twice and said in a loud, steady voice, 'Activate Bertha.' All at once, the ground rumbled beneath them; the walls vibrated gently. 'You might want to watch this.'

Becky and Joe raced to the banister. Their eyes widened as the Time Room floor separated in the middle and began to disappear into the wall. Something was emerging from the level below. A few moments later the floor had been completely replaced by a revolving platform. Standing on it, gleaming under the strips lights was a green and white campervan.

'My lovely Bertha,' Uncle Percy said as if introducing an old and very dear friend.

Becky's jaw dropped open.

Joe, on the other hand looked slightly disappointed.

Uncle Percy noticed. 'She might not look much, Joe, but I've made plenty of minor modifications.'

Becky couldn't help but smile. She remembered only too well the last time Uncle Percy had made minor modifications to a vehicle.

Uncle Percy descended the steps, and ran his hand fondly across Bertha's bodywork. 'You see most travellers build their time machines out of their favourite vehicles. Mine happens to be the 1963 Volkswagen Campervan.' He inserted the Gerathnium into a slot to the rear the van and slid open its door. 'Come on.'

Becky and Joe clambered in and sat opposite each other. Uncle Percy closed the door and climbed in the front, settling himself onto the driver's seat. He leaned over to the dashboard and typed a destination code onto a small keypad. Almost immediately, the campervan rumbled, shuddering as a surge of power resonated beneath them.

'Nervous?' Uncle Percy asked.

'Excited,' Joe replied.

'And you, Becky?'

Becky's heart threatened to burst through her chest. 'Terrified.' Her knuckles clung tightly to a handrail below the window.

Uncle Percy nodded kindly. 'Don't worry. I've done this more times than I care to remember.'

'So where are we going?' Joe shouted over the escalating noise.

Uncle Percy grinned. 'Kansas.'

'And when?' Joe pressed.

Before Uncle Percy could reply, fizzy blue and white light spilled from the front panel. Becky clamped her eyes shut. All of a sudden, twisting torrents of light surrounded them, extending to every inch of Bertha's interior. Becky covered her ears, bracing herself for the explosion she knew would come.

And with a BOOM, Bertha disappeared.

Chapter 8

Otto Kruger

In a fraction of a second it was over. Becky forced open her eyes and stared at Joe, disorientated and somewhat disappointed. She'd expected more. Other than a flashy light show and a loud bang nothing else suggested they weren't still in the Time Room at Bowen Hall. That was until – splat - an enormous dragonfly careered into the window. Looking round, she saw they were in a thick bushy glade, enveloped by soaring trees that stabbed the sky.

Uncle Percy turned to face them. 'You are now officially time travellers - unregistered, of course.'

'And we're in Kansas?' Joe asked.

'We most certainly are.'

'When?' Becky asked.

'Let's just say the Big Mac won't exist for another twelve thousand years.'

'T-twelve thousand years?' Becky spluttered.

'Wow,' Joe gushed.

'Wow, indeed, Joe,' Uncle Percy said, grabbing his backpack. 'Welcome to the last Ice Age - the Pleistocene epoch, to be precise.' He opened the door and stepped on to the soft, damp turf. Sliding Bertha's side door open, he said, 'Now, whatever you do, no wandering off.'

'Err, why?' Becky's eyes flicked to the undergrowth. 'It's not dangerous, is it?'

'No, but it is we who are out of our time. You just have to be careful.'

'Careful of what?'

'Well, it is a forest. Forests have animals. But don't worry - '

'What kind of animals?'

'Mostly the harmless kind, but -'

Becky was getting alarmed now. '- But?'

'But you may get the odd snake, wild boar, grizzly bear and …' - his voice dropped to something of a mumble - '… Sabre-tooth tiger.'

'Sabre-tooth tiger!' Becky exclaimed.

'It's the Ice Age, what do you expect?' Uncle Percy shrugged. 'Don't worry, you've met Milly and - '

'But Milly's your pet! She's tame, and -' Becky's voice rose to fever pitch. '- And this is the wild!'

'Stop being such a wuss,' Joe said, earning himself a twanged ear.

'Wild and wonderful!' Uncle Percy said with a smile.

Suddenly Becky wasn't quite so sure as to what was so wonderful about it.

*

The moment Bertha left the Time Room, a cold and unusually heavy wind swept the shingled path behind Bowen Hall kitchens. A violent explosion of swirling scarlet light cut the air and a huge coal-black Daimler car appeared. Four heavily built men sat in it, each wearing a finely tailored suit and floor-length, leather trench coat, their emotionless faces masked behind black, steel-rimmed sunglasses.

Otto Kruger stepped out of the time machine with surprising elegance for a man of his size. Standing six foot five inches tall, with icy green eyes and a pale, square-jawed face, he was perhaps the most fearsome looking man to step foot in the grounds of Bowen Hall.

Kruger surveyed the lawns. The information he'd received had been correct: the groundsman and the Sabre-tooth cat were in the outermost field. Good. If truth were told, he wasn't sure why his employer had warned him about the groundsman, no matter whom he was or claimed to be. There wasn't a man, woman or child he couldn't kill if he wanted to. And he'd had plenty of practice.

Still, he had received his orders and killing the groundsman wasn't one of them. It would therefore not happen. Not today, anyway. And that was precisely why his employer had sought him out and recruited him. Otto Kruger always followed orders.

As he moved towards the Hall, Kruger felt extremely pleased with himself. The plan was finally moving forward. Furthermore, for the second time in his life his orders came from a man he truly respected. And the rewards when the plan was complete - well, they were more than he could have ever dared imagine.

Yes, if the artifact were here, at Bowen Hall, then he would certainly find it. And nothing and nobody could stop him.

*

'But, Jacob, they are children,' Maria pressed, angrily jabbing a feather duster at a rather fragile looking vase. 'This is too much danger for them. They are too young. They are too special.'

Jacob winced. He knew only too well the vase was over a thousand years old. But he also knew that there was no point enraging his wife further.

'And they are babies, just babies,' Maria continued, lip quivering. 'And this silly travelling may get them killed.'

'The master would never let them come to any harm,' Jacob replied. 'He is the wisest of men. He knows what he is doing.'

'Pah!' Maria huffed. 'All of this bad, terrible business with Mr Preston has jumbled his brain, I think. He hardly sleeps … he works like a mule… his thinking is wonky.'

'He is fine, Maria.'

Maria was about to contradict when she saw something in the corner of her eye. She stopped dead, her insides ablaze as if doused in boiling oil.

'Guten Morgen,' Otto Kruger said without emotion. 'We meet again, so I believe. Now you will tell me where the children sleep or I will kill you like dogs as I should have in our former lives.'

Maria turned pale, then deathly white. She was staring at the devil himself.

An ugly smile curled on Kruger's lips as he pointed a pistol at Jacob's head.

Chapter 9

A Mammoth Event

'Let me show you the real reason we're here,' Uncle Percy said.

Becky looked at Joe and gave a glum shrug. They had been walking through dense jungle for some time and seen nothing vaguely interesting. If truth be told, she was bored stiff.

'Just through here,' Uncle Percy said, disappearing through a gap in the trees.

Becky followed. As she emerged from the other side, sunlight blinded her. When her eyes adjusted, she found herself on the top of a cliff overlooking a vast canyon at the base of which were thousands of large animals, covered with long, shaggy, dusty-brown hair and huge curved tusks.

'A - are they woolly mammoths?' Joe asked, astonished.

'They are indeed. I call it Mammoth Gorge. Do you like it?'

'It's amazing,' Joe replied. 'Isn't it, Becky?'

Becky said nothing.

'Are you all right, Becky?' Uncle Percy asked.

She remained silent.

'Becky?' Uncle Percy repeated, sounding anxious now. Then his face cracked into a knowing smile.

Tears were spilling down Becky's face. 'I'm okay,' she slurred, turning away so Joe couldn't see.

Uncle Percy leaned into her ear and whispered, 'It's quite all right, my dear. That's exactly how I reacted when I first saw it...'

*

A few minutes later, Uncle Percy spread a picnic blanket on the ground and emptied the contents of his backpack. 'I trust everyone's hungry? Maria's laid on quite a spread.'

They launched into the food with gusto, and then lay on their backs, watching condors weave the velvet blue sky. Soon, the only sound that could be heard was the soft, rhythmic purr of Joe sleeping.

Becky saw this as an ideal opportunity to raise something that had been bothering her. 'Who's Bernard Preston?'

Uncle Percy sat up sharply. 'What?'

'That Keith bloke last night mentioned something about Bernard Preston's murder and a manuscript. I was wondering who he was. It's just... I'm sure I've heard that name before.'

'Well, it's a common name, but it's unlikely you'll know this Bernard Preston. Remember when I said that at Oxford, Professor Locket told my class about the existence of time travel?'

'Yes.'

'Bernard Preston was one of that group.' Uncle Percy arched his eyebrows, as if welcoming the opportunity to reminisce. 'There were nine of us in total: myself, Bernard, Stef Calloway, Mary Blyton, Emerson Drake, Ricardo Nero, Malcolm Everidge, Ian Cuthbertson, and Sally Everard. We called ourselves The OTTERS - The Oxford Time Travel Exploration and Research Society.'

'And are they all time travellers?'

'They certainly were. Malcolm, Ian and Sally are still active. Unfortunately, Emerson Drake was killed in a plane accident. Stef passed away quite some time ago. Ricardo died last year, and Mary stopped travelling when her children were born. And then, of course, there was Bernard.'

'And how was he…' Becky hesitated, 'killed?'

Uncle Percy fell silent. 'He was shot in the back.'

'And you're trying to find out who shot him?'

'Something like that.'

'So how does the manuscript fit in?'

'It's related to something I believe he was working on.'

'And what was that?'

'You really are an inquisitive young lady, aren't you?'

'Mum reckons I'm just plain nosey,' Becky replied. 'And that I get it from my dad.'

Uncle Percy nodded. 'Yes. I believe you do. Anyway, Bernard was searching for something … searching through time.'

'What?'

Uncle Percy hesitated for a moment, his voice lowered to a whisper. 'A relic. A very old, very important, very powerful relic.'

'What relic?'

Uncle Percy tilted forwards, his eyes meeting hers. 'The Golden Fleece.'

Becky had to suppress a laugh. The Golden Fleece – she'd heard of it, of course. In fact, it was one of her dad's favourite stories, one he would often recite to her at bedtime. It was about a man called Jason who gathered fifty of Ancient Greece's mightiest warriors, the Argonauts, and embarked on a dangerous quest to find the Golden Fleece, fighting dragons and other monsters along the way. 'But wasn't the Golden Fleece just a -'

'A fairy story? A myth?' Uncle Percy interrupted. 'That's certainly what I thought until I studied Bernard's research. No, incredible though it may seem, there is quite compelling evidence to suggest that the Fleece existed.'

Becky wanted to continue her questions when a croaky voice interjected.

'Any more butties left?' Joe said, yawning.

'I think you've polished them off, young man,' Uncle Percy said, glancing at his fob watch. 'Deary me, is that the time? I think we'd better be getting back.'

But Becky didn't want to go home yet. She wasn't nearly satisfied. How could she be? A murder. A mysterious document. A search through history for a fabulous relic. She needed to know more. As her mum always said, she was plain nosey.

Just like her dad.

*

The campervan reappeared back in the Time Room, the return journey being as uneventful as the outward one. No headaches, no travel sickness, no Elton John CDs – as far as Becky was concerned, it really was the only way to travel.

Walking back to the Hall, Joe talked excitedly about the trip, but Becky wasn't really listening. Instead, she was processing all she'd been told about The Golden Fleece and Bernard Preston's murder.

As they entered the kitchen door, Becky was about to dash to her room to start researching the Golden Fleece on her phone, when she noticed that Uncle Percy had come to an abrupt halt, his gaze set on the far wall. Fear engulfed her. 'What's going on, Uncle Percy?'

'Silence, please,' Uncle Percy said firmly, hand raised in a halting gesture.

Becky tracked his eye line to see a portrait on the far wall had been slashed from left to right, exposing the canvas beneath.

Becky glanced anxiously at Joe, who had frozen to the spot. Then, through the silence, she heard something. A crunching sound. Staring into the parlour, a shiver shot down her spine. A plastic shopping bag hung from the light fitting.

It was moving.

Straight away, Uncle Percy raced over, quickly detached it and ripped it open.

Appearing at his side, Becky felt sick to her stomach. Sabian was lying at the bottom of the bag, his jaws tied together with rope, wriggling like a fish in a net. She choked back a scream.

Uncle Percy untied the rope and wrenched Sabian to his chest, who yelped wildly with relief. 'There, there, little one ... everything's okay now.'

'W - who could've -?' Joe began.

'Shhh,' Uncle Percy said, handing the trembling cub to Becky. His face burned with anger. 'I want you both to take Sabian to the tree house. Find Will, I believe he's with Milly in the archery field. Tell him there's trouble. And wait there until I come and get you.'

'I'm not leaving you,' Becky said defiantly.

Uncle Percy shook his head firmly. 'Now's not the time for rebellion,' he replied decisively. 'You must do as I say. Get to the tree house. Tell Will I need him. And stay there. RUN!'

'But –'

'Please, Becky, Maria and Jacob could be in grave danger.'

Becky glanced fearfully at Joe. Although her every instinct told her not to leave Uncle Percy's side, she knew if there really was trouble he needed Will and Milly. Seizing Joe's arm, they raced off.

*

Watching them leave, Uncle Percy's face grew fierce. Marching through the parlour and down the passageway, he stopped midway at a sword hanging on the wall. Unsheathing it from its scabbard, he continued purposefully into the Entrance Hall and scanned the area. Nothing.

Then he heard something: a muffled whimper. It was coming from the morning room. The sword tightened in his grip and he paced over, and threw open the door.

What he saw repulsed him.

Maria and Jacob were lying on the floor, squirming, their hands, feet and mouths bound by thick rope. Uncle Percy hurried over and removed Maria's binds. In a flood of tears, she flung her arms around his neck.

'He is here. HE IS HERE!'

'Who's here?' Uncle Percy replied, moving over and untying Jacob.

'Otto Kruger,' Maria cried.

Uncle Percy's body stiffened. 'Otto Kruger?' he repeated, clearly recognising the name.

'And three others. They are after the children.'

'The children?' Uncle Percy said disbelievingly.

'Yes, sir,' Jacob said, taking his panic-stricken wife in his arms.

Uncle Percy struggled to catch his breath. 'Why the children?'

'He didn't say,' Jacob replied. 'But he wanted to know where they slept. You must take them at once. You must flee. This man is evil in its purest form.'

'I know only too well who Otto Kruger is, Jacob.' Uncle Percy stood up, the incredulity on his face replaced by rage. 'But no one is leaving. I can assure you of that.' And with that, he walked over to a chest of drawers on the far side of the room. He opened the top drawer and cupped two small objects into the palm of his hand. Then he sharply moved towards the door.

Jacob looked petrified. 'Sir, they have guns.'

Uncle Percy didn't blink an eye. 'Guns are for amateurs...' And with that, he sharply exited the room.

Swiftly, Uncle Percy went from door to door, checking each room, but found each one empty. Then he heard footsteps. Whipping round, sword raised, he saw Will emerge from the passageway, his bow and quiver of arrows across his back, a sword in his right hand.

'I was in the far field,' Will said. 'I heard nothing.'

'Not to worry, Will,' Uncle Percy said. 'I'm glad you're here. There are four of them. They'll be well-armed.' Then, to his frustration, he saw three familiar shapes race into the Entrance Hall. Becky and Joe stood there, panting, Milly at their side. 'I thought I told you to stay at the tree-house.'

'We wanted to help,' Becky said.

'That's right,' Joe added.

Uncle Percy's expression softened. 'Then go and comfort Maria and Jacob in the morning room. They've been through a terrible ordeal.' He turned back to Will. 'I've checked the downstairs rooms. Let's try upstairs. If we're lucky, they're still here. Just remember, Will. They're very dangerous.'

Fury crossed Will's face. 'As am I.'

Uncle Percy moved swiftly upstairs, Will to his rear. They stole down the corridor, and promptly stopped.

Becky's bedroom door was ajar. In a flash, he kicked the door open. His eyes bulged. The room had been ransacked. Bed linen had been torn and strewn on the floor, pillows ripped apart, drawers emptied, cabinets overturned, clothes and jewellery scattered everywhere.

But there was no sign of Kruger.

Will left the room, only to return moments later. 'Joe's chamber has been ravaged, too.'

Uncle Percy stood there, confused, speechless. He surveyed the chaos, desperately trying to make sense of what had happened. The intruders had looted Becky and Joe's rooms. But why?

For the next hour, Uncle Percy and Will scoured the rest of the Hall looking for clues that would explain why Kruger had broken into the Hall. They found no other damage, with the exception of a painting that had been ripped from the banquet room wall and impaled on a figurine. A portrait of the German industrialist responsible for saving over a thousand Jews in the Second World War, and one of the finest men Uncle Percy had ever met.

It was a portrait of Oskar Schindler.

*

By early evening Becky and Joe had searched their rooms thoroughly to find nothing had been taken. At seven, everyone gathered in the parlour. It was a chilly night and a shocked Maria sat by the fire, shivering, her blank eyes locked on the dancing flames, a thick woollen blanket coiled tightly round her shoulders. Jacob sat alongside his wife, stroking her hands tenderly. Will stood by the window, clearly furious the intruders had escaped.

Becky was sitting at the table, her gaze fixed on the wall. After a few minutes of confused silence, she spoke, 'Why us? Why our rooms?'

'I don't know, Becky,' Uncle Percy said softly. 'I really don't. But there is one thing I do know: it's not safe for you here. I'll phone your mother and drive you back to Manchester tonight.'

Becky looked mortified. 'No way. We want to stay here. Don't we, Joe?'

Joe nodded. 'Too right.'

'But it's not safe,' Uncle Percy said. 'There are things happening that I can't -'

'We don't care,' Becky said. 'We want to stay with you!'

'I'm sorry, but if Otto Kruger and his thugs are -'

Becky interjected. '- Are after us, then we're best staying here.'

'I don't think they are after you. I don't see how they can be.'

Becky sat up sharply. 'Well they were after something. And that something was in our rooms, right?'

'It appears so.' Uncle Percy sighed. 'That's why you should be at home with -'

'With who, mum?' Becky interrupted. 'What's she going to do if they turn up, hit them with a baguette? Here we've got you to protect us, and Will, and a prehistoric tiger with massive fangs. Back home we've got no one.'

Uncle Percy's eyes searched out Will's, eager for advice. Will deliberated for a few seconds, and then nodded coolly. Uncle Percy turned back to Becky. 'Very well, you can stay.'

Becky beamed at Joe.

'What do you think they were looking for?' Joe asked.

'I'm afraid, Joe, I have absolutely no idea.'

'It's to do with the Golden Fleece, isn't it?' Becky said sharply.

A tense silence swept the kitchen.

'The Golden Fleece?' Joe blurted. 'What're you talking ab - '

'Shhh,' Becky snapped back. 'It is, isn't it?'

Uncle Percy hesitated for a moment. 'It may be. Although for the life of me I can't imagine what.'

'I knew it!' Becky said, sounding triumphant.

'Knew what?' Joe barked. 'Will somebody tell me what is going on.'

Uncle Percy gave a heavy sigh. 'Perhaps we should go to the library, and I'll tell you all I know.'

Maria spun round, trembling with anger. 'Sir … NO!'

'Maria,' Uncle Percy said calmly. 'Otto Kruger came looking for something. Something, it seems that concerns Becky or Joe. Now you know Kruger better than anyone, and the horrors he's capable of, it's only fair they know what we know. Who knows, they may even be able to help…'

Chapter 10

Bowen Library

Becky had never entered Bowen library before. A sprawling room on the top floor, it had tall walls and an ornate rococo ceiling. Thick with dust, a stale smell emanated through the room. She had the feeling it was the one room she'd seen that was off-limits to Maria's thorough cleaning regime. Books of all shapes and sizes, old and new, filled the bookshelves, with the uppermost tiers occupied by ancient ragged scrolls, coiled up, and tied with string.

Uncle Percy ushered Becky and Joe to a large, circular table in the centre of the room. He moved to a corner shelf, pulled out a thick leather bound volume and returned to the table. 'Where to begin?' He placed the book down on his right. 'About a month ago, a good friend of mine, Bernard Preston, turned up at the Hall. He'd been shot and was dying. Now according to his time machine, he had travelled to London on the 15th January 1900. Upon examining the bullet, however, it was clear that the gun from which it was fired was not made until many years later. Therefore, he had to have been murdered by a time traveller.'

The words made Becky shiver.

'Now just before he died, he told me to see someone named Aubrey. Later, I discovered he was referring to the seventeenth century writer and antiquarian, John Aubrey. Now, Aubrey's specific area of expertise was Stonehenge. You've heard of Stonehenge?'

'Of course,' Becky said.

'I went there with the school.' Joe crumpled his nose. 'It was naff.'

Uncle Percy shot Joe a disapproving look. 'I assure you, Joe. Stonehenge is far from naff. In fact, I believe somehow the monument lies at the very heart of this mystery. Anyway, I visited Aubrey, and he told me that Bernard had indeed been to see him to discuss a legend associated with Stonehenge.'

'What legend?' Becky asked excitedly.

'Well, as you may know, Stonehenge took hundreds of years to build. Anyway, there is an ancient legend that states that when it was finished, God was so delighted he rewarded its makers with a powerful object. A divine object.'

'The Golden Fleece,' Becky said.

'Precisely. Now, of course, stories like this are common throughout history, and more often than not are total poppycock. I didn't see why this one would be any different. That was until I scrutinized his research. His investigations, both academic and in the field, have convinced me that the legend was indeed based on some semblance of fact. To what extent, I'm not sure, but I am in no doubt that the Golden Fleece existed. You've heard of the Golden Fleece, Joe?"

'Course,' Joe said, 'Dad used to read it to me. It's an awesome story.'

Uncle Percy continued. 'Yes, it is. Anyway, as Stonehenge was finished so long ago, before recorded time, no one knows precisely when it was completed, or indeed who completed it.'

'Couldn't you just use the time machine and go and get it,' Becky said.

'To do that, you would need an exact date, time, location and who it was presented to. I have none of these. Anyway, Bernard believed, as with the popular legend, it was taken to Ancient Greece. But he had no idea as to where or when. So he started investigating more contemporary sources.'

Uncle Percy pulled the book closer. He pressed three letters on the padded cover and the book's title illuminated red. Suddenly a bookshelf creaked open, exposing a compact wall safe concealed behind it. Becky and Joe looked at each other in astonishment. Uncle Percy approached the safe and typed nine digits into a keypad. The safe door sprang open.

From what little Becky could see, the safe contained tattered documents, an old watch, a necklace, a small non-descript wooden box, rolled up blueprints and other assorted valuables, but Uncle Percy closed the door before she could get a better look. He returned carrying just two items: a scrap of paper and an object wrapped in cloth. He passed Becky the piece of paper. 'I found this note in Bernard's pocket.'

A.J E
17 Cromwell Gardens

6768956665
SS?

Uncle Percy studied Becky and Joe's enthralled faces. 'I believe A.J.E. to be the initials of the Victorian archaeologist, Arthur John Evans. Now, Evans lived in Oxford, but he did keep a place in London. The address is that of Evans' apartment in Westminster.'

'And what about the numbers?' Becky asked.

'I believe they're the combination to his wall safe. To cut a long story short, knowing Evans was in Oxford at the time, I believe Bernard broke into number 17 Cromwell Gardens, found the safe and stole its contents.'

'And what was in the safe?' Joe asked eagerly.

Uncle Percy lifted the package. 'This.' He removed the cloth to reveal an orange disc about seven inches in diameter.

'What is it?' Becky asked, engrossed.

'I don't know. The metal is unlike any I've seen. The marks, well, they bear no resemblance to anything I can find in history. This disc is a true enigma.'

'So where did Arthur Evans get it?' Becky asked.

Uncle Percy shrugged. 'Much of this is speculation, but I know for a fact that in January 1900 he'd recently returned from an archaeological dig at Knossos on Crete. Perhaps he found it there. Anyway, as well as being an archeologist he was also the curator of Oxford's world-renowned

Ashmolean Museum. And that's where I'm going tomorrow, to January 16th 1900, to talk to him about it.'

'Can we come?' Becky said immediately.

Uncle Percy walked to the far side of the room and stared out of the window.

Becky could see he was struggling to give his consent. 'We're involved now, whether you like it or not,' she said. 'It was our rooms that were done over.'

Uncle Percy continued gazing into space. As the seconds passed by, Becky glanced anxiously at Joe. Then she watched as her uncle's mouth edged open. 'I suppose it may benefit your education to see Victorian England.'

Becky and Joe gaped at each other. They were going on another journey in time, to meet Arthur Evans and to find out about the mysterious disc.

Uncle Percy returned the disc to the wall safe, when Becky remembered something. 'Uncle Percy, on the note, what do the letters 'SS' mean?'

Uncle Percy's expression grew solemn. 'Well, I'm still not completely sure, but judging by today's events I think we may have found our answer. You've heard of a rather notorious figure called Adolf Hitler?'

'Er, yeah,' Becky said sarcastically.

'The SS, or the Schutzstaffel, were originally formed as Hitler's personal guards. One of the men who broke into the Hall today was Otto Kruger, a founding member of the SS, and one of Hitler's most brutal bodyguards. In fact, Kruger was so notorious for his cruelty, his ruthlessness, and his unwavering loyalty to the Nazi Party he ended up being so powerful he only took orders from Hitler himself.

I know for a fact he was personally responsible for sixteen murders on June 30th 1934; a diabolical night in German history infamously known as 'The Night of The Long Knives.' Obviously I won't go into details of his atrocities, but let me just say that even the most high-powered members of the Nazi Party were afraid of Otto Kruger.'

Becky had turned white. 'So what happened to him? Why is he in our time? And what on earth was he doing tearing our rooms apart?'

'I'm afraid I can't answer any of those questions. All I do know is that Otto Kruger disappeared sometime in the summer of 1940 and was never heard of again. Until now, that is…'

Chapter 11

A Victorious Revelation

The following morning, Becky stared jadedly at the mountain of eggs and buttered toast piled high on her plate. She had hardly slept. Despite Uncle Percy's appeals not to research Kruger, she had found a black and white photo of him on the net and his face had plagued her all night.

At that moment, Uncle Percy breezed into the kitchen dressed in a single-breasted morning coat and glossy black top hat, a walking cane tucked securely beneath his arm. 'Morning all,' he said brightly. 'Wonderful day, isn't it?'

Maria glared at him. Joe had told her about the trip to Victorian Oxford and she'd been smashing crockery ever since.

'Morning.' Joe glanced up. 'You look great'

'Thought I'd better look the part,' Uncle Percy said, kissing a growling Maria on the cheek. 'Now, are you both ready to try on your costumes?'

A wave of nausea passed over Becky. Going back in time was one thing but wearing a daft costume was another thing altogether.

Minutes later, Becky and Joe followed their Uncle to the morning room where they saw two very different outfits laid out for them. Becky stared at hers in horror: a brown and white striped cotton dress, cream bonnet with matching woollen shawl and parasol. Her throat dried up.

Uncle Percy noticed her shock. 'Well, Becky. If one wishes to venture in time, one must dress as others dress.'

'I AM NOT WEARING THAT!' Becky roared, as Joe giggled loudly. She spun round to face him. 'I don't know what you're laughing at? Those are knickerbockers. You'll look more like a girl than me.'

Joe shrugged. 'Don't care.'

'Well, if you wish to accompany Will and me this is exactly what you will wear,' Uncle Percy said cheerily. 'It is not open to debate.'

'Will's coming?' Becky asked.

'Yes.' Uncle Percy bent forward and whispered, 'Between you and me, he's not particularly happy with his apparel either.'

At that moment Becky heard a shuffling sound. Will entered the room, head down. He wore a brown suit, wide britches and knee-high stockings. His long hair was tied in a bun under a cloth cap and he carried a silver ball handled cane. His sullen expression spoke volumes.

Becky choked back a burst of laughter.

'Ready?' Will muttered.

Uncle Percy winked at Becky. 'When Becky and Joe are dressed, William.'

Minutes later, Becky paced her room. As far as she could remember, she'd never worn a dress in her life, and didn't really want to start with one that made her look like a Cornetto. However, she dearly wanted to see Victorian

England and if this was the price she had to pay, so be it. She began to dress.

As the clock rang eleven, Uncle Percy, Will and Joe gathered at the foot of the staircase in the Entrance Hall. Joe wore a black jacket, baggy blue short trousers and a rather gnarled black cap (Gump and Sabian had taken it in turns to nibble at it.)

As the clock finished chiming, they heard movement from above and Becky appeared, stomping noisily down the stairs. She glared at Joe, who was on the verge of laughing. 'If you say a word, I'll strangle you with your own knickerbockers.'

Uncle Percy ignored her outburst, his face glittering with pride. 'You look quite beautiful, my dear.'

'I look like a bog roll with legs!'

'No, Miss Becky,' Will said. 'You look enchanting.'

Becky felt a sudden rush of blood to her cheeks. Maybe the dress wasn't so awful, after all.

*

Although it was an extremely muggy day, the Time Room felt cool and fresh as an eager Becky watched Bertha emerged from the lower levels. She turned to Uncle Percy, who inserted a small cube of Gerathnium into the time machine. 'If we're only going back a hundred years, what are we going to do with Bertha? She'll stand out like a sore thumb.'

'I'm glad you asked me that, Becky,' Uncle Percy replied. 'All time machines are equipped with a standard Invisiblator. Observe…' He withdrew a device from his trouser pocket and pressed a button marked with the letter 'I'. At once, Bertha vanished.

'Whoa!' Joe exclaimed.

'It's invisible,' Becky panted.

'Indeed,' Uncle Percy said, rapping his knuckles against where Bertha's doors used to be. A resounding metallic clank echoed through the room. 'The effect is achieved using a series of expandent mirrors and nanocameras that record and broadcast the immediate area around the machine. It's the image playback that gives the illusion of invisibility. It's rather old technology, but still effective.' He pressed the button again and the campervan reappeared. 'Anyway, best make tracks. Next stop - the Ashmolean Museum, Oxford, 16th January, 1900…'

*

Bertha materialised in a narrow side street. Thick snow shrouded the deserted street and a scrawny black cat clawed a dead mouse in the gutter. The cat glanced up at the campervan, temporarily puzzled, but then turned back to its lifeless quarry.

'Out, please.' Uncle Percy opened the door and retrieved the Invisiblator remote. 'Quick as you can.' He leapt out. Everybody followed.

Straightening his hat, Uncle Percy pressed the 'I' button and the campervan disappeared. Pulling out his fob watch, he turned to the waiting group. 'It's due to snow again in precisely forty-eight minutes, so we need to return by then otherwise there'll be a campervan shaped snowman.'

Becky's first thought was that Victorian Oxford didn't seem much different from any modern city, until they entered the main street and saw a wooden cart, brimming with coal, being drawn by a gigantic shire horse. Dozens of people trudged the long, bustling road, some in formal attire, others wearing little more than rags. A red-haired woman with a dirt-stained face shivered on the street corner, clutching a bucket brimming with wilted flowers.

A short while later, Uncle Percy stopped and pointed at a very grand building. 'The Ashmolean Museum.'

Becky glanced at Will, whose eyes were bright and alert, flitting in all directions. She noticed he maintained an unusually firm grip on his walking cane.

Entering the high doors, Uncle Percy strode purposefully to the front desk. Finding it deserted, he slapped a brass bell, which sent a echoing clang through the large, airy lobby. A middle-aged woman scrambled from a door behind the counter. 'I'm sorry, I just -'

'No matter, dear lady,' Uncle Percy said in an unusually pompous voice. 'I'm Colonel Igidor Puffbury from the Royal Academy of Antiquities. I have an appointment with Arthur Evans regarding his recent excavation at Knossos.'

Becky held back a giggle.

The woman stared at Uncle Percy blankly. Placing her glasses on the tip of her crooked nose, she opened a leather bound volume to her left. 'You do, sir?' She studied a page carefully. 'Colonel Puffbury, you say? I'm afraid I don't seem to have- '

'Nevermind,' Uncle Percy said, with a flick of his hand. 'Arthur and I go way back. It's this way, isn't it?' Before the woman could protest, he was leading the others down a winding passageway with a succession of wooden doors on either side. Seconds later, they were standing beside a thick oak door with a polished brass sign that read Arthur J Evans, Chief Curator. Uncle Percy knocked vigorously on the door.

Arthur Evans sat behind his mahogany desk, polishing a ceramic figurine with a worn brown cloth. Evans, a slim, affable looking man with a thick moustache and short, curly brown hair tinged with flecks of grey, looked up, surprised. 'Come in!' He set the figurine down.

Uncle Percy opened the door and marched into the room.

Becky noticed a strong smell of stale tobacco as she followed.

Arthur Evans looked up. 'Can I help you?'

'Good morning, Mr Evans,' Uncle Percy said. 'I'm Colonel Igidor Puffbury.'

'Good morning, Colonel Puffbury,' Evans said, slightly bewildered.

'May I introduce you to my manservant, Shakelock.' Uncle Percy nodded at Will, who glared back at him. 'And my two charges, Rebecca and Joe.'

'Hey up,' Joe grinned.

'Hiya,' Becky said.

Evans didn't really know what to say. 'Err, hello to you all,' he said. 'I'm afraid I wasn't expecting you.'

'Well, you wouldn't be, Mr Evans. I never make appointments because I never like to break them. And I'm such a busy fellow I surely would.' Uncle Percy nodded at the figurine. 'Wonderful piece you have there. A Cycladic statuette of Amorgos unless I'm very much mistaken. One of your finds?'

'Y-Yes,' Evans replied, surprised. 'How did you -'

'I'm in the game,' Uncle Percy said nonchalantly. 'As a matter of fact, that's why we're here.' He withdrew the disc and positioned it carefully on the table. 'I was wondering if you could tell me anything about this.'

Evans' brow furrowed as he picked up the disc. 'W-w-where did you get this?' he stammered. He pulled an eyepiece from his jacket pocket and fixed it over his right eye.

'Cairo. I was leading a dig there.'

'Cairo, you say?' Evans said sounding astonished. 'But this is amazing. I have an identical piece. It's at my apartment in London waiting for a metallurgist friend of mine to examine it.'

'Really?' Uncle Percy said, feigning surprise. 'What an astonishing coincidence. And, if I may be so bold, where did you find yours?'

'At Knossos. On the island of Crete,' Evans replied, flipping the disc over and allowing his fingers to glide over the surface markings. 'This is quite remarkable. I thought mine was unique.'

'Knossos, you say? Where exactly at Knossos?'

'It was lying on the bed of a lagoon.'

'How interesting,' Uncle Percy said. 'And where was this lagoon?'

Evans removed his eyepiece. 'I found a tunnel that connects the city of Knossos to the Aegean Sea. Anyway, there were dozens of caves leading from this tunnel, and the lagoon was in the largest of those caves.'

'Well, isn't that just fascinating,' Uncle Percy said.

'It's more than that,' Evans added. 'I believe the tunnel to be one of my most important discoveries.' He cleared his throat. 'You see, I actually believe – well, I believe the tunnel is the site that legend has termed The Labyrinth.' Evans broke eye contact and focused rather uncomfortably on his inkwell.

'The Labyrinth?' Uncle Percy expressed with genuine interest. 'As in the fabled location where Theseus slew the Minotaur?'

Becky heard Joe gasp. And she knew why - if memory served, Theseus was one of the fifty Argonauts that accompanied Jason in the search for the Golden Fleece. Could Theseus have actually existed?

'If you believe that kind of thing, yes.' Evans replied. 'That, in fact, is why I've named it The Theseus Disc. So you found your disc in Cairo; may I ask where?'

'In a pyramid,' Uncle Percy replied, rather unconvincingly. 'A very small pyramid occupied by a very minor Pharaoh.'

Becky had to stop herself from laughing.

'Really?' Evans said. 'Amazing.'

Uncle Percy smiled weakly. 'Anyway, any ideas as to the origin of your disc?'

'I'm afraid not,' Evans said. 'To my knowledge, these discs are like nothing found before. They bear no physical relation to any civilisation that has ever existed. The metal is unlike any I've encountered. The markings are utterly unique in any cultures I've encountered. It's safe to say this disc, and yours now, of course, may be the some of the most important finds in the history of archaeology.'

Becky stared at Evans and a wave of guilt swept through her. Arthur Evans appeared genuinely thrilled by his discovery. Yet he would never see that discovery again. He would never learn the disc's story. He would not be a part of its future.

The Theseus Disc would from now on only ever exist in his memory.

*

Becky, Joe, Will and Uncle Percy retraced their steps down the main road, satisfied expressions on their faces. Even Will had become more relaxed as they approached the time machine.

Becky had never seen Joe more animated.

'Theseus was an Argonaut, wasn't he?' Joe said excitedly.

'According to legend, yes, Joe.'

'And what was that about a Labyrinth?'

Uncle Percy smiled. 'It's another Greek myth. Theseus supposedly entered the Labyrinth, a kind of maze, which existed beneath King Minos' Palace and fought a creature called the Minotaur, a fearsome beast that terrorised the city of Knossos.'

'What type of beast?' Joe asked.

'A monster with the body of a man and the head of a bull,' Uncle Percy replied. 'The Minotaur was thought to be one of the fiercest beasts of the Ancient world. If you believe that sort of nonsense.'

'Have you seen one?'

'No-one's seen one, Joe. They never existed,' Uncle Percy replied. 'I doubt Theseus did either, or any of the so-called Argonauts, for that matter. Stories like this tend to blend fact, fiction, gossip, and good old-fashioned codswallop. However, I'll soon be able to tell you one way or the other.'

Becky's ears pricked up. 'How?'

'Because I'm going there,' Uncle Percy replied simply. 'And Will if he's up for it. What do you say, Will?'

Will gave a decisive nod. 'I would insist on it.'

'You're going to Ancient Crete?' Becky asked keenly.

'That's right.'

'Can we come, too?' Becky asked at once. When Uncle Percy didn't respond, she added, 'I mean … we've established we're safest with you.'

'That's right,' Joe agreed. 'And if we stay at Bowen Hall with you and Will gone, Kruger might break in again and hack Becky to bits. And you wouldn't want that would you?'

Becky frowned at Joe. 'All right, squidley. I think he gets the point.'

Joe ignored her. 'Then it would be your fault if he cut her head off and impaled it on one of Gump's horns.'

'Seriously,' Becky grumbled. 'Stop speaking.'

'Or if he sliced off her hands and –'

Uncle Percy had heard enough. 'That's quite enough, Joe,' he said. 'You really do have a disturbingly gruesome imagination, young man.'

'But it might happen if you didn't let us go with you,' Joe said. 'No, I think it's best for everyone if you take us with you, especially Becky.'

Uncle Percy looked troubled as he took out the remote and activated the Invisiblator. An instant later, Bertha appeared. Taking a long, pensive breath, he said, 'I don't know why you have to be so dramatic about everything, Joe. Of course you're both coming…'

*

As they boarded the campervan, not one of them noticed a tall, sallow-faced, middle-aged man studying them intently from across the road. Neither did they see the considerably taller, broader, younger man standing to his left.

The traveller's venomous blue eyes narrowed. Just looking at Percy Halifax sickened him to his core.

'He did bring the children,' Otto Kruger said. 'Just like you said he would.'

'Of course,' the traveller hissed. 'Halifax is as predictable as the tides. Unfortunately for him, I certainly am not.' He didn't even blink as the campervan vanished. He'd seen hundreds of them in operation. 'Now, let us pay this ridiculous curator a visit. I'd like to know precisely what was discussed.'

And Otto Kruger's powerful fingers curled round the dagger nestled in his overcoat pocket.

Chapter 12

Will and Marian

Becky awoke to find Sabian purring lightly at the foot of her bed. For a moment she lay there recalling the events of the previous day. Rolling to her left, she fully expected to see Joe in the spare bed moved to her room since the break-in, but it lay empty. Her first thought was a horrible one: he'd been abducted! She dismissed it at once. Not only had Milly been standing guard outside her bedroom door all night, but Uncle Percy had installed a series of security systems the previous night, which made it impossible for an unsanctioned time machine to materialise within the grounds of the Hall.

Still, where was he?

Becky dressed quickly and checked the bathroom and upstairs bedrooms. No sign. Hurrying downstairs, she checked the ground floor rooms. Nothing.

Finally, she marched through the parlour and into the kitchen, where she saw Jacob sitting on the doorstep, chipping mud from the soles of his boots. 'Jacob, have you seen Joe?'

'No, Miss Becky.' Jacob's kindly expression changed to one of worry when he saw her reaction. 'What's the matter, child?'

'Oh, nothing,' Becky replied. Then her gaze fell on to the half-eaten plate of sausages, bacon, egg and baked beans on the table. 'Is that Joe's plate?'

'I think so, Miss Becky,' Jacob replied. 'Tell me what's wrong?'

'What's wrong is there's food on it!' Becky was alarmed now. She had never seen Joe leave so much as a single bean on a plate, particularly at breakfast. Telling herself she was worrying needlessly, she marched out of the kitchen and crossed the rear path. Shielding her eyes from the brilliant sun, she scanned the area. He was nowhere to be seen. She ran to the front of the Hall. Still nothing. Feeling slightly anxious now, she was sprinting over to Will's tree house when, silhouetted against the turquoise sky, she spied two figures in the archery field: a boy wielding a bow and the distinctive outline of a three-horned dinosaur.

The relief that swept through her was replaced by anger. She stomped over to Joe, arms folded and barked, 'Why didn't you tell me you were up?'

At hearing her raised voice, Gump looked up, strands of grass dangling from his mouth like green spaghetti.

Joe looked confused. 'What?'

"Why didn't you tell me you were up? And why didn't you eat all your breakfast?'

'My breakfast? What's that got to do with anything?'

'You left your breakfast. I've never seen you do that before.'

'It was a third helping,' Joe said. 'Maria wouldn't let me leave the table until I couldn't physically move. Have you really come over here to yell at me for not finishing my sausages?'

Becky didn't know what to say to that. 'You should have let me know you were up, that's all I'm saying.'

'Why? What's it got to do with you?'

'I'm your big sister, and that means I'm your boss! And the other day a bunch of nutters trashed our rooms.' Her face turned red. 'SO IT'S GOT EVERYTHING TO DO WITH ME!'

'Don't get your knickers in a twist. I was here, and besides, you were snoring. I didn't want to wake you.' Facing the target, he positioned his fingers on the bowstring, pulled back and released. Whoosh. The arrow landed dead centre.

Becky was impressed at the shot. Her temper faded. 'I don't snore,' she mumbled. Then she heard another voice.

'Your aim is much improved…'

Becky whirled round to see Will emerging from the trees.

'I've still got a long way to go to be as good as you,' Joe replied.

'In time, young sir, you will better me, of that I am sure. Now, before you do each other harm, would you join me in a drink?'

'Yes, please,' Joe said.

'In the tree-house?' Becky asked eagerly. Unlike Joe, she had never been there before.

'Aye,' Will replied. 'I'd like you to meet an old friend of mine.'

Becky and Joe looked at each other, puzzled.

'Who?' Becky asked curiously.

'Why, the Lady Marian, of course…'

*

A few minutes later, deep in the forest, Becky and Joe were standing on a wooden platform at the base of an oak tree. Thick with age, its huge, gnarled roots clung to the ground like giant fingers. Becky looked up and marveled at the structure above; lodged between the tree's branches, the tree house was the size of a small bungalow. Will stood beside her, clasping a lever attached to a series of wheels, pulleys and ropes that scaled the trunk like vines.

'Ready?' Will asked.

Upon Becky's nod, the platform took to the air. Climbing higher, she grew breathless as the Hall, the lake, the maze and even the distant village of Addlebury unfolded before her. She followed Joe off the platform onto a spacious verandah, her eyes soaking up every bit of detail.

'So where's Marian?' Joe asked impatiently.

'I'll get her.' Will whistled loudly and looked over blanket of treetops that lined the horizon. A treetop stirred and, to Becky's surprise, a giant bird rose into the air.

'This -' Will said, '- this is Marian.'

Hiding her initial disappointment, Becky watched as the bird soared towards them. Extending its claws, it landed on the balcony rim and gave a triumphant yelp. Becky stepped backwards, stiff with fear.

'Do not be alarmed,' Will responded, as Marian pecked affectionately at his fingers. 'She will not harm you.'

'What kind of bird is she?' Joe asked.

'A Golden Eagle. Stroke her. She will approve.'

Becky and Joe gathered their courage and inched towards her, their hands outstretched, until they touched the eagle's neck.

'She's beautiful,' Becky said.

'Methinks she knows,' Will whispered.

Becky and Joe coddled Marian for a few minutes and then watched as she flew off into the forest. Will brought a jug of fresh apple juice and three goblets and together, they settled back to enjoy the cool morning air.

'Do you ever miss your own time?' Becky asked.

'I miss my friends,' Will replied without a hint of sadness. 'The untouched countryside, the purity of the air. It was a simpler time. Things have changed a great deal in eight hundred years, much of it for the worse.'

'So what's it like being Robin Hood?'

'I would not know, miss.' Will laughed. 'I am not he.'

'I know that,' Becky said. 'But you're the basis for him. And he's, like, one of the best heroes ever.'

'I am no hero,' Will replied simply.

'You must have done something pretty major to become Robin Hood,' Becky added. 'Has Uncle Percy told you about him, about the legend?'

'He has.'

'So what's true and what isn't?'

'I shall confess to never wearing tights of Lincoln green. What else are you keen to know?'

Becky pondered this for a few seconds, but Joe beat her to it.

'I saw a film where it said you were the son of a rich nobleman. Is that true?'

'My father was a blacksmith,' Will replied. 'An esteemed man but lowly of standing.'

'What about the Sherriff of Nottingham and Guy of Gisbourne,' Becky asked. 'Were they real?'

Will's expression hardened. 'Aye,' he replied bitterly. 'The Sheriff was a Norman aristocrat, William de Wendenel, a spineless, cruel, rodent of a man. But it was Guy of Gisbourne who was evil incarnate. One of my regrets is leaving my time without dealing him the brutal justice he had dispensed to so many others.'

Becky thought Will so full of bitterness and regret she should change the subject. 'And were you an outlaw?'

'I was a soldier …a soldier who became an outlaw through duty and wish - a duty to a people, and a wish to honour an absent King.'

'And you did steal from the rich and give to the poor?'

'In 1189 I left England for foreign shores. When I returned Prince John, King Richard's cowardly brother had proclaimed himself King of England. Moreover, he was crippling his people with taxes and laws that denied all liberty. Myself, and a few of my friends stood against that.'

'So you did rob the rich?' Joe pressed.

A smile split Will's face. 'We attempted to distribute the wealth more squarely, yes.'

'Awesome,' Joe exhaled.

But there was one question Becky was burning to ask. 'So was there a Maid Marian? I mean one without a beak...'

Will paused. 'There was another Marian, yes.'

'And were you two, well, you know?'

'We were but acquaintances. That is all.'

'But the story goes that Robin Hood falls in love with -'

'But as I have stated, it is just that – a story. Furthermore, Marian was betrothed to another …' Will's gaze shifted to Becky's neck. 'Perhaps, if I'd have been a wealthy man and could have presented her with such gifts -' he nodded at the pendant, '- then our fate would have been very different…'

Becky teased it between her fingers. 'It's my lucky pendant,' she said proudly. 'My dad gave it to me before he died. I've never taken it off since.'

'Tis a most beautiful trinket.'

She looked down at the stone and her smile faded. But then a thought struck her. A wonderful thought! 'I've got to go,' she said abruptly. 'Joe, you stay here!'

'What's the matter?' Joe said.

'Just stay here!'

Moments later, a bewildered Will lowered Becky to the ground. Before the platform reached the bottom, she had leapt off and disappeared into the forest. Bursting out of a gap in the trees, she sprinted over the archery field, over the lawn, and into the kitchens, hurtling past a baffled Jacob.

'Did you find your brother, miss?' he asked anxiously. 'Is everything well?'

'Couldn't be better,' Becky replied ecstatically. 'Where's Uncle Percy?'

'The library,' Jacob replied. 'I believe, he's - '

But Becky had gone. She scaled the stairs in record time, and was soon at the library door. She hurled it open to see

Uncle Percy surrounded by books and an unfurled scroll of brown parchment. He looked up.

'What's the matter, Becky?'

Becky marched over. 'I want you to take me back in time.'

'I am taking you back in time. In fact, I've got a -'

'No,' Becky interjected. The widest of smiles crossed her lips. 'I only want to go back six years. I want us to stop my dad going on that boat trip. We can stop my dad from dying...'

Chapter 13

The Omega Effect

Uncle Percy exhaled slowly. 'Becky, please sit down.'

Impatiently, Becky sat, her feet tapping the floor. She didn't understand. Why wasn't he as excited as her?

Uncle Percy rolled up the parchment slowly. 'What I'm about to say will be difficult to hear.' His eyes found hers. 'But I did travel back to try and save your father…I did try to stop his boat setting out to sea. It didn't work. Nothing worked. No matter what I did, no matter how far I went back, your father set sail, a storm set in and he never came back.'

Becky's face dropped. A dull silence cloaked the room.

Uncle Percy continued, his face growing wearier with each word. 'You see, what happened every time I tried to change the events of that day is the single most inexplicable occurrence in time travel. Furthermore, I have no answers that will make this any easier for you. All I can say is that sometimes things can be altered, and sometimes they can't.'

'You tried to save him?' Becky whispered.

Uncle Percy nodded miserably. 'Many times. I thought the world of your father, and ever since your grandfather died, I felt a paternal responsibility for him. Yes, we had our disagreements, but I never once stopped loving him. So when I was informed of the boat accident, the first thing I did was travel back in the hope of preventing it. But I failed …'

Becky's bottom lip started to quiver.

'So I kept travelling back to different points in that day to see if that made any difference. It didn't. I even sent Bernard Preston to try. He failed too. No matter what I did, I could not change the outcome.' He sounded defeated. 'Some would argue it was fate, that he was meant to take that boat trip. All I know is, again and again, I travelled back to stop him but the Omega Effect prevented it.'

'The what?'

'The Omega Effect. It's what travellers call a very common phenomenon in time exploration - essentially, where events can't be changed, even with a traveller's interference. To put it simply, fate insists some things happen and others do not. It's a very strange feeling when it occurs, like you're there but not there. It's quite bizarre and really does suggest that fate has a most inflexible design.'

'B-but -' Becky spluttered, 'you saved Will, and Maria, and Jacob. You saved their lives? Why couldn't you just -'

'- But I didn't have to travel back in time specifically to help them,' Uncle Percy said softly. 'They hadn't died. I just happened to be there to assist. It was luck more than intention.' He heaved another sigh. 'I know this must be soul-destroying for you. I'm afraid, for some reason, your father was destined to go on that journey and not return.

And there is nothing that I, or any traveller, can do to prevent it. I am sorry. I'm truly sorry.'

A tear spilled down Becky's cheek. Uncle Percy stood up and held her tightly.

Joe entered the room. 'What're you blartin' for, Becky?'

Uncle Percy released her.

Becky mopped her eyes and gave a weak smile.

'Joe,' Uncle Percy said. 'You really do have the sensitivity of a scab.'

Joe gave an indifferent shrug and surveyed the cluttered table. 'So what year are we going to?'

'In accordance with Bernard's research, we will be travelling to the year 1634 BC,' Uncle Percy said. 'Saturday, July 12th 1634 BC, at 2.00pm to be exact - so I don't want anyone skimping on the sun cream.'

'Great,' Joe said. 'When are we going?'

'Tomorrow morning. So it's an early night for everyone. Let's face it, it's not every day you travel back almost four thousand years in the quest for a legendary relic, is it?'

Joe punched the air. He turned expectantly to his sister.

Becky forced another smile, but couldn't quite share his enthusiasm. For a few delicious minutes she had been convinced she would see her dad again. And to have the one thing she desired most in the world snatched away seemed too cruel for words.

*

The following morning, Uncle Percy changed into his outfit while Becky and Joe finished breakfast. He wore a black hooded cloak, brown tunic with leather belt, brown sandals and held a crooked wooden staff.

As Uncle Percy gave them a twirl, Becky noticed a series of peculiar bumps and bulges beneath his tunic (although when questioned about them, he seemed surprisingly evasive). He then escorted Becky, Joe and Will to the morning room where he presented them with their costumes.

Becky's outfit consisted of a white linen tunic that draped over her right shoulder and was pinned together with a bronze brooch in the shape of a dolphin. Although hardly flattering, she felt it an improvement on the silly meringue thing she wore to Victorian Oxford. Joe's outfit was similar to Uncle Percy's, although in grey, and even Will appeared more at ease with his costume - a short brown, woollen tunic, bronze breast plate, a leather kilt and long black cape. He also carried a selection of weapons, including a bronze short sword and a circular shield.

A tense air surrounded them as they said their goodbyes to Jacob and Maria (who proceeded to burst in to an uncontrollable fit of drool and tears,) and made their way to the Time Room. Uncle Percy, carrying a backpack of provisions, led the way, followed by Joe, Becky, and finally Will, who had added a bow and quiver of arrows to his arsenal.

The Time Room seemed livelier and more boisterous than usual with the sounds of bleeps and buzzes and hums at full volume. Becky saw a freshly polished Bertha standing in the centre of the room. Then something occurred to her. 'Uncle Percy, how're we going to talk to anyone?'

'What do you mean?'

'Obviously, people in Ancient Crete didn't speak English. We won't understand a word they're saying and they won't understand us.'

'An excellent point, Becky,' Uncle Percy agreed. 'And one that for many years caused severe headaches for the travelling community.' He opened a drawer and pulled out an oblong box that resembled a pencil case. 'Take a look at these …' He opened the box.

Becky leant over and saw a series of shiny metal nodules, each one no bigger than the head of a small drawing pin.

'These are transvocalisors,' Uncle Percy said. 'I invented the prototypes over twenty-five years ago. Now, I'm proud to say, they're an essential part of the traveller's kit. Let me put them on for you.'

He placed one on Becky's throat and one behind her left ear. He repeated the process for Joe.

'What's a transvocalingy?' Joe asked.

Uncle Percy passed a pair to Will, and then put a pair on himself. 'A transvocalisor, Joe, well, it's a very powerful translation device. Inside each transvocalisor is a very powerful microchip that, with regards to the one on your ear, will translate any language, ancient or modern, into English for you; whilst the one on your throat will automatically convert anything you say into whatever language you need. In short, you will both understand, and be understood wherever and whenever you are.'

Becky immediately decided to secretly borrow a set for her French exams the following year.

'Right then, shall we make a move?' Uncle Percy took a wedge of Gerathnium and inserted it in to the campervan. Becky and Joe clambered aboard.

'Are you going to register the trip?' Becky said, sounding slightly anxious.

Opening the driver's door, Uncle Percy tossed the bag and staff into the back. 'Not this time, Becky. I'm aware it's not an ideal situation, but I'm afraid we're going to have to break a few rules.' Will joined him up front.

'But what if something happens to us?' Becky asked.

Joe shot Becky a disparaging look. 'Like what - you losing a scrunchie?'

'I don't know,' Becky snapped back at him. 'An emergency! What if the campervan packs up? What if we need to get back in a hurry? What if something massive and hairy bites your fat ugly head off?' She sounded quite hopeful with her last example.

'Now, now, we'll have less of that,' Uncle Percy cut in firmly. 'Charlie Millport at HQ knows where and when we're going - off the record, of course. I've also left details with Jacob. He knows what to do if there's a problem. Does that reassure you, Becky?'

Becky nodded but still felt rather uneasy. After all, they weren't the only ones searching for the Golden Fleece, and their rivals were pretty much as dangerous as could be. However, before she could reply, a power surge from below stopped her in her tracks.

'Okay, everyone … next stop, Crete, 1634 BC,' Uncle Percy shouted, his voice swelling to counteract the mounting volume.

'And the Minotaurs,' Joe shouted back, grinning widely.

'Im afraid you may be disappointed there, Joe,' Uncle Percy answered with a grin. 'There'll be no dragons - no bogeymen - no fabulous monsters of any kind. But, with any luck, we may find some answers...'

Chapter 14

Harpy Attack

Bertha materialised on a dusty path in the middle of a narrow ravine. Immediately, Becky felt a blistering heat envelop them. She looked through the window and saw towering bleached white rocks, a thousand foot high, on either side.

'Andrana's Valley,' Uncle Percy said, marveling at the natural spectacle. 'It's an outstanding example of -' He glanced in the wing mirror and cut short his sentence. 'Blimey!'

Becky heard the shock in his voice. She whipped her head round and her mouth dropped open.

A gangly boy was hurtling towards them, his sweat drenched face etched with terror. Two huge winged creatures were chasing him, taking it in turns to swoop down.

Becky screamed.

Instinctively, Will grabbed his bow and quiver and seized the door handle. Uncle Percy pulled him back. 'No, Will!' The boy veered past the campervan, too frightened or perhaps disorientated to notice it.

'W-what are they?' Joe hollered.

'Well - err -' Uncle Percy spluttered. 'My - err - knowledge of Greek Mythology is somewhat limited, but I believe they might be -' He slammed his foot down and Bertha sped off.

'- They're the Harpies!' Becky yelled, recalling the story of the Golden Fleece.

Uncle Percy fought to control the wheel. 'It seems so.'

Becky glared at Uncle Percy. 'No monsters, eh?'

Before Uncle Percy could reply - CRAAASH - the larger of the two Harpies collided with them, momentarily knocking Bertha off her wheels.

As she clutched the handrail desperately, Becky's gaze locked on the window. The larger Harpy had moved parallel to them. It was as long as the campervan, with gigantic scaly wings, a deep green leathery torso, and the face of a disfigured old woman. Two muscular arms tipped with curved claws hung down as it thrashed the air.

Becky's blood turned to ice as the Harpy's eyes found her. A wicked grin curled on its mouth.

Petrified, Becky's fingers inched to her lucky pendant, when - CRAASH - the second Harpy struck the van from the opposite side, throwing her headfirst to the floor. She landed hard, blood filling her mouth.

Uncle Percy wrestled Bertha to the left. Immediately, the Harpies took to the air, disappearing from sight.

Uncle Percy scanned the skies. Nothing. Slowing down, he drove toward the boy. 'Becky, open the door!'

'Are you bonkers?' Becky yelled at him, scrambling back to her seat.

'Open the door,' Uncle Percy said. 'Grab the boy!'

With trembling hands, Becky slid the door open.

Uncle Percy weaved over to the boy, whose pace had slowed to a jog. 'Get in,' he shouted. 'You'll be safe!'

Dazed, the boy stared at the campervan, wide-eyed.

'Here. Take this,' Joe said, extending his hand.

Disorientated, the boy was about to take it when - SHRIIIEEEEK – a sickening howl rang out. From nowhere, Talons seized the boy's tunic, lifting him off his feet. He squirmed and wriggled, but it was no use. The larger Harpy had got him and was ascending.

'Drive under the boy,' Will insisted.

Uncle Percy whipped Bertha to the right as Will scooped up his bow.

'What're you -' But before Uncle Percy could finish, Will had heaved open the door. In one acrobatic movement, he hurled himself on to the roof. Steadying himself, he loaded two arrows onto his bowstring, and aimed at the Harpy above. He fired. The two arrows, separated in mid air, and pierced the Harpy's thick arms. It screeched and dropped its haul. The boy crashed on to the roof.

Will knelt beside him. 'Are your injuries severe?'

'N-no, sire,' the boy whimpered.

'Then forgive me.' Will grabbed the boy's shoulders and threw him through the open door, safely on to the seat. Then he slammed the door shut.

'What's he doing?' Becky cried with disbelief.

Will looked up at the circling Harpies. With a screech, the injured Harpy attacked, swooping down at him, its rotted teeth bared. Will fixed another arrow to the bowstring. He fired again. This time, the arrow pierced the Harpy's breastbone. It howled in agony and swerved away.

The second Harpy hung in mid air for a second. Then pounced. Will reached for another arrow, but there wasn't time. Claws stabbed his shoulders and blood showered his face. Heaved into the air, he dropped the bow. The wounded Harpy joined its companion. Together, they let out a jubilant wail and flew off into the canyon, carrying their prize.

'They've got Will!' Becky shouted hysterically. 'Uncle Percy. Do something!'

'Oh, I intend to,' Uncle Percy said coolly. He powered Bertha in the direction of the canyon. 'Joe, my staff, please.'

Confused, Joe scooped up the walking staff and passed it over.

'Here, take the wheel,' Uncle Percy said to the boy, who complied though it was clear he had no idea what to do.

Keeping his foot firmly on the accelerator, Uncle Percy leaned from the open window. Holding the cane with his left hand, his right hand inched towards the grip. He aimed at the Harpy holding Will. BOOM - a laser blast erupted from the cane.

Becky and Joe stared at each other, astounded. Uncle Percy had a weapon!

The blast slammed into the cliff; giant hunks of rock rained down onto scorched earth.

BOOM. Uncle Percy fired again, this time missing Will by a matter of inches.

'Stop it. You'll hit him!' Becky yelled.

Uncle Percy looked quite put out. He paused for a moment, pulled the staff inside and muttered, 'Sadly, Becky, you're almost certainly right.'

*

The Harpies rose higher and higher. Through blurred eyes, Will saw Bertha in the distance. The higher the Harpy carried him, the less chance he'd survive. He knew that. Slowly, pain scorching his shoulders, he edged his sword from its scabbard. The blade glistened in the blazing sun. He took a deep lungful of air and thrust upwards, burying the blade deep into the beast's underbelly. Blood smothered his hands. The Harpy gave a hideous squeal. It released him. He fell.

Twenty-five feet.

Twenty-feet.

Fifteen-feet.

Suddenly, pointed branches tore at his skin. More pain shot through him as a tree slowed his descent. Flung from branch to branch, he landed with a dull thump on the unyielding earth. Struggling to his knees, bleeding, battered, he watched the Harpy thrash wildly in agony as it crashed to the ground. Dead.

The second Harpy saw its lifeless companion then pivoted towards Will. With a blood-curdling shriek, it thundered towards him.

Calmly, Will closed his eyes and waited for impact.

Chapter 15

Phineus

'Hold on to something!' Uncle Percy bellowed, pressing a large scarlet button on Bertha's dashboard.

At once, a rumbling sound echoed throughout the van.

Becky had heard the sound once before. An ultra-booster. Her heart pounded as she watched Uncle Percy aim the campervan at the charging Harpy. Then they raced off like a missile.

Becky didn't have time to shut her eyes when - SMAASSSSH – the campervan ploughed into its target, shuddering violently as metal crunched bone. The Harpy was pitched into the cliff-face, its body landing in a twisted, motionless heap.

Uncle Percy swung Bertha round and slammed on the brakes. He leapt from the driver's door and sprinted over to Will. 'Are you all right, Will?'

'Aye,' Will replied, his hand pressed firmly against his left shoulder. Uncle Percy removed the hand carefully to reveal a deep gash. He examined it closely. 'I can fix it.' Jumping to his feet, he raced back to the campervan.

Becky rushed over, Joe close behind, his face colourless.

'Will!' Becky said softly, dropping to her knees. 'Are you -'

'I am fine, child.' Will watched as tears formed in Becky's eyes. 'Worry not. This is nothing your uncle cannot heal.'

A moment later, Uncle Percy returned clutching a bottle of orange liquid and what looked like an electric toothbrush. 'Now, this might hurt a tad, Will.' He switched on the device. It hummed faintly and a glittering blue beam shot from its tip.

Becky and Joe watched helplessly as Uncle Percy ensured the light crossed every cut, every graze, every bruise, before applying thick drops of the liquid. After a few minutes he looked up, satisfied. 'He'll be fine.'

After setting Will in the shade to rest, Uncle Percy returned to the boy, who was looking more bewildered than ever. 'I'm Percy Halifax,' he said with a kindly smile. 'This is Becky and Joe. And that man over there is Will Shakelock. We are visitors to these shores and mean you no harm.'

The boy returned a feeble smile. After a few uncomfortable moments where Becky thought the transvocalisors had been damaged, he spoke in a rather edgy squeak. 'I - I am Phineus of Athens.'

'A pleasure to meet you, Phineus,' Uncle Percy said. 'Would you care for some water?'

Phineus nodded. 'Please, yes, water.'

Uncle Percy returned a moment later with a plastic water bottle. Phineus' face turned white. 'What kind of sorcery is this?'

'It's quite all right, Phineus,' Uncle Percy said. 'It's what we call plastic. Where we come from plastic is very common.'

Phineus eyed the container warily. Hesitantly, he took a drink.

'So, Phineus, do your parents live around here?'

'My parents are with the Gods,' Phineus replied. 'Like you, I am not of this place. Our boat is moored here.'

'Your boat?'

'The Argo … alas, she suffered damage passing the Clashing Rocks of Izos, my comrades are making repairs whilst I explore the island. I was gathering olives when the sky-beasts attacked.'

But Becky only heard the first two words: The Argo. The Argo was Jason's legendary boat in the quest for the Golden Fleece. Uncle Percy clearly couldn't believe it either. 'The Argo – so you're an Argonaut?'

'I am,' Phineus replied proudly.

'And the captain of your ship is … Jason?'

Phineus looked surprised. 'You know of my master?'

'Only by reputation.'

'As you should.' Phineus' chest ballooned with pride. 'He is a remarkable man, a great leader and a fierce warrior. I doubt whether there is a braver man in the breadth of Mycenae.'

'Will you take us to him?'

Phineus took a side-ways glance at the dead Harpies. 'Well -' he bowed his head. '- I owe you my life. It is the very least I can do.'

Uncle Percy turned to Becky, a glint in his eyes. She smiled back. They had been blessed with the most extraordinary luck. According to legend, Jason, the Argo, the Argonauts, and the Golden Fleece were inextricably linked. And, although she knew Uncle Percy rarely found truth in legends - well, perhaps this time could be the exception.

Perhaps this was more than coincidence.

*

Uncle Percy decided they would need a substantial lunch, and Will a few hours convalescence, before they set off to meet the Argonauts. And as Becky protested at eating beside two fly-ridden Harpy corpses, they drove deep into Andrana's Valley, stopping beside a shallow brook.

After lunch, Uncle Percy conducted safety checks on Bertha to ensure everything was in working order. As he did this, Phineus wandered over and began to study Bertha's damaged bodywork, his eyes filled with wonder.

'What manner of chariot is this?' Phineus asked.

'It's a new model,' Uncle Percy said cagily. 'They'll be all the rage this time next year.'

'But how does it move?' Phineus asked. 'There are no horses.'

Uncle Percy thought it would be pointless to explain the finer details of automotive engineering. 'Oh, there are horses. They're actually underneath.'

'Underneath?' Phineus said incredulously. 'But what breed are they?'

Uncle Percy checked he was out of earshot. 'They're a British breed: Devonshire Bunny Horses.'

'My Uncle Alpheos was a breeder of horses,' Phineus replied. 'I thought I knew all varieties of the creature. But I have never heard of a Devon-shire Bunny Horse.'

'Well, they're rare,' Uncle Percy replied unconvincingly. 'Even in Devon.'

Phineus nodded. 'But how are they harnessed beneath such a - '

'Oh, its not hard. They're actually very small,' Uncle Percy interrupted. 'No bigger than rabbits, hence the name…'

'How many are there?'

Uncle Percy was blushing now. 'Ten.'

Phineus fell to the ground, keen to examine the van's undercarriage. 'Where are they?'

'Oh, you won't be able to see them,' Uncle Percy said, heaving a disappointed Phineus back to his feet. 'When I start the chariot, their legs lower and they start running. They have incredibly long legs for such tiny things.'

'May I see one?'

'I'm afraid they don't respond well to strangers. They're likely to bite.'

'Bite?'

'Oh, yes, this breed is renowned for its nipping. They have very sharp teeth.'

'Perhaps they would be happier if they ran free.'

'Ah, that would be bad. They hate sunlight, you see. It sends them into a violent frenzy. If I set them free it could turn very nasty. A bloodbath! I'll let them out tonight when it's dark.'

Phineus looked sad. 'Perhaps that would be best.'

Uncle Percy gave a loud sigh of relief.

By the time it came to leave, Will had made an excellent recovery. In fact, it had been a pleasant few hours, the only sobering moment occurred when Phineus examined Uncle Percy's cane and nearly blew his head off. But after the panic had faded, they left feeling refreshed and ready for their trip to the coast.

*

However, what none of them had realised was that since their arrival on Crete, an enormous black bird had been following them, studying their every move. And, as the campervan disappeared from sight, the bird's pitch-black eyes snapped shut. The ambo-processor in its head had stopped recording - its homing device had been activated.

Its creator was waiting.

As the bird approached a clearing at the peak of a white mountain, a tall, slender man in a dark cloak met it, a thick hood masking his face. He held a device showing, in total clarity, everything in the bird's eye-line. He turned a toggle and the bird collapsed soullessly at his feet. He picked it up and placed it into a satchel. Then he turned to a limousine parked ten foot away - a limousine that once belonged to the Russian dictator, Joseph Stalin … a man who arrested, imprisoned and executed millions of his own citizens.

The traveller rubbed his hands with anticipation. He had a short but crucial journey in time to make. It was a trip that, regardless of the outcome, would bring him a great deal of amusement.

Chapter 16

Argonauts

Even with the air conditioning at full blast, the campervan felt like an oven. Becky watched Phineus who was lying spread-eagled on the floor, his ear tightly pressed against the metal panelling. 'Phineus, what are you doing?'

'Listening,' Phineus replied, a faraway smile on his lips.

'To what?'

'To the horses.'

'The what?'

'The little horses. They are most wondrous.'

Uncle Percy gave an unusually loud cough. 'Phineus, if you could return to your seat, please.'

'What horses?' Becky probed.

'The Devonshire Bunny Horses,' he said. 'I can hear them.'

'Your seat, Phineus …' Uncle Percy said awkwardly.

'What're you going on about?' Becky continued.

'Beautiful scenery, isn't it?' Uncle Percy said at the top of his voice, before bursting into a peculiarly enthusiastic bout of whistling.

Reluctantly Phineus returned to his seat, his eyes exploring every inch of the campervan as though a new discovery waited in every corner. Joe stared at Phineus, with the same bemused expression as his sister. This was an Argonaut?

'This is the most uncommon chariot I have ever seen,' Phineus said. 'This Brit-ain from which you hail must be a wonderful place.'

Joe looked at the campervan with indifference. 'S'pose. We've got loads better stuff than this, though.'

'Better?' Phineus asked. 'But what could be better?'

Joe pondered for a moment. 'Err, Manchester City.'

'And what is Man-chest-er City?'

'It's a football team,' Joe said. 'The best team in the world.'

'What is football?'

'It's a game. Eleven men versus eleven men - one ball.'

'What is ball?'

'It's a round object, full of air.' Joe spread out his hands as if holding an invisible ball. 'You kick it.'

'Why?'

'So you can score.'

'What is score?'

'When you kick the ball in the net.'

'What is net?'

'It doesn't matter,' Joe scowled, his tone suggesting he hoped the other Argonauts were a significant improvement on this one.

Becky smiled, turned to the window and caught sight of the Aegean Sea. The crystal-blue water extended to the horizon, bordered by a blanket of rambling white sand. And, as the valley merged into the shore, she noticed a boat anchored fifty feet from the beach.

Phineus bolted upright. 'The Argo.'

An air of anticipation swept through the van. They all strained to get a better look at the celebrated ship. The closer they came, however, the more Becky sensed disappointment and with good reason. The Argo was, without doubt, the smallest, shabbiest looking vessel imaginable. A crooked wooden mast rose from the deck with a dirty green sail that hung limp like a soggy piece of lettuce.

'Is that it?' Joe said, loudly. 'It's tiny.'

'Tis big enough,' Phineus said defiantly.

'For fifty men?' Joe blustered.

'Fifty?' Phineus snorted, offended by Joe's tone. 'But only four undertook the journey.'

Joe slumped miserably in his seat. 'Four? But I thought there were fifty - '

Uncle Percy interrupted, 'Phineus, about the Argo, is it sinking?'

'No.' Phineus tried to sound positive. 'Jason said -'

'What-a-flippin'-shock,' Joe growled, folding his arms.

Becky could see Uncle Percy was right. The Argo was sinking and sinking fast. The prow tilted down, half submerged in water and she could make out two small figures scurrying around the deck, emptying buckets over the side.

Uncle Percy steered Bertha into a small cave and urged them to exit as quickly as possible.

'Can we not ride the chariot on to the beach?' Phineus asked. 'I am certain my comrades would be keen to see it.'

Deeming the fewer people who saw Bertha the better, Uncle Percy leant towards Phineus, careful of being overheard. 'I don't like to talk about it in front of Becky and Joe, it upsets them, but the horses hate sand. In fact, they're allergic to it. They develop green boils all over their little bodies if they come into contact with it.'

Phineus nodded with concern. 'That sounds most worrisome.'

'Oh, it is,' Uncle Percy said. 'Anyway, they'll be fine as long as we keep them away from the beach.'

'Wise, indeed,' Phineus said gravely.

Then Joe appeared. 'Are we going then?'

'Of course, Joe,' Uncle Percy said. 'Come, Phineus, you must introduce us to your friends.'

Phineus took a lingering look at the time machine and sighed. Then he sprinted out of the cave.

'Off his box,' Joe mumbled to Becky, as Phineus disappeared over a dune.

As they trudged across the sand, Becky saw a large man sitting on a boulder, his brown eyes swirling round in their sockets, streams of slobber trickling down his stubbly chin.

'Hail, Theseus,' Phineus said. 'Has your condition improved?'

Becky's ears pricked up. Theseus - the slayer of the Minotaur. Her stomach sank. This man was a slobbering wreck.

Theseus raised his head. 'H-hail Phlinumbleness.'

'What's the matter with him?' Joe blurted.

'His head was struck when we hit the clashing rocks,' Phineus replied. 'Jason believes he shall recover in a day or two.'

Becky stared doubtfully at Theseus, who had tilted back on the boulder, his legs dangling, when his eyes rolled white and he collapsed with a heavy thud.

Will ran over and hoisted him back onto the rock.

'Ooops. My head hurts,' Theseus gurgled.

'Here, let me take a look.' Uncle Percy lifted Theseus' straggly black hair to reveal a bluish lump the size of a conker. Becky winced.

Fortunately, Uncle Percy knew exactly what to do. After a few minutes of gentle probing, he finally spoke, 'There's nothing broken, just severe concussion.'

'Are you my mother?' Theseus said in a swirling drawl.

'Err, 'fraid not,' Uncle Percy said, turning to a mortified Phineus. 'We need to get him out of the sun.' Struggling, they hauled Theseus to the shade and Uncle Percy spent the next ten minutes treating him with implements from the campervan's medi-box. As soon as the swelling had reduced they left him to rest and returned to the beach.

Becky, Uncle Percy, his hood shielding his face from the sun, Will, Joe and Phineus gathered at the shore. The stern rose higher and higher into the air as the Argo tilted at a steep angle.

'Jason … Jason… I have returned!' Phineus yelled.

A small head popped over the side of the boat. Soaked in sweat, Jason stared at the smiling group of strangers. For a brief moment, his bearded face displayed shock, but this quickly disappeared. 'Phineus?' Jason shouted back, intrigued. 'Who accompanies you?'

'These are my friends. They saved my life,' Phineus replied. 'Master, I have so much to tell you. I was attacked!'

Jason whispered something to his fellow Argonaut and they nodded in agreement. Conceding their cause was lost, they pitched the buckets into the sea, jumped overboard and approached the shore. Phineus dashed through the lapping waves to his mentor.

'Attacked, you say?' Jason said. 'Then it pleases me you are safe.'

As Jason stood upright, Becky noticed something quite unexpected. Phineus towered above him.

'Jason's an elf!' Joe whispered in Becky's ear.

'Shhh,' Becky replied. Nonetheless, she couldn't help but agree. Jason, the famous leader of the Argonauts, was indeed a very, very tiny man.

The second Argonaut approached Phineus. He was very tall, reedy, and his round balding head made him look like a spoon.

'Hercules,' Phineus said. 'It pleases me to see you.'

'Hail, Phineus,' Hercules replied. 'You say you were attacked by demons? They're not still around are they?' He looked nervously at the distant valley.

'No. My friends slew them.'

'Oh, good,' Hercules replied with relief.

Joe struggled to maintain a respectful silence. 'That's Hercules?'

For once, however, Becky could quite understand her brother's incredulity. Of all the legendary Argonauts,

Hercules had to be the most famous. But this Hercules, however, could not have looked more different from the Hercules of legend.

'Is the Argo doomed, sire?' Phineus asked Jason.

'That slab of rotting timber,' Jason muttered angrily, 'tis not fit for firewood. You wait 'til I get my hands on that dung beetle Argus…master shipbuilder, my stumpy rump!' He scooped up a floating bucket and hurled it at the ship.

'But what of our quest?' Phineus asked anxiously. 'The Fleece of Gold?'

Becky's heart slammed in her chest. She heard Joe gasp loudly. The Argonauts were searching for the Golden Fleece.

'Fear not,' Jason said, reaching up on tiptoes and patting Phineus firmly on his shoulder. 'Something will arise. Anyway, who are your companions?'

'They are my new friends,' Phineus said, trailing Jason out of the water. 'They are strangers here, too. They hail from a far-away land called Brit - ain.' At these words Jason's expression changed. Oblivious, Phineus continued, 'I was gathering olives when I was attacked by sky demons. These fair people rescued me, and - '

But Jason had stopped listening.

Becky knew something was wrong. She stared at Jason, but it was clear he was focused on one thing, one person: Uncle Percy.

Uncle Percy had noticed it too. Slowly, he removed his hood.

Jason gasped loudly and fell to his knees. 'It's you … It's you… Hercules, Phineus, to your knees at once!'

Bewildered, Hercules and Phineus dropped to the sand. Becky watched in amazement as the three Argonauts groveled before them.

For a brief moment, even Uncle Percy was at a loss for words. 'May I ask what you're doing?'

'The gods foretold of your coming, sire,' Jason said, his eyes never leaving the sand. 'But I didn't believe it. Please, forgive me.'

'There is nothing to forgive,' Uncle Percy said. 'Please, stand.'

Jason ignored him. 'We are your humble servants, my master.'

Becky glanced at Joe, then Will. She had a sudden urge to laugh, but resisted it. Something very strange was going on.

'It was foretold?' Uncle Percy asked curiously.

'Yes. The stranger told me. The messenger of the gods. He came to me as I slept. He said I would meet you - the silver haired one, the traveller from Brit - ain, that you - you are his trusted envoy - the rightful owner of Nephele's Fleece. He said we must beg to be your servants.'

A curious look crossed Uncle Percy's face. 'Then it is my wish that you stand.' Leaning over, he guided Jason to his feet. 'Let us move to the shade, you must tell me everything...'

Becky wondered whether to laugh or not. Then she glimpsed her uncle's expression and a sense of dread enveloped her. Any thoughts of how amusing the situation was instantly vanished, because, for the first time since she'd met him, she saw utter confusion and perhaps even fear in his eyes.

Chapter 17

The Messenger's Message

A puzzled silence engulfed them. The Argonauts gathered their possessions and moved to the sheltered cluster of trees where Theseus lay, snoring like a bagpipe.

All the while Becky couldn't take her eyes off a troubled Uncle Percy. She knew he was contemplating the identity of the messenger. It had to be a time traveller. But who? Friend or foe? And why visit Jason? And then the real complexity of time travel struck her. The messenger could even be Uncle Percy - an Uncle Percy from the future travelling back in time for some, as yet, unknown reason. What a bizarre thought!

By late afternoon, the smell of cinnamon filtered on the heavy air. Becky and Joe were sitting on the gnarled grey trunk of a fallen tree; Phineus and Hercules sat opposite, cross-legged, on the sandy ground. It was obvious from their puzzled looks this was the first time they had heard about Jason's messenger.

Uncle Percy removed his cloak and gave Jason a kindly smile. 'Please, Jason, I need you to tell me everything about this messenger. Every detail. Leave nothing out.'

Jason surveyed at his captive audience. 'Seven days ago, the first night of the full moon, I was asleep in my hut on Iolcus having an agreeable dream about very tall women, when I woke to find the earth growling and a noise like the snap of an ox-skin whip met my ears.'

Becky glanced at Joe, who gave a nod of silent recognition. Jason was describing an operational time machine.

Jason continued. 'The door opened, and a man stood before me. A tall man, like yourself.'

'What did he look like?'

Jason deliberated for a moment. 'I could not see. His features remained in shadow. He wore a cloak, much like yours, his face hidden.'

Uncle Percy hesitated. 'Now, I want you to take your time answering this. You said the messenger wore a cloak like mine, that he was a tall man like me. Could it have been me? Was I the messenger?'

Jason's head jerked up sharply. 'Is this a test, sire?' he said, sounding confused. 'Are the Gods testing me?'

'Yes,' Uncle Percy said. 'It's a test. Now, think back. Was it me?'

Jason paused again. 'It may have been you, master. It was too dark to be certain.'

'Very well,' Uncle Percy said. 'Did he sound like me? Was the accent the same as mine?'

'A week of sleep has blurred the event, sire. But his accent was unfamiliar to me - it may have been your voice. Was it you who visited me that night, master? Have I passed the test?'

'You're doing well.' Uncle Percy smiled sympathetically. 'Now, please, tell me what was said.'

'He said I was to embark on a great journey. A mission decreed by the Gods. I was to gather a mighty crew and go in search of the Fleece of Gold, the divine prize presented to Queen Nephele by the God, Hermes. He told me to first land upon Crete where he would send his herald, a silver-haired man from a distant land called Brit - ain. He said that I must assist the herald in finding The Golden Fleece.' Jason stopped, dreading his next words. 'And the messenger ordered I bestow upon you a message. He said you must leave Crete before two moons passed. That should you remain, your lives would be taken, and the Fleece of Gold lost forever. Then he left.'

A tense silence hung in the air.

Only Uncle Percy, who looked somewhat relieved, had something to say. 'Thank you, Jason. That was most helpful. Now, shall I make everyone a nice pot of tea?' He walked off in the direction of the cave, leaving the three Argonauts baffled as to what a pot of tea was.

Becky watched Uncle Percy leave, countless questions filling her mind. Was the messenger Uncle Percy or someone else? Were they really in danger on Crete? If so, why? Then her thoughts were interrupted by an deafening creaking sound. Staring out, she watched as the Argo disappeared from view, swallowed by the hungry sea.

Chapter 18

In the Shadows of the Past

After deciding they would camp there for the night, Uncle Percy spent rest of the afternoon finding reasons to isolate himself from the group. He would go for lengthy walks along the gorge admiring the griffon vultures and picking wild orchids. He would paddle in the shallow sea, gathering shells and placing them in a small leather pouch, claiming to be a keen conchologist.

Becky knew this was all a front. He needed time to consider Jason's story and think about their next step. As she watched him pluck the umpteenth shell from the damp sand, she felt a powerful sense of helplessness.

Joe, on the other hand, seemed oblivious to her concerns and decided to lighten the mood by teaching the Argonauts to play cricket. He found a stained cork ball in the campervan (which judging by the deep grooves in its surface belonged to Milly) and whittled some stumps out of olive branches, whilst Will carved a makeshift bat.

Joe soon came to the conclusion the Argonauts were the worst cricketers he had ever seen. Phineus stood more chance of catching the ball with his ears than his hands. Hercules was even worse, and Jason launched himself with such gusto at his first delivery that the bat flew out of his hands and crashed into Hercules' forehead, knocking him out cold.

By the time Uncle Percy had returned daylight had bowed to a comfortable dusk. The solitude seemed to have rejuvenated him and he joked with Becky as they lit a fire and watched as fine wisps of smoke slithered into the sky.

Dinner was a jovial affair, and Becky found herself enjoying the company of the Argonauts immensely. She watched as Theseus, his condition much improved, Phineus and Hercules, (Jason remained oddly quiet) took centre-stage and entertained them with folk songs and fantastical tales of the Gods. Before long the sun had set and a full moon cast a silver flush over the camp.

An hour later, Becky lay under a blanket, taking in the glittering stars above. Despite the day's revelations, she felt remarkably at peace. Listening to the crackling embers of the fire, her eyes searched out Uncle Percy. She found him sitting on a rock, staring blankly out to sea. She walked over, her bare feet welcoming the coolness of the sand.

'Mind if I join you?' Becky said.

Uncle Percy looked up. 'I believe this rock was made for two.'

'It's beautiful, isn't it?' Becky said, sitting down and gazing out at the water.

'The sea is always beautiful,' Uncle Percy replied softly. 'It's one of life's constants. No matter when or where you are, the sea remains the same - wonderful, elegant, dangerous and vast.'

Becky hesitated for a second. 'The messenger's worried you?'

'Well, granted, it was unforeseen,' Uncle Percy replied, 'but when travelling you come to expect the unexpected. After all, it is we who are the trespassers. You must never forget that.'

Shocked to hear him use a word like trespass, Becky said, 'I prefer to think of it as visiting…visiting the best museum in the world.'

'But you can't take museum exhibits home with you. Visiting a museum is a passive activity. Time travel is as active as can be. That's precisely why it's the most potentially destructive power the world has ever known.'

'You sound like you wish it didn't exist?' Becky said.

'Age changes a man.' Uncle Percy said without a hint of sadness. 'Believe me, I have enjoyed every journey - well, almost…' his eyes dimmed, 'but I have devoted my life to travel, and that's not always a wise thing to do. Sometimes it's too easy to dwell on the past and ignore the present.'

'But look at the life you've lived,' Becky said. 'It must've been brilliant. You've seen things people would kill to see.' As soon as the words left her mouth she knew she'd said the wrong thing.

Uncle Percy looked sad. 'And people are being killed. And if we don't put a stop to this, more will die. That is why I'm prepared to take the risks I'm taking.'

'Good,' Becky said resolutely.

'But it's not just me who's in danger, is it? Believe me, I wish it was, but there's you, Joe, Will, Maria and Jacob to consider, too. The people I care most about in the world.

I'm growing old, it doesn't really matter what happens to me.'

'It matters to me.' Becky gripped his hand. 'Besides, you're not that old, and you shouldn't worry about us. We'll be okay. I just know we will.'

Uncle Percy turned his head towards the water. 'I don't know, perhaps it was a mistake inviting you to Bowen Hall. Perhaps you should have stayed at home with your mother. At least you'd be safe.'

'Please, don't say that,' Becky replied. 'And besides, you don't know that. After all, it was our rooms those freaks trashed.' She paused. 'To be honest, I didn't want to come and stay with you at all. I thought it was going to be the worst summer of my life. And I was wrong. It's been the best.'

'That's very kind of you to say.'

'But I am angry with you…'

'Why?'

'Because I'm thirteen.'

'And?'

'And it's taken you all this time to let me back into your life. And that's not fair...' She could feel her entire body begin to shake.

'I know,' Uncle Percy said quietly, 'and I am very sorry.'

But Becky hadn't finished. 'So, if Joe and I are your only family, why didn't you want us around?'

Uncle Percy sighed. 'You've got every right to be angry with me, Becky. The reason I've not seen you is -' He hesitated, unable to find the words.

Becky stared at him impatiently. 'Well?'

'The reason is complex…'

'Okay.' Becky found her temper rising. 'I'm not a child. You might think I am, but I'm not. I can handle it. What was it?'

Uncle Percy took a grave breath. 'It was your father's wish. He ordered me not to see you …'

The words hung in mid-air like the echo of a distant bell. He ordered me not to see you! Becky whirled with shock. 'I - I don't understand.'

Uncle Percy's eyes found hers. 'How could you understand? In retrospect, I'm not sure I do. There was a time when your father and I were close, you see. Very close. He was my favourite nephew, and we spent a great deal of time together.' He smiled fondly. 'Anyway, some time before he died, we had a disagreement - a particularly heated disagreement. And, as often happens in the fervor of the moment, we both said things perhaps we shouldn't have said. Anyway, the upshot was he asked me to never to see him or his family again. I had no choice but to respect his wish.'

Becky's brow furrowed. 'Mum told me about your argument. I mean, she didn't know what it was about, but she knew dad really regretted it.'

'As did I. Of course, you always think you have time to fix these things. Unfortunately, in this instance, time was the one thing we didn't have. I am aware of the irony. Anyway, after he died, I didn't know how to introduce myself back into your family. Naturally, I offered your mother financial assistance, but she wouldn't take it. I invited her to bring you to live at Bowen Hall. Again, she declined. She's an honourable woman. I respected that.'

'What was the argument about?'

'I can't say,' Uncle Percy said sadly, breaking eye contact for a moment.

'Why not?'

'I just can't. It was merely a difference of opinion. He thought a situation should've been handled one way. I thought something else.'

Becky remained unsatisfied. 'Well, I can't see how any argument was worth having nothing to do with us when dad died.'

'I said I didn't know how to introduce myself back into your family. I didn't say I had nothing to do with you.'

'What - what do you mean?'

Slowly, Uncle Percy turned to Becky and his gaze met hers. 'I was always there for you and Joe. You just didn't know it.'

'I don't understand?'

'I used my time machines to journey back to see you and Joe as you were growing up. To ensure you were both safe and well.'

'You did?' Becky whispered.

'Many times. I was there on your first day at that new school … you made friends with that small, freckly girl who was crying because she was cold. You gave her your duffel coat. '

Stunned to silence, Becky remembered the incident well. The girl's name was Kelly Martin.

Uncle Percy continued. 'I was there when you visited Chester Zoo and were scared by the chimpanzees. Your teacher wanted you to leave the ape compound but you stayed until you conquered your fear. You even ended up buying a book about them from the gift shop. I could name dozens of other things I've seen you do.'

Becky felt her eyes dampen. She remembered these events as clearly as if they happened yesterday. And Uncle Percy had been there? Silently watching, standing in the wings like an understudy in a play.

Becky exploded into tears. She covered her face, ashamed of her outburst.

Leaning over, Uncle Percy placed his arm gently around her shoulders. 'Please, don't cry. Just believe me when I say I was always there for you. And Joe. I just couldn't let you know.'

But she had stopped listening now. The sound of weeping muffled any words. All her life, Uncle Percy had been her guardian angel. It was the saddest, most touching thing she'd ever heard.

*

Hours later, as dawn approached, the camp lay as still as a cemetery. A cool sea breeze had swept in and finally extinguished the dying fire. Everyone was in a deep sleep. Everyone, except Jason. He'd been awake for hours, his stomach churning with guilt and confusion. Surely, he couldn't do it? But he knew he must. He had no choice.

The Gods had spoken.

Silently, he stepped away from his bed. It was late now, and the gentle breaths from the sleeping group floated throughout the darkness. He eased past Phineus, Hercules, and finally Theseus, until he stood over his target. Feeling his fingers tremble, he gazed down at the sleeping man. What was he doing? Surely this was a good man? A worthy man?

But no, he could not be what he seemed. The Gods had told him the truth. Drawing his bronze dagger, he whispered 'Hestia, forgive me...' And he plunged the blade towards Uncle Percy's heart.

Chapter 19

Capture

With a gentle swish, an arrow sliced the air. It connected with the blade, sending it flying from Jason's hand. Will leapt from the blackness. He loaded another arrow and pointed it at the small man's throat.

'P - P - Please don't kill me,' Jason whimpered.

Will drew back the bowstring, fury creasing his face.

Uncle Percy's eyes snapped open. Shocked and disorientated, he saw the dagger. He scrambled to his feet, creating a human shield between the two men.

'WILL…NO!'

The turmoil caused Becky to wake. She screamed. Joe, Theseus, Phineus and Hercules jolted up simultaneously.

'Forgive me.' Jason curled into a quivering ball.

'I think you can lower the bow now, Will,' Uncle Percy said assuredly. 'He is no longer a threat, are you, Jason?'

'N-no,' Jason whined.

'You were just carrying out orders, weren't you?'

'Y-Yes … I am sorry.'

'No harm done. Will, please, sit down.'

Reluctantly, Will complied, but never once took his steely gaze from the tiny man.

'Now, Jason,' Uncle Percy continued. 'You were told to kill me. Why?'

Jason lowered his head. 'The messenger said you were a cruel man. That you had travelled here to secure the Fleece of Gold and use its sacred power to destroy these lands. He claimed to be an emissary of Zeus himself. That it was Zeus' decree that I carry out a divine mission: your execution. And if I failed, my soul would forever be condemned to an eternity in Tartarus.'

Uncle Percy's face shone with compassion. 'Your soul is safe, Jason. You have been the victim of a deception, that is all. This so-called messenger is not godly in any way. He is but a man...'

'But only a God could foretell your coming.'

'There are other ways, believe me,' Uncle Percy said simply. 'The messenger was just someone that wants me dead. He tricked you into doing it for him.'

'Can this be true?'

'I swear,' Uncle Percy said. 'He is the dangerous one. And that is why we have travelled a great distance to be here. We are trying to stop him. Now, tell me … what exactly did he want you to do?'

Ashamed, Jason turned away. 'He said I must gather a crew and boat, and then journey to Crete. That soon after our arrival, I would meet you and your companions, that I was to gain your trust. I was to wait until you slept, then … then slay you.' Jason paused. 'Then I was to kill him …' He inclined his head towards Will, who responded with a derisory grunt.

Jason seemed unable to continue his admission.

'Please, go on,' Uncle Percy said.

Jason hung his head. 'I cannot.'

Uncle Percy's eyes narrowed suspiciously. 'What was to happen to Becky and Joe?'

'He ordered they remain unharmed.'

Uncle Percy nodded sharply as if this confirmed what he already knew. 'And what was to happen to them?'

'He said I was to take them with me.'

'Take them where?'

'To Hypatia Point in the Grey Mountains.' Jason pointed into the distance.

Everyone turned to chart the direction of the finger. The night was lifting and in the early morning light they could just make out a sprawling mountain range. One mountain towered above the others.

'The messenger said that there would be an olive grove at the base of the mount. He said he would meet me there. He would take charge of the child from then on.'

'Child?' Uncle Percy asked. 'You mean children?'

'If possible, both children, yes …'

'Go on,' Uncle Percy pressed.

'The messenger demanded I deliver both children to him, but if they became troublesome …' he faltered, 'then only the girl mattered. I was to kill the boy…'

*

Becky watched as Joe's face turned white.

Kill the boy!

Joe took a moment to digest this. Then he exploded with rage, his hands balling into fists. 'I'd like to see you flippin' try!'

'But I couldn't have seen it through. I could never harm a child.'

'But you could kill Uncle Percy?'

'But I couldn't -'

Joe was about to shout again when Uncle Percy held up his hand and stopped him. 'Please, calm down, Joe. Jason was fed a pack of lies.'

'I don't care if he was fed cabbage,' Joe roared. 'He was going to kill you, then Will, probably me, and kidnap my sister.' His eyes flicked to Becky before returning to Jason. 'If you ever lay a hand on my sister … I'll - I'll come back when I'm fifteen and kick your - '

'That's enough, Joe,' Uncle Percy said firmly.

Becky placed her hand gently on Joe's arm. Then she shuddered as an alarming thought entered her mind. It was definite now: the traveller wanted her. And only her. But why? What possible use could she be? Uncle Percy didn't seem to know either … or did he? Perhaps he had known the whole time? Had this been why he invited her to Bowen Hall for the summer, for her protection? Then something else occurred to her: they could use this to their advantage?

'Let him have me!' Becky said.

All went silent.

Joe stared blankly at his sister. 'What're you talking about?'

Becky stared at Uncle Percy. 'It makes sense. Let the messenger have me. Let Jason take me to the Grey Mountains. You can use me...'

'Oh, no way, Becky,' Uncle Percy blustered. 'Not - a - chance!'

'No, this is the chance,' Becky said. 'The chance to finish it. To stop all this for good. Let's have Jason take me to Hypatia Point, and have Will follow us. When the traveller comes into the open, it will only take Will one shot - one shot and this whole thing is over.'

'I am not using you as … as bait!' Uncle Percy said with disbelief. 'That's the most ridiculous thing I have ever heard.'

'Why is it?' Becky replied. 'You know what's at stake here. Give me one good reason we shouldn't do it?'

Uncle Percy looked flustered. 'There are a thousand reasons, all of them involving your demise.'

But Becky wasn't about to give up. 'That's not going to happen.'

'And how do you know that?'

'Because I've got Will on my side and he's the best there is.'

'Well - err - what if Will misses?'

Becky glanced proudly at Will. 'Will never misses. Your words not mine. Come on, you know it makes sense. This man has to be stopped. If this stupid Fleece is as powerful as you think, then imagine what he'll do if he gets it. Besides, if anything does go wrong, you can always use the -' she scanned the Argonauts' faces, '- the you-know-what and change things.'

Uncle Percy sighed heavily. 'I've told you about the Omega Effect. You can't always change things. It doesn't work like that.'

Becky held firm. 'It's worth the risk…'

'Listen, Becky,' Uncle Percy said. 'I appreciate what you are suggesting. Your proposal is very brave, but I am not prepared to risk your life. Besides, we're not here to kill anyone. We're the good guys remember. We're just here for the Fleece.'

'I'm not saying kill him,' Becky clarified. 'Just capture him.'

'Well,' Uncle Percy said defiantly, 'it's not going to happen. End of story!'

Becky gave a loud snort. She turned her attention to Will, hoping for a sympathetic ear. 'Will, you know that I'm right?'

'I agree with your uncle,' Will said softly. ''Tis a valiant gesture, miss, but far too dangerous.'

'Pah!' Becky huffed. Why couldn't they understand? It was her life that was at stake.

Uncle Percy sat beside Becky, placing his hand on hers. 'I'm sorry, but I'm not prepared to risk losing you again.'

Becky, however, refused to let it rest. 'But twenty minutes ago I nearly lost you, and that's all right, is it? You're dispensable? Well you're not to me…' Tears of frustration welled inside. 'You know I'm right about this. You should use me and -'

But Becky stopped herself. The soft shafts of first sunlight had highlighted Will's face. He appeared anxious, his eyes locked firmly on the valley behind them. Swiftly he jumped to his feet, his bow raised high.

'What is it, Will?' Uncle Percy said as the ground shuddered and a rumbling sound filled the air.

'Horsemen are approaching …'

*

Everyone scrambled to their feet, their heads rising over the dunes to see a billowing cloud of dust and sand.

Within seconds, a dozen men riding giant warhorses galloped into view. The Argonauts panicked. Phineus tripped over, falling flat on his face. Hercules fumbled for his sword, terrified.

Only Theseus demonstrated a hint of courage as he gripped his short sword. 'Argonauts. Arm yourselves!' He raised his sword high. 'Be brave, my brothers!' Then – thump - a spear punctured the patch of ground between his feet. His courage deserted him. 'Surrender, my brothers. We are defeated!'

The lead rider halted and gestured for the soldiers to gather in line on the dunes. 'Lower your weapons!' he shouted, drawing his sword.

The Argonauts dropped whatever they were holding with a resounding clank.

Becky watched as the lead rider threw his huge legs over his warhorse and dismounted. The horse looked relieved at shedding the weight. He took off his plumed helmet to reveal a tangled mass of black hair and a enormous cherry-red face. She wasn't sure where his head stopped and his neck began.

The lead rider strode self-importantly towards the group. 'You are now the prisoners of King Minos,' he yelled. 'I am Helladius. Captain of the Night Guard.'

Uncle Percy took a step forward. 'Good morning, sir. I'm Percy Halifax. My friends and I mean you, your king or your country no harm, and would like to -'

'SILENCE!' Helladius roared. Then he slapped Uncle Percy brutally across the face.

Becky gasped with horror.

Will made to launch himself at Helladius, when Uncle Percy's hand pulled him back.

'No, Will!' Raising himself to his full height, he pivoted back to face Helladius. 'Now that wasn't particularly friendly, was it?'

Straightaway, Helladius hit him again. A thick smear of blood dampened Uncle Percy's bottom lip.

'Leave him alone,' Becky yelled.

Helladius swung towards her. 'Silence, girl! Lest I show you the back of my hand.'

Will had heard enough. 'It takes a big man to threaten a young girl. And there are few bigger than you. Or uglier.'

Helladius turned menacingly to Will. 'You are a brave fool to offend me, stranger.'

'Then let me be a stranger no more. I am Will Shakelock, and if you touch any of my friends again you will not see another sun rise.'

At once, Helladius threw a mallet-like fist at Will.

With lightning speed, Will caught it and, teeth gritted, crushed it powerfully in his grip.

Helladius howled.

Will heaved the huge man close and leaned coolly into his ear. 'Wail like a newborn all you will. It matters not how many men you have in your little army, you will not harm my friends again. Do you understand?'

Eyes streaming, Helladius' legs buckled and he tumbled to his knees, simpering. At the same time, a soldier raced behind Will.

'Will!' Becky yelled. 'Behind you.' But it was too late. Lifting his sword high, the soldier smashed its hilt on to Will's skull. Will fell, clutching the back of his head.

Clasping his swollen hand, Helladius got to his feet, glared fiercely at Will before kicking him in the face.

'Please,' Becky cried. 'No.'

Helladius rounded on the floored Will. 'A quick death would be too easy for you,' he growled, although his voice lacked conviction. 'It pleases me the last thing you will smell will be the Minotaur's rotten breath as it feasts on your innards.'

Uncle Percy's expression changed. For a moment, even Becky forgot her fear and stared at Joe with disbelief. The Minotaur?

'Timaeus, Perticus - bind him,' Helladius bellowed. 'Bind them all. The King will appreciate our spoils, and the Minotaur will welcome fresh meat.'

A few soldiers leapt from their horses, coils of rope in their hands. They approached the Argonauts who offered themselves freely. Becky watched horrified as a guard tied Uncle Percy's wrists behind his back. Then Timaeus and Perticus bound a dazed Will.

Becky froze as a thickset guard approached her and Joe. He smirked cruelly and lifted them on to his horse.

'My cane,' Uncle Percy said to Helladius. 'I need my cane...'

Helladius picked up the staff. In one swift movement, the cane shattered across his knee. 'You have no cane.' Then he threw himself onto his warhorse. 'The King will be pleased,' he shouted, fat globs of saliva showering his horse's ears. 'TO KNOSSOS…'

Chapter 20

Dungeons and Dragoons

A golden sun inched over the mountains as the party marched into the mouth of Andrana's Valley. Becky watched as Uncle Percy trudged on. He looked surprisingly at peace, content even. She couldn't understand it. What was he thinking? It almost looked as if their capture had been a part of some master plan. But he couldn't have planned it. Could he?

'What are we going to do?' Joe asked Becky. 'Did you hear that nutter mention the Minotaur? It's real. I know it is.'

Becky said nothing. She didn't know what to think anymore.

'I'm worried,' Joe said quietly.

'Well don't be,' Becky replied. 'Uncle Percy isn't worried, so I don't think we should.'

'Yeah, but he's deranged.' He looked at his uncle who had begun to chunter happily to himself. 'He'll be more bothered about spotting a pink Blubber Frog than us being captured by a hairy psychopath. Anyway, what's the Omega Effect?'

'What?'

'The Omega Effect. I heard Uncle Percy mention it. What is it?'

'Oh, nothing.'

'Well it must be something. And how come I don't know about it?'

'He trusts me more than you,' Becky said. 'He thinks you've got a big gob.'

'No, he doesn't.'

'Okay, he doesn't, but I do. Now, shut up!'

They had been marching for more than an hour when they came to the Grey Mountains. Although it was perhaps a mile to their left, Becky could see Hypatia Point clearly. As she looked for the olive grove, she found herself wondering - would the traveller be there, waiting for Jason to deliver her safely? Did he know the assassination attempt failed? Was he watching them right now?

The temperature rose and the Argonauts were wilting as the party left Andrana's Valley and entered a desert of green scrub and fine sand. Then Becky saw something that left her breathless. In the distance, rising into the sky like a mirage, stood a colossal pearl-white structure: Knossos.

As they drew closer, Becky saw a stream of ox-drawn carts being steered through an archway, standing atop of which was a giant stone Bull's head; its painted yellow eyes appeared to follow them as they approached the towering city walls. Once through the arch, Becky felt a knot form in her stomach. They were in a vast courtyard full to bursting with hundreds of people, gathered for an outdoor market. She watched an old, craggy-faced woman in a ragged smock chase a runaway chicken that squawked loudly in a fruitless bid for freedom. Peering over at Helladius, whose red, pitiless face was sopping with sweat, she thought the chicken stood a better chance of getting it than they did.

Then something caught her eye: a face that didn't fit. A slender man wearing a dark cloak with an oddly fair complexion studied them intently. She looked over to see if Uncle Percy had seen him, but he was too busy saying 'Good Morning' to the bemused onlookers to notice anything. By the time she looked back, the man had gone, consumed by the jostling crowd.

*

They passed through a smaller archway into a quiet square. Helladius dismounted and turned to the guard on his right. 'Eustathious, take this scum to the dungeons. I will meet with the King and enquire as to his wishes.'

Helladius stood before them, his legs wide apart as he drew a wheezy breath that caused his massive stomach to rise above his belt. 'Do not get accustomed to the comfort of your cell. I am hopeful to see you dead before nightfall.' He disappeared into a five-tiered building.

Becky assumed they were at the Palace, for it was, without question, the most imposing structure within the city walls.

Eustathious leapt from his horse. 'PRISONERS, FOLLOW ME!' He marched to a smaller building to the rear of the courtyard.

They were guided through the dungeon entrance, down a series of steps, into a tunnel lit by flickering torches. Muffled laughter could be heard from the market above.

Becky turned to see the Argonauts, their heads bowed, plod down the steps. She heard Theseus mumbling about how he should have been in charge in the first place and if Hercules didn't stop whining he would punch him in the face. As they entered the cells, she saw a short, grubby-looking man, a few strands of wiry hair poking out of his bald head, his chest damp with grime and sweat. He was sitting on a stone slab, a plump finger inserted up his nose.

Even Eustathious appeared to think the gaoler was revolting and avoided eye contact when speaking to him. 'Prisoners, Galdeus.'

The gaoler pulled his finger from his nostril and wiped it on his shoulder. Then he stood up, his back hunched and burped.

'Ooh, lovely fresh prisoners,' Galdeus wheezed, unhooking a set of wooden keys from his belt. 'They look tasty. The Minotaur will feast well.' He threw them a toothless smile, and nodded at Becky. 'Especially on your pretty bones …'

Becky turned away. What a scumbag.

Galdeus turned towards a rear door and hobbled into an antechamber. 'Follow me.'

They found themselves in an airless room that contained a wide iron-barred grille that framed the entrance to a narrow cell. With a grunt, Galdeus slid it open and gestured for them to enter, cutting them free as they passed.

'Most kind,' Uncle Percy said, twisting his freed wrists. 'Galdeus, about this Minotaur, it wouldn't happen to live in a tunnel round here, would it?'

'It dwells in the Maze of Kyros, far beneath the ground.' Galdeus smirked. 'Only Daedalus' Gate, at the Maze's mouth, prevents the beast from rising and devouring us all. You will not be so lucky.'

'I'm sure,' Uncle Percy said. 'How do we get to the gate?'

Galdeus gave a cruel laugh. 'You will see the gate soon enough. The Minotaur is owed a feed, and the King dare not disappoint. There is no doubt … Death is coming for you.'

'Terrific,' Uncle Percy said brightly. 'We've all got to go sometime.'

'Mock all you will, stranger.' He slammed the grill shut. 'Will you jest when the beast has the girl's head between its teeth?' He locked the padlock, broke wind loudly and left the room.

'Charming fellow…' Uncle Percy said.

As a tense stillness cloaked the cell, the gravity of the situation occurred to Becky. Twenty-four hours ago, she would have dismissed the idea of an actual Minotaur as nonsense, but after the Harpies she wasn't sure of anything. And what if they didn't survive? Her mum wouldn't even have an explanation as to where they were, or what had happened.

For the next ten minutes no one said a word. Will paced round the cell like a caged animal; Becky and Joe sat making circles with their toes on the floor.

Uncle Percy, on the other hand, wore a bemused smile as if it was all an amusing game. Upon noticing Joe's anxious expression, he turned and said, 'Don't worry, Joe. I've been in considerably worse scrapes than this and always managed to get out of them in one piece.'

'Oh yeah, like what?' Becky snapped. Sometimes her uncle's constant optimism was really quite annoying.

Uncle Percy paused for a moment. 'Let me see - well, many years ago, Malcolm, Bernard and I, celebrated our graduation by going on a little jaunt to 1686 to visit King James II court. Malcolm always nursed an ambition to be a Royal Dragoon guard, you see.' He smiled fondly. 'Anyway, our costumes were perfect, our boots polished, our muskets gleaming. We thought we really looked the part, and, of course, we were young and convinced we wouldn't be caught.'

'What happened?' Joe asked.

'Caught within ten minutes,' Uncle Percy chuckled. 'By a rather grumpy Captain named Edward Blakely. Thinking we were spies for William of Orange, he imprisoned us as traitors. Anyway, we contacted the Trackers and they rescued us that very afternoon.'

'Trackers?' Becky said, puzzled. 'What are Trackers?'

'Oh, they're an invaluable part of GITT operations. A rescue service for time travellers. If, on a registered trip, a traveller finds himself or herself in trouble then they contact GITT headquarters with their pagidizor, and a team of Trackers is dispatched to give assistance.'

'What's a pagidizor?' Becky asked.

'Well, it's nothing spectacular to look at, rather like a calculator,' Uncle Percy said. 'But, in fact, it's a most ingenious piece of kit. When pressed, the pagidizor engages a series of temporal waves that stimulates sequential displacement and emits what we call a spatial flare.'

'Uh?' Becky grunted.

'Basically,' Uncle Percy said, 'it sends a distress signal to our time, so the Trackers can come and get you. It's a wonderful gadget, really.'

'Then use your pagidiwotsit and get us out of here.'

'I can't,' Uncle Percy said simply. 'It's in Bertha. Besides, the trip isn't registered so they wouldn't know when to come looking for us even if I did use it.' He smiled weakly. Sensing her despair, he injected enthusiasm into his voice. 'But anyway, we're not ready to go back yet, are we? We've still got a legendary relic to find.'

'We don't particularly want to be eaten by a dirty great monster, though,' Becky added sullenly.

'It won't come to that, I promise. Besides, we need to get into that Maze, no matter what's in there. Unless I'm very much mistaken, the Maze is Arthur Evans' Labyrinth.' Uncle Percy whispered, 'How else will we find out more about the Theseus Disc? Furthermore, the Fleece might even be in there.'

Becky huffed. 'Along with a dirty great monster.'

'Well, we don't know that for sure, do we?'

'Everyone around here seems pretty convinced.'

'Ah, don't worry,' Uncle Percy said. 'To be honest, I don't think that the Minotaur exists for one second, history is full of mythical beasts that never existed.'

'Like Harpies,' Becky said.

Uncle Percy's face dropped. 'Fair point. Anyway, if the Minotaur does exist I have come very well equipped.' He patted his chest mysteriously. 'You'll just have to trust me when I say - '

The dungeon door opened. 'Well, well, Percy Halifax. It looks as though you've landed yourself in a right old pickle, doesn't it?'

Even in the half-light, Becky could see Uncle Percy's face had drained of colour as though he'd seen a ghost.

And in a sense he had.

Chapter 21

A Young Old Friend

The man stepped out of the shadows.

'Bernard?' Uncle Percy said in little more than a whisper. 'Bernard Preston?'

'The very same,' the man said. 'Hello, my friend.'

Becky recognised the name. Bernard Preston, the traveller who met with John Aubrey and discovered the legend of Stonehenge. The traveller that was searching for the Golden Fleece. The traveller who died at Bowen Hall just over a month ago.

But as the torch opposite flickered on Preston's face, Becky gave an involuntary gasp. This wasn't possible. Preston studied at Oxford University with Uncle Percy, they would be a similar age, but this was a young man.

'It's happened, hasn't it?' Preston said, astonished. 'Lockets Syndrome, I mean. I never thought I'd see it.'

'I think it has.' Uncle Percy stood silently. 'And I've never seen it before either.'

Becky stared at Joe. Lockets Syndrome?

'You're from my future aren't you?' Preston whispered. 'Well, obviously you are. I only saw you last week and you were twenty six, same age as me.'

'I grew old.'

'So when are you from?' Preston asked.

'Let's just say I am from your future, shall we, Bernard? The details are unimportant.'

The Argonauts looked at each other, bewildered. Becky doubted she could explain even if she tried.

'Wow!' Bernard clapped his hands with delight. 'It's funny, you know. I was only saying to Emerson yesterday - what would we do if genuine Lockets Syndrome happened to us? And you know what a miserable beggar he can be … he just gave me a dismissive look as if to say it was impossible. But it's happened. It's really happened...'

'Yes, it has,' Uncle Percy replied. 'What are you doing here, Bernard?'

'Oh, you know me. I've always been fascinated by Ancient Greece. I come to Knossos quite often, particularly on Saturdays, like today. It's market day, in case you hadn't guessed.'

'I thought so.'

Preston smiled. 'So there I was, standing at my favourite stall, and who comes though the gate but that buffoon, Helladius, and my good friend, albeit slightly older, Percy Halifax. I couldn't believe my eyes.'

'I bet you couldn't,' Uncle Percy said.

'Anyway, I just bribed Galdeus with a packet of cheese and onion crisps and he let me right in.' Preston clapped his hands again. 'It's remarkable. Only last week, I made a decision to stay away from this timeline for a while, but for some reason, thought I'd visit Knossos one last time, and look what's happened: a genuine case of Locket's

Syndrome. Anyway, that's enough about me. What're you doing here?'

Uncle Percy paused. 'We're just having a family day trip. This is Becky and Joe, my niece and nephew. I just thought I'd show them what Crete was really like. You know, help them with their schoolwork and all that.'

'Real history, eh kids?' Preston waved at Becky and Joe. 'I wish I'd had a time traveller for an uncle when I was a nipper. It beats reading stuffy old books, eh?'

Becky and Joe smiled politely, although neither of them could think of anything to say.

'So how come you've landed yourself in jail?'

'Just a touch of rotten luck,' Uncle Percy said.

'Do you want me to bust you out?' Preston asked eagerly. 'A jailbreak would be so exciting. I can pop back to my time and get a couple of squid grenades from Charlie Millport. I wouldn't even need to inform headquarters, he owes me a favour. I'll have you out of here in no time at all.'

Becky's heart leapt. A jailbreak. However, a firm shake of Uncle Percy's head dashed the idea.

'No, thank you,' Uncle Percy said. 'We're going to see the King.'

'Are you sure?' Bernard said. 'I could always round up a couple of other Otters to help. I know Steffers would definitely do it, and Malcolm, he's always up for a rumble. Not too sure about Emerson, he doesn't seem to like you much and Ricardo is probably swanking around as a sixteenth century conquistador somewhere, but I could try - '

'No,' Uncle Percy asserted. 'Actually, would you do me a favour? In fact, it's more than a favour, it's a deeply felt appeal.'

'Anything.'

Uncle Percy took a heavy breath. 'You must not tell a soul about our meeting. Not anyone. Do you understand?' There was sadness in his voice. 'I know the fact that you've encountered Lockets Syndrome must be desperately exciting, but, please, I beg of you, you cannot tell anyone.'

Preston was clearly disappointed. 'But - but I'm sure that the younger you would love to hear that you're still travelling at your age. Surely -'

Uncle Percy's expression turned grave. 'Especially not the younger me. That would be very bad. Please, Bernard, you must respect my wishes on this. Besides, I know you do as I ask, and I thank you for it.'

'How do you know?' Preston asked.

'Because if you had told me, I would have known that we were to meet here, in this very dungeon, for twenty odd years, and, as I'm as surprised by this as you are, then you can't have mentioned it.'

Bernard Preston laughed heartily. 'That is a very good point, old chap. Well, if you're sure, then we'll make this our little secret.'

'Thank you, Bernard,' Uncle Percy said. 'It's more important to me than I could ever begin to explain.'

A mischievous twinkle appeared in Bernard Preston's eyes. 'Well, if I'm to do that for you, then perhaps you should do something for me.'

Uncle Percy sighed.

'How do I turn out?' Preston asked. 'Do I get married? Do we stay friends? What happens to me?'

Uncle Percy's mouth creased into a wide smile, careful not to display a trace of sadness. 'You turn out just fine, Bernard. In fact, you prove yourself to be one of the noblest men to have ever walked the earth. We are, and always remain, the best of friends. And that is all I'm prepared to say on the matter. It's never good to know too much about one's future.'

Bernard Preston exhaled. 'You're right. I don't want to know any more. That's the beauty of the future. Let it unfold as it may. But, I do thank you for those words.'

Becky saw Uncle Percy's bottom lip tremble slightly.

'That's perfectly all right, my dear friend,' Uncle Percy said quietly.

'Now are you sure you don't want me to get you out of here?'

'No. We'll be fine. Now you - you go get back to your time safely.' He smiled. 'I know for certain that you will.'

Bernard Preston extended his open hand through the iron bars and the two men shook. 'Goodbye, my friend.'

'Goodbye, Bernard.'

Then Preston turned to Becky and Joe and grinned. 'See you in twenty something years, kids. I'll know you before you ever know me. Good luck, everyone.' After giving a final bow, Bernard Preston left the dungeon.

When Uncle Percy arched round he was shaking like a leaf. He staggered to the far corner of the cell and slumped to the floor, his head cradled in his hands.

Becky wanted to reach out to him, to help. But what could she do? She couldn't begin to understand the grief he must be feeling. After all, it had only been a matter of weeks since Uncle Percy had watched that young man die in his arms.

Chapter 22

All the King's Horses

The stale air hung heavy as the minutes crawled by. Everyone tried not to stare at Uncle Percy, who remained as still as a statue. Becky turned to guidance from Will, but even he looked uncertain as to what to do. Deciding she had to at least try and help, she took the initiative and walked over to him, sat down and placed her hand gently on his arm. 'Are you okay?'

'I'm fine,' Uncle Percy said, raising his head. 'Good fellow, Bernard. Thoroughly decent. And handsome too, don't you think?'

Becky shrugged. 'Not really my type.'

Uncle Percy smiled weakly. 'Perhaps not. Nevertheless, he was a virtuous, warm-hearted chap.'

Becky felt close to tears. It was the first time she'd seen her uncle so vulnerable. She decided to change the subject. 'What's Lockets Syndrome?'

Taking a moment to collect his thoughts, Uncle Percy whispered, 'Well, it's a very, very rare occurrence. You see, the world is an enormous place. And time - time as you are doubtless aware, is infinite. Therefore, the chances of two travellers casually bumping into each other, unplanned, at a specific place at a specific time are - well, the odds are astronomical. Of course, there are certain events throughout history where it is common for travellers to gather at the same time and place, but that's not genuine Lockets syndrome. Not like what we've witnessed today.'

Becky looked puzzled. 'Uncle Percy, can I ask you something? You cared about Bernard Preston, didn't you?'

'Very much.'

'Well, couldn't you -' Becky paused for a moment, unsure whether to continue or not, '- couldn't you travel back and stop his murder?'

Uncle Percy sighed. The glow from the nearby torches accentuated the deep sorrow on his face. 'I tried,' he said. 'I travelled back to London on the afternoon he was killed. But I couldn't get close to him or the events that transpired. I'm sure you can probably guess why.'

'The Omega Effect.'

'Correct,' Uncle Percy said sourly. 'It was exactly like when I tried to help your father. It nearly always happens if you try and prevent a human death, for some reason.'

Then something occurred to Becky. 'Did you see him get shot? Or who shot him?'

Uncle Percy bowed his head. 'I'm afraid not. I returned time and time again, but the Omega Effect prevented me getting close enough to see anything. After the seventh attempt failed, I had to accept the painful truth…'

'And what was that?' Becky asked.

'That, for whatever reason, fate had determined that he should die that day and that the killer should escape.'

Becky shuddered. 'I'm sorry.'

'Don't be,' Uncle Percy said. 'Many lives may have been saved because of his sacrifice. I'm sure he would've wanted that.'

A sudden CRASH shook the dungeon walls as Helladius threw open the door, an ugly expression fixed on his face. 'Right, filth... The King wishes to see you!'

'Oh, goody,' Uncle Percy muttered.

Helladius stepped aside and Galdeus shuffled in. Unlocking the wooden padlock, he slid the grille open. They all trudged out of the cell, the Argonauts leading the way.

'Farewell, my tasty friends,' Galdeus growled.

Uncle Percy winked back. 'And farewell to you, Galdeus. You have been a most charming host.'

'I hope your death is a brutal one, white hair,' Galdeus rasped, shoving Uncle Percy roughly through the doorway.

As he straightened the creases from his cloak, Uncle Percy muttered, 'It seems like everyone wants me dead lately...'

*

The prisoners surfaced into daylight. Becky felt nervous as the blast of light stung her eyes. What were they walking into?

They were marched through the courtyard to an open-planned corridor with brilliant, multi-coloured murals lining the walls.

'The Corridor of Processions,' Uncle Percy said, his eyes glazing over. 'Look at the detail in those frescoes - wonderful.'

Finding it impossible to share his enthusiasm, Becky shrugged. The last thing she cared about were stupid paintings.

Making a sharp right at the far end of the corridor, they passed a shaded propylaeum, and found themselves in a grand hall at the end of which stood a large staircase, patrolled by the Palace Guard.

As they followed Helladius up the staircase, Becky couldn't help but wonder why Uncle Percy did not take Bernard Preston's offer of a jailbreak? She understood he wanted to enter the Labyrinth, but surely there must be a safer way … a way that didn't involve pleading before a possibly merciless King.

Helladius led them through a series of magnificent rooms until his giant frame wobbled to a standstill. 'Wait here!' He disappeared through a doorway, only to reappear a few seconds later. 'The King will see you now. Move!'

'Don't be afraid,' Uncle Percy said to Becky, before stepping into the Throne Room. 'I've got a good feeling about this.'

'Of course you have,' Becky mumbled and Becky followed him inside, head bowed. When she looked up, she gulped noisily. Sitting on an enormous gold throne was a well-groomed man with a bearded face that resembled a hairy sprout. He wore a shining ruby necklace and a snow-white tunic that just about concealed his gigantic tummy. A crown of lilies sat upon his unruly raven black hair.

Helladius took a pace forward. 'King Minos, my lord.' He bowed. 'I give you the prisoners...'

For a few moments, King Minos sat there in silence, studying the group with a fierce expression. Then broke into a grin. 'Welcome, my prisoners, to The Great Palace of Knossos.'

Helladius frowned.

Uncle Percy stepped forward. 'Thank you very much King Minos. I'm - '

'SILENCE, PRISONER!' Helladius bellowed, striding up to Uncle Percy and grabbing him by the hood. 'You will only address the King, if, and when, you are addressed.'

Uncle Percy nodded dutifully. 'My apologies.'

'Now, now, Helladius,' King Minos said cheerily. 'Today we forgo all formalities. Today is a happy day. A momentous day!' The King's eyes gleamed. 'Please, stranger, speak, you have nothing to fear.'

Helladius scowled again.

'We thank you, King Minos. My name is Percy Halifax, and these are my friends. We are strangers to your kingdom, and have come here to do you a service.'

King Minos studied Uncle Percy, bemused. 'A service you say, prisoner? What possible service could you perform that others already do not?'

'We are here to slay the Minotaur,' Uncle Percy replied simply.

There was silence. Then, with a crashing thud, Hercules fainted.

King Minos hesitated. He smiled, then chuckled, then began to laugh. His crown fell off as it turned into an uncontrollable fit. After a few seconds, in which time Will had helped Hercules to his feet, King Minos spoke., 'You, grey hair?' His face swelled to the size and shade of a basketball. 'You believe you can kill the Minotaur?'

'Yes, sir, I do.'

Becky stared at Uncle Percy with disbelief. This was his plan?

'Oh, what a joyous day,' King Minos gushed. 'First, Pasiphae has agreed to be my wife, then the King of Athens has presented me with a wonderful new pet, and now this ... Tell me, stranger, what makes you think you can succeed where so many others have failed?'

'We have means,' Uncle Percy replied mysteriously. 'All I ask is that should we succeed, you give us our freedom. That these men -' He gestured towards the Argonauts, '- will be given safe passage throughout your lands, and that, if necessary, you give us a ship, the fastest in your fleet.'

King Minos waved flippantly. 'Of course.' He leant forward. 'You are aware that I have sent many of my finest warriors into the Maze of Kyros to complete that very task, that scores of men and women have been sent as sacrifice to prevent the beast leaving its lair - that none have returned!'

'I am now,' Uncle Percy said. 'Do we have a deal?'

'Certainly, stranger.' King Minos slapped his thigh joyfully. 'Certainly we do. And as you have continued my excellent mood, you may see my new pet, a creature of such beauty as to rival Aphrodite herself. Castor ... bring me the beast!'

Everyone looked to the rear doorway as a young boy entered carrying a loop of rope. With a firm jerk, he pulled a snow-white foal into view. Becky felt her heart skip a beat.

Murmurs of wonder filled the room as everyone caught sight of the most astonishing thing. Tucked snugly beneath the foal's shoulder blades were a small but well-defined set of wings.

King Minos rolled off his throne. 'Prisoners, this is Pegasus - The Horse of the Gods. Of course, she can't fly yet, but when she's older she will take to the skies like an eagle. That's if I allow it, of course.' He snatched the rope from the boy and yanked the horse closer to him. 'I may just have her wings clipped.'

It was then Becky noticed the tiny horse was trembling with fear. She couldn't stop herself. 'HOW DARE YOU!' Her angry voice filled the room.

'What?' King Minos replied with a mixture of surprise and amusement.

Uncle Percy held up his hand, gesturing her to stay silent. 'No, Becky.'

Becky ignored him. 'How dare you talk of clipping her wings. And don't drag her like that, you're scaring her.'

King Minos looked bewildered. 'Are you really addressing me in such a manner, child?'

'Yes, I am,' Becky said boldly. 'Shame on you! Some King you are.'

King Minos glared at her. 'SILENCE!'

'Quiet, Becky,' Uncle Percy said.

Becky looked desperately at her uncle. 'But -'

And for the first time, Uncle Percy raised his voice to her. 'Becky, that's enough!'

Becky was about to object, but his angry tone and a sharp shake of his head made her think otherwise.

'Muzzle the child,' King Minos roared at Uncle Percy. 'If she speaks again, I will have your heads where you stand.' With an incensed breath, he returned to his throne. 'Castor. Take the beast to the Hall of the Colonnades. Flog her if she whimpers.'

The boy nodded dutifully. He dragged Pegasus through the rear door and into the far room. The small horse arched its head sadly towards Becky and then disappeared.

Becky boiled with anger. Then, as she stared at the spot where Pegasus had stood, something very strange happened. She experienced a very strange sensation, as if a droplet of water had trickled onto the top of her head, then she saw something move in the opposite room - a cloaked man, his back pressed against the wall, his hooded face twisted left and right as if watchful of an unseen enemy. She blinked to double-check, but the man had gone. The strange sensation had gone too. She turned to Joe, then Will, and finally Uncle Percy, but their faces were expressionless, as if they hadn't seen a thing.

Impossible, Becky thought. How could they not see him? The man was right in front of them. She was baffled now.

Meanwhile, King Minos continued his rant. 'Now, look what you've done. You have vanquished my fine humour.' He huffed loudly. 'Very well, face the Minotaur … Helladius, make an announcement in the marketplace, Daedalus' Gate is to be opened. Now … Get them out of my sight!'

'Weapons,' Uncle Percy said. 'We'll need weapons.'

The King hesitated. 'Very well, Helladius, arm them. I will join you at the Gate in one hour. Now … leave me.'

'I trust you know what you're doing?' Will said to Uncle Percy as they exited the Throne room.

'Haven't the foggiest,' Uncle Percy whispered back.

All the while, as a much cheerier Helladius led them through the Corridor of Processions, Becky's eyes remained fixed on Uncle Percy. Eventually he noticed and said, 'Is something the matter, Becky?'

'It's nothing,' she said, looking away.

'Something happened in there, didn't it?' Uncle Percy probed, lowering his voice so the Argonauts were out of earshot. 'Something you can't explain?'

'Why'd you say that?' Becky said. 'Did you see something?'

'No,' Uncle Percy replied. 'But I saw your face.'

Becky sighed. 'I thought I saw something in the far room.'

'What?'

Becky's face creased. She knew her suspicions were unbelievable, but then the unbelievable had become quite commonplace lately.

'Well, at first, I thought I saw … well – you.'

'I think he was with us,' Joe mocked.

'I know he was, dimpling,' Becky snapped at him.

'Let your sister speak, Joe.'

Becky turned back to Uncle Percy and whispered, 'I mean - another you! '

'Another me?' Uncle Percy replied.

'Yes, or -' Becky said, '- or someone looked like you. I mean, whoever it was wore a hood, I didn't see their face, but - well, it was either you - or -' she paused, '- can I ask you something?'

'Of course,' Uncle Percy replied.

'Your brother,' Becky whispered. 'Was he a time traveller, too?'

'Yes.' An unusual expression crossed Uncle Percy's face. 'But he's dead.'

'But so was Bernard Preston, yet he was here an hour ago.'

'True. Perhaps your mysterious stranger was Bernard, then?'

'I don't think so,' Becky said assuredly. 'No, the more I think about it, the more I'm certain it was you.'

'Or maybe you're just seeing things?' Joe said.

Becky shot him an angry look. 'Why don't you just go and eat your own bum!'

Uncle Percy frowned. 'What a delightful image,' he said. 'Anyway, Becky, why do you think it was me?'

'The same thing that made her think she saw George Clooney in Kebabland last year,' Joe sneered.

'Will you … shut up!' Becky turned to Uncle Percy. 'I don't know, it just felt like you. It was actually the strangest feeling I've ever had, like - '

'Like the one you had when you saw George?' Joe interrupted. A moment later, he nursed a very sore arm.

Becky never did finish the sentence.

Chapter 23

Edgar

Thirty minutes later, Becky stood before a huge iron gate in the Central Court. The gate merged into solid rock behind them. Will stood to her right, fully armed with a sword, bow, and a quiver of arrows. Thousands of eager eyes watched them as if lined in a bizarre beauty pageant. Word had travelled fast that Daedalus' Gate would be opened.

Uncle Percy had obviously decided to not go quietly either. Waving madly at the crowd, he acted like a very desperate, aged rock star, trying unsuccessfully to start a Mexican wave and, every now and again, launching into a dance routine that looked suspiciously like the hokey cokey.

'What's he got to be in such a good mood about? Joe asked Becky. 'If this Minotaur is as nasty as everyone tells us then what chance do we have?' He looked at the Argonauts and sighed. Phineus' looked deathly white; Theseus stared blankly at the ground; Jason looked as though he'd wet himself, and Hercules had just vomited for the fourth time in as many minutes. 'Let's face it … they're a waste of space.'

Becky nodded. 'I'm sure Uncle Percy knows what he's doing,' she said unconvincingly as she watched him start breakdancing.

A hush rippled through the crowd.

King Minos mounted a podium, took a mighty breath and bellowed, 'Fair citizens of Knossos, salutations to you all! As you will have heard, Daedalus' Gate is to be opened.'

The crowd roared with pleasure.

'These eight prisoners will enter the Maze of Kyros to face the great beast that lurks within. Today, so they inform your King, their valour, their mettle and their lethal skills will purge our great city of the dreaded horned beast that has plagued out nightmares for so long.'

King Minos sniffed scornfully. 'These are to be our champions. Now have you ever seen a more dismal band of warriors?'

Hercules retched loudly.

King Minos pointed at Hercules and laughed wildly. 'Witness for yourself the courage of our defenders.' His dampening eyes returned to the crowd. 'Anyway, I shall delay these proceedings no more. Let the - '

His speech was interrupted by a distant snapping noise, like a popped balloon. Slivers of silvery smoke billowed out from a window in the west wing of the Palace. A collective gasp echoed through the courtyard.

Becky glanced at Uncle Percy, as a strangely satisfied expression crossed his face.

King Minos huffed. 'Is that a fire?' he snarled at the guard on his right. 'Put it out and find out who's responsible. I want them flogged. Do not fret, good people, he yelled, even louder than before. 'The matter is in hand.' He waited until all eyes returned to him. 'Without further ado, let the spectacle commence … OPEN DAEDALUS' GATE!'

A dozen guards scurried to the gate, lifting an enormous iron chain off the ground. The guards heaved it tight and the gigantic gate inched open.

Becky whispered in Uncle Percy's ear, 'Promise me, whatever's in there won't eat us.'

'Don't worry,' Uncle Percy replied. 'If the Minotaur exists it will rue the day it messed with us.'

'Why do you say that?' Becky asked.

'Because I have a Tracker Pack strapped to my chest!'

Becky remembered the bumps and bulges under his tunic. 'A what?'

'A Tracker Pack. Trackers wear them when they go on rescue missions. It's got all sorts of exciting stuff.'

'What sort of stuff?'

Uncle Percy gave a mischievous grin. 'Oh, a veritable smorgasbord of devices: K17 stun bombs, a memoraser, squid grenades, spatial vaporisers, smoke pellets, a temporaliser and suction balls. I'm positively a lethal weapon.'

'You have bombs strapped to your chest?'

'Yes.'

'W-what if you went off?'

'Well, then none of us have to worry about being eaten, that's for sure?'

Becky regretted asking.

The hum from the crowd rose to fever pitch as King Minos faced the prisoners. 'You will now enter the Maze of Kyros, and may the fortune of Hermes shine upon you.'

'Thank you so much,' Uncle Percy said, taking a flaming torch from a servant boy and waving merrily at the crowd. 'Cheerio then, everyone. Have a smashing day.' Then he turned briskly and entered the gateway.

One by one, the rest followed.

The temperature fell sharply as Becky placed her foot on the first step. She saw Uncle Percy ignite a series of torches set on the wall, which revealed hundreds of steps that led deep underground.

'Well, thanks a bunch, white-hair,' Theseus growled to Uncle Percy. 'Our deaths are on your hands.'

'Ah, don't worry, Theseus,' Uncle Percy said with a wink. 'I wouldn't be surprised if you, in particular, didn't come out of this as something of a hero.'

'I'll come out of this as Minotaur dung,' Theseus replied sourly.

A few seconds later, Becky heard a shattering clang from above. Daedalus' Gate had been closed again. She felt sick. They were off to battle the infamous Minotaur! Terrific, she thought sourly.

By the time they reached the final step they were at least two hundred feet below ground. It was damp, musty and very cold.

'It must lead under the Grey Mountains,' Uncle Percy whispered.

Becky didn't care where it led.

Five minutes passed and Becky found Arthur Evans' words ringing in her head. "I found a tunnel that connects the city of Knossos to the Aegean Sea." Hope filled her. Perhaps they would just walk to the sea without incident;

perhaps there would be no Minotaur at all. Then, just as she began to relax, she heard a rumbling sound, as if the tunnel walls had woken from a heavy sleep. The group froze. Hercules squeaked.

They were not alone.

*

Becky watched as Uncle Percy reached into the folds of his tunic. He pulled out two tiny objects, no bigger than marbles. Will loaded an arrow and aimed into the darkness. The noise rumbled through the tunnel again. Becky felt her stomach flip.

Uncle Percy pointed the torch ahead. The light showed the tunnel forked right; whatever was coming was round the corner.

WUMP. WUMP.

They were footsteps. Becky felt sure of that. Heavy footsteps. Just how big was this creature? Then she saw a glittering orange light. Will pulled back the bowstring and took aim.

WUMP.

Becky muffled a scream as a very definite silhouette swelled on the far wall. The Minotaur did exist. The outline was clear: an enormous human body and an animal's head with two long, twisted horns that jutted from either temple. It was carrying something in each of its massive hands.

The Minotaur turned the corner and drew to a halt. It was colossal - at least fifteen feet tall, with a muscular physique, a gigantic bull's head and lifeless ebony eyes.

Frozen, Becky watched the Minotaur approach, in its mighty grip, a flaming torch and a bunch of flowers.

A bunch of flowers?

'Good afternoon,' the Minotaur said, grinning from ear to ear.

The group was stunned to silence.

The Minotaur moved forward. Suddenly his footsteps didn't seem as loud or scary. 'Oh, please, do lower your weapons.' He spoke softly, rather like a well-mannered country vicar. 'What's the matter with you lot, anyway? Never seen a giant with a bull's head before?' He let out a belly laugh.

At once, the tension of the moment evaporated. Soon the tunnel rang with laughter.

'See, isn't that better,' the Minotaur said. 'These are for you, little lady.' He presented the flowers to Becky.

'Er, thank you very much,' Becky replied.

'My absolute pleasure.' The Minotaur resumed his full height. 'First of all, I'd like to welcome you to my home. It's not much but we like it. I do so hope you do too. Anyway, I'm Edgar.'

A long pause followed. Everyone stared at each other with astonishment.

Uncle Percy stepped forward. 'Thank you, Edgar, we're delighted to be here. My name is Percy Halifax, this is my niece, Becky, my nephew, Joe, my friend, Will, and these are the Argonauts: Phineus, Jason, Hercules and Theseus.'

'Welcome,' Edgar said. 'I'm dreadful with names, but please give me time. I'm not a completely mindless Minotaur.' Edgar let out another very loud chuckle. 'Now, you must all be ravenous. We're just about to have a spot of afternoon tea. It would be an honour if you'd join us.'

'We?' Uncle Percy said.

'Yes,' Edgar said. 'My friends and I. I'm sure they'll be keen to meet you. Now, personally, I'm a vegetarian, but there's plenty of meat for those that prefer it. Anyone hungry?'

'I'm starving,' Joe said.

'Terrific,' Edgar replied. 'Now, it is a bit of a hike so would anyone care for a piggy-back?'

'I will,' Joe said eagerly.

'Excellent!' Edgar beamed. 'Climb aboard, then.' And the Minotaur sank to his knees and lifted Joe on to his shoulders. 'Just hold on to the horns, and mind your head.' Rising to his feet, he traced his own steps back into the tunnel.

Becky breathed a sigh of relief and watched as Joe bobbed up and down. The infamous Minotaur, the scourge of Knossos was, in reality, nothing more than an oversized teddy bear, with sparkling black eyes and a temperament to match.

*

They walked for a further fifteen minutes with Edgar leading the way, when they came to an abrupt halt, their mouths all falling open at the same time.

'Welcome to our home,' Edgar announced proudly.

A gobsmacked Becky stared at a gigantic cavern with a lagoon in its centre. Enormous stalactites, of every colour, hung from the ceiling like chandeliers, nearly touching the surface of the clear, green water. But the most surprising thing was the sixty or so people gathered there, some basking on leather towels, others swimming in the lagoon, the rest cooking food on an open fire. She knew at once these were the warriors dispatched to kill the Minotaur, the human sacrifices sent into the Labyrinth. They had chosen to stay and formed a community. A community dedicated to relaxation and pleasure.

Becky remembered something else: Arthur Evans found the Theseus Disc in a lagoon.

Edgar lowered Joe to the floor.

'Where do you get all this?' Uncle Percy said with amazement, nodding at the tables buckling under the weight of huge piles of food.

'There's a direct path to the surface,' Edgar replied. 'Actually, there are three paths, including one to the sea. Ionoclus, over there runs a farm on the surface so we never run short. And do you see Darius …' He pointed at a large man whose cloth apron barely covered his generous tummy. 'He's an excellent chef. He's even invented something he calls the Doner Kebab, which I am assured is an excellent delicacy following a goblet of ale. Anyway, enough of my chitter-chatter, would you like to eat now?'

'Please,' Joe replied.

And eat they did. Course after course, with every taste catered for.

Halfway through the meal, Becky scanned the mass of contented faces as they talked, laughed, and swapped stories, and she came to a single conclusion.

It really was the happiest of homes.

Chapter 24

The Minotaurs Mark

'Why don't you all stay?' Edgar said to Uncle Percy, polishing off his last baked mushroom stuffed with soft cheese. 'It would be so much fun to have you live with us.'

'I'm afraid we can't,' Uncle Percy replied.

'But why?' Edgar replied. 'Your friends seem very happy.' He pointed a giant finger at Phineus, who was swimming with two girls in the lagoon, his face beaming like a cat with a bucket of cream.

Uncle Percy smiled kindly. 'I'm sure the Argonauts would love to stay, but I'm afraid we must move on. We're looking for something.'

'How exciting.' Edgar's eyes glistened. 'What are you looking for?'

'Information.' Uncle Percy removed the Theseus Disc from his cloak.

'Where did you get that?' Edgar said, sounding alarmed.

'That's a long story,' Uncle Percy said.

'You know what it is?' Becky asked Edgar.

'Of course I do,' Edgar wheezed, becoming more and more distressed. 'My grandfather made it - but, how did you get it? Oh, Lordy! It's out isn't it? It's free!' His gigantic body began to tremble.

'What's free?' Uncle Percy asked.

'The dragon with nine heads. The Hy -' His voice failed him.

'The Hydra!" Joe exclaimed.

Becky shivered as she recalled her dad's book. The Hydra was a fearsome nine-headed monster and supposed guardian of the Golden Fleece.

'You know of the great beast?' Edgar whimpered. 'I thought that -'

'Only from stories,' Uncle Percy interrupted. 'Listen, Edgar, it's rather difficult to explain, but the Hydra may not be free.'

'But this is the key.' Edgar said, nodding at the disc. 'Well, part of it ... '

'The key?' Uncle Percy said. 'The key to what?'

'To the Great Gate in the Red Caves.' Edgar struggled to find the words. 'To the Lair of the Beast.'

Becky's head reeled. They were getting somewhere.

'You said it was part of a key?' Uncle Percy said.

'Yes,' Edgar replied. 'The key was forged in two parts - the disc and the Eye of the Bull. One will not work without the other.'

'The Eye of the Bull?'

'It is a powerful jewel,' Edgar said. 'The only one in existence - a Suman Stone.'

Uncle Percy turned pale. 'A Suman Stone?'

Becky heard the shock in his voice. 'What's a Suman Stone?'

'I don't know,' Uncle Percy replied. 'But Bernard Preston's last words were "Find Suman". I always assumed it was a person, but never found anyone of significance with the name. Come to think of it, do you remember the letters 'SS' on his note. Perhaps now we can see what he meant by them.'

'What's so special about the Suman Stone, Edgar?' Joe asked Edgar.

'It is a magical jewel, an enchanted jewel. Its power harks back to my brethren's earliest days, in the age of the ancients. It is the stone of my people. The Minotaur's Mark. My grandfather used it for the key because of its mystical properties. You see, when placed in the disc's centre the two become one – metal and jewel. Only then will the Great Gate open.'

'Tell me, Edgar,' Uncle Percy said. 'Did your grandfather ever mention a Fleece? A Golden - '

Before Uncle Percy could finish, Edgar made an ear splitting squeak and his thick black lips quivered. 'You know of the Great Fleece? I thought that my brothers and I were the only ones who knew...'

Uncle Percy looked grave. 'No, there are others. And they are searching for it.'

'They must not find it,' Edgar said desperately. 'The Fleece is a powerful object. My grandfather said that it should not be trifled with, particularly not by manfolk. That is why he hid it in the Red Caves, with the beast as its protector.'

Uncle Percy sighed. 'I'm afraid that's not going to happen. These men will find it, at whatever cost. That is why we are here. We intend to find it first, and - '

Edgar's nostrils flared the size of golf balls. 'NO!' he shouted. 'You are good people. The Fleece is a bad thing! It is not for humans! Humans cannot be trusted with that much power. Humans are corruptible. Humans are -' His eyes glistened with tears.

'Please lower your voice,' Uncle Percy said. 'What I'm going to tell you now must go no further, do you understand?'

Edgar stared ahead, miserably. 'I'm sorry. I didn't mean to shout.'

'That's quite all right,' Uncle Percy replied, glancing round to make sure he couldn't be heard. Leaning forward, Uncle Percy told him everything - of the invention of time travel, of Bernard Preston's murder, of the failed assassination attempt. He left nothing out.

Considering the remarkable nature of this information, Becky thought Edgar took it very well. He listened intently and, save for the odd gasp, whoop and whimper, digested everything.

'So you want the Fleece so you can hide it again?' Edgar clarified.

'That's right,' Uncle Percy said.

'But will not the protection of the Hydra be enough?'

'I don't think so,' Uncle Percy said. 'You see, in our time we have many formidable weapons. Weapons you could not begin to comprehend.'

'But the Hydra cannot be killed by the weapons of manfolk,' Edgar said, sounding relieved. 'They are akin to Minotaurs. Only a weapon built by the Gods, or one forged from the metal of the motherland can kill it.'

Uncle Percy looked skeptical. 'I don't know about any of that. But I do know these are dangerous men we are dealing with. They will find a way to kill it.'

Edgar didn't appear to believe him. He blew out an enormous squall of air. 'Lordy!' His lopsided mouth broke into a wide smile. 'This is a lot to take in.'

Becky smiled at him. 'We thought that, too.'

'Please, Edgar,' Uncle Percy said. 'Where are these Red Caves?

'They are on the Island of Kera, many leagues from here.'

'Could you draw us a map?' Uncle Percy said.

'Indeed,' Edgar replied. 'But you are forgetting the real problem: The Great Gate. My grandfather was the shrewdest of our kind and an extraordinary craftsman. It would be impossible to open without both pieces of the key.' As he scanned their faces, his mighty jaws fell open and he stopped breathing.

'What is it?' Uncle Percy asked immediately.

Edgar didn't reply.

'Edgar?'

Edgar couldn't take his eyes off Becky. 'B-but y-you have it?' he stammered.

'Have what?' Uncle Percy replied.

'The Eye of the Bull. You already have it. But how?'

Uncle Percy's eyes traced Edgar's and he, too, found himself looking at Becky. 'What do you mean?'

'The g-girl,' Edgar spluttered.

Becky felt confused. What was Edgar talking about? 'I'm the Eye of the Bull?' she said. 'I don't think so.'

'Not you -' Edgar pointed at her neck, at her lucky pendant. 'That is the Eye of the Bull. That is the Suman Stone.'

Becky looked down. The pendant's stone shed a soft green reflection across her neck.

At once, for each of them, a heavy mist lifted. All recent events clicked into place: the break-in at Bowen Hall; Jason's orders to abduct her.

Someone wanted her lucky pendant.

A pendant she had owned since she was seven years of age – a pendant given to her by her late father.

Chapter 25

Uncle Percy's Wish

Becky's fingers trembled as she traced the central stone. How could it be part of the search for the Golden Fleece? It was just a worthless trinket she'd been given for coming last in a particularly aggressive egg and spoon race. 'You're mistaken.'

Edgar stared fixedly at the necklace. 'The Suman Stone is the stone of my ancestors. There is no mistake. Where did you get it?'

'My dad gave it to me,' Becky replied, her voice barely audible. 'Just before he died.'

Uncle Percy closed his eyes. 'Edgar, may we go somewhere private?'

A few minutes later they were huddled on the floor of a musty cave, far away from the crowded lagoon. Becky refused to look at anyone, her eyes locked on the far wall as she waited for someone to speak.

'Becky, please, pass me the pendant,' Uncle Percy said.

Her fingers tightened around it. 'No.'

'Please, Becky.'

'Give it to him,' Joe snapped.

Becky's eyes dampened. She knew she had no choice. Slowly, she coiled it over her head and passed it over.

'When this is over, I swear I will fix this.' Uncle Percy took the pendant and pulled a penknife from his pocket. As he sliced the stone from its cluster, Becky squeezed her eyes shut. He cupped the Theseus Disc in his right hand and inserted it into the disc's central groove.

Becky heard Joe gasp. Forcing her eyes open, she saw thin feathery shards of misty green light pulsating into the disc. It seemed alive. And then the light was everywhere, shooting out like lightning, illuminating the far reaches of the cave.

'Whoa!' Joe yelled as bolts of lightning coiled round Uncle Percy's outstretched hand like blazing tentacles.

'The key is complete,' Edgar breathed.

Uncle Percy removed the Suman Stone and the cave fell into darkness.

'That was excellent!' Joe said. 'Do it again.'

'No, Joe,' Uncle Percy said solemnly, holding the Suman Stone between his fingers. 'I'm afraid, Becky, I'm going to have to keep this.'

'You can't,' Becky growled. 'It's mine.'

'I know,' Uncle Percy said. 'And I'll keep it safe. I swear I will.'

Becky looked to Will, but his face offered sympathy not support. She folded her arms and turned away.

Moments passed. All the while, Joe couldn't take his eyes off the Suman Stone. 'Where would dad get something like that?'

Uncle Percy paused. 'I have absolutely no idea.'

As the words lingered in the air, Becky felt anger welling inside. Was it really possible Uncle Percy had no idea about where it came from? Had he truly never heard of the Suman Stone?

Uncle Percy looked at Edgar. 'We need your help. We need you to tell us how to find the island of Kera. Unless I'm very much mistaken, we're running out of time.'

Edgar swallowed hard. 'I will take you.'

'You will?'

'I give you my word.' Edgar forced a smile. 'My family's home is on a neighboring island. Perhaps it is time I paid my brothers a visit.'

'Thank you, Edgar,' Uncle Percy said. 'We'll need a boat. I shall return to the Palace and talk to the King.'

'No!' Edgar said at once. 'If you return he will believe I am dead, the community will be doomed. We will take my boat. We will leave at first light. With the wind on our side the journey should take three days.' He sighed heavily. 'But you will arrive at Kera. And may the Gods protect you from what you find there.'

*

That night Becky lay under a blanket, staring at the inky lagoon. She felt tired - exhausted even - but her mind ached with questions. Her thoughts, however, were disturbed by a groggy voice.

'Becky,' Joe said. 'Are you awake?'

'No.'

'It's weird, innit?'

'What is?'

'You having the Suman Stone.'

'I guess.'

'How do you think dad got it?'

'How should I know?'

'Do you think he knew what it was when he gave it to you?'

'How should I know?'

'Well, I suppose we'll never know.' Joe yawned.

'I suppose not.'

But Becky did know, at least she thought she did. And tomorrow she would confront Uncle Percy about it. She knew her suspicions were unbelievable, but surely there could be no other explanation? But just how much did he know? Certainly, if what she now believed were true, then he was a manipulative liar. And if that was the case, she never wanted to see him again.

*

'Oi, get up,' Joe said, pushing his sister. 'We're going!'

Becky's eyes sprang open to see Joe standing above her. 'You touch me again and I'll tear your head off.'

'Lordy. Look who's been bitten by Mr Grumples?' Edgar said.

'Sorry, I didn't sleep well,' Becky replied. Then she heard another voice and her stomach churned.

'Good morning, Becky,' Uncle Percy shouted over.

'Morning,' Becky mumbled, refusing to look him in the eye. Casting her blanket aside, she watched four figures emerge from a nearby cave. The Argonauts gathered in line before Uncle Percy, sad but resigned smiles on their faces.

Jason stepped forward. 'So you will not stay?'

Uncle Percy placed his hand on the small man's shoulder. 'I'm afraid we can't, Jason. We have a Fleece to find. But I think you will all be very happy here.'

'Thank you,' Jason said.

'We would accompany you, but would be of no aid,' Theseus said guiltily. 'We are not warriors.'

'But you are great men,' Uncle Percy said kindly. 'And history will remember you as such. I promise you that.'

Phineus leant over and whispered in Uncle Percy's ear. 'And I am sad I never witnessed the Devon-shire Bunny horses.'

Uncle Percy turned pink. 'Next time,' he whispered back.

The next few minutes were filled with hugs and warm exchanges of good luck. After their goodbyes, Uncle Percy, Will, Becky and Joe collected their possessions and turned to Edgar who stared sadly at his sleeping friends.

'Let us depart…' Edgar said, and holding a torch in one hand, a sack in the other and two water urns dangling from his horns, he lumbered towards the tunnel.

*

For ten minutes, they followed the bobbing flame of Edgar's torch along a narrow, sandy path flanked by a saltwater river and the damp tunnel wall. The sound of the ocean grew louder all the time.

'Nearly there,' the Minotaur said, his spirits improving with each step. Then, as the path curved, Becky glimpsed a most welcome sight. Daylight.

Gathering pace, the group emerged into a cove. Water lashed against rock giving the impression the sea was much rougher than it was.

Edgar came to a halt, pointing below. 'There...'

Becky looked down and saw a boat, painted gold and maroon, bobbing on the water like a fishing float. Two giant wooden oars were raised on its helm like matchsticks. In no time at all, the ship was loaded with provisions. Edgar had lifted the stone anchor, settled his mighty frame into a large wooden seat in the center of the deck and seized the oars.

'Can we help, Edgar?' Uncle Percy said. 'Will and I could take an oar and -'

Edgar chuckled. 'Thank you for the offer, Perce, but I'm rather looking forward to the exercise. It's difficult enough to attract the ladies when you have a bull's head - the last thing I want is a sagging tummy.'

With a splash, Edgar launched the oars into water and the ship creaked to life. Before long, Edgar was powering them out of the cove, towards the open sea. Within the hour, Bertha had been loaded onto the boat.

Edgar stared in wonder at the strange looking vehicle. Unfortunately, when he climbed inside his horns became stuck in the upholstery and it took twenty minutes to set him free.

By the time they set off to sea again everyone was in good spirits. Everyone, that was, except Becky. The novelty of the boat trip had worn off and all she could think about were the events of the previous day - that, and a series of increasingly bizarre theories about Uncle Percy. Isolating herself as best she could from the others, she watched as Edgar broke into song.

Becky smiled. It was such an extraordinary sight to see this man-monster singing what sounded like a gentle lullaby. Indeed, Edgar's singing made her eyes heavy and within minutes she fell asleep. When she awoke, she saw a sail had been raised, inflated by a keen sea breeze. Edgar stood at the rear of the ship, Joe hanging from his horns, as he completed dozens of squats. Then she heard a voice she no longer trusted.

'Sleep well?' Uncle Percy said.

'Yes, thank you,' she replied curtly.

'Perhaps, Becky, it's time you and I had a little chat.'

'I'll get Joe,' Becky said. 'What I've got to say concerns him, too.'

'That's as maybe,' Uncle Percy said simply. 'But why don't we talk first, just the two of us. Perhaps, then, you can decide if he's ready to know what I've got to say.'

Becky thought for a moment then nodded silently.

A few seconds later, they were standing at the prow, staring out at the empty horizon.

'Now, I know that you are angry with me,' Uncle Percy said, 'that perhaps I've kept things from you. And, to some extent that's true. But I believe you'll understand why. Now, why don't you ask me what I know you're longing to ask?'

'You've used us, haven't you?'

'What do you mean?'

'You've used us,' Becky repeated. 'Joe and me. You knew I had this Suman Stone. You knew that when you invited me and Joe to stay for the summer?' Her voice cracked. 'You acted like you cared about us, like you wanted to get to know us, but it was all a lie. You just wanted the stone…'

Uncle Percy paused to digest her words. 'Is that what you think? That's why you're angry with me?' He let out a relieved laugh.

'Don't you dare laugh at me!'

'I'm sorry,' Uncle Percy said sincerely. 'Becky, now you must believe me. I swear I had no idea you possessed the Suman Stone. No idea at all.'

She searched his eyes, looking for the truth. Her voice softened. 'Then why did you invite us this summer, of all summers? You've had plenty of time to see me, yet you never have. Me, who just happens to own the one item that you need to get that stupid Fleece.'

Uncle Percy sighed. 'I never wanted you to become involved in any of this. I certainly had no idea about the Suman Stone. Don't forget, it was you who discovered I was a traveller. I didn't tell you. I was never going to tell you. Well, not yet anyway.'

'What do you mean, not yet?'

'Because -' Uncle Percy fell silent '- Because I won't be around forever. And no matter how much I can manipulate time, time is also manipulating me. Now, you and Joe are the only family I have. And furthermore, you are such extraordinary people and both possess the qualities that are needed -' He hesitated.

'Needed for what?' Becky pressed.

'To run Bowen Hall,' Uncle Percy said honestly.

A look of shock crossed Becky's face.

Uncle Percy continued. 'You see, I want you and Joe to inherit all I have: Bowen Hall, the other properties, the inventions, the patents. I want you to have everything. That is why I invited you this summer - to get to know you again, and for you to know my world.'

'But you're not…' Becky couldn't finish the sentence.

'Dying?' Uncle Percy cut her off. 'We're all dying, Becky. That's the one thing in life that is certain. But that's not the point. The point is I want to make contingencies for the future. And I want to give Bowen Hall to the two people I know would cherish it as I do.' He threw her a warm smile. 'That's if you both want it, of course?'

Becky felt moved to silence.

'You see,' Uncle Percy said, 'the running of Bowen Hall may be a responsibility you're not willing to bear. To run Bowen Hall, you must recognise what it stands for, and preserve it as best you can. Now that is asking a lot of anyone. However, all I wanted to do this summer was to introduce you to it. Then we could have taken it from there…'

A tear trickled down Becky's face. So this was why he had invited them to stay for the summer. His legacy.

'I'm so sorry,' she said. 'I just - I just never understood.'

'How could you?' Uncle Percy replied. 'But it is I who should apologise. And I do. However, the story doesn't end there, and I think you know it.' His expression grew serious again. 'I have lied to you. Well, at least, I haven't told you the whole truth. And I think this is also what you're wanting to talk to me about isn't it?'

'There is something else, yes...' Becky replied nervously.

'Then, please, ask. I'll be as truthful as I can.'

'It's about my dad.'

'I know.'

Becky felt her body tremble. 'He was a time traveller too, wasn't he?'

Uncle Percy paused. 'One of the finest...'

Chapter 26

Bird's Eye View

To Becky's surprise, the confirmation her father had been a traveller didn't shock her at all. It had been the only answer from the moment Edgar had recognised the Suman Stone. 'Did you know he had the stone?'

'No,' Uncle Percy replied honestly. 'Don't forget, he and I hadn't talked for some time.'

'D'you think he knew what it was when he gave it to me?'

'Absolutely not,' Uncle Percy said assuredly. 'I'm sure he thought it was just a very unusual necklace. That's all.'

'So how did he get it?' Becky said.

'I'm afraid I have no answer to that.'

Becky gulped. Then something else occurred to her; something that sent a chill through her bones. 'Did mum know he was a traveller?'

'No. I don't think so,' Uncle Percy said. 'I'm certain she didn't. You see, when your father first met your mother he was the happiest I'd ever seen him, so content in his own time that his journeys became less frequent. He just wanted to spend as much time with her as he could. The more their relationship grew, the less incentive he had to travel. In fact, although your father was a very brave man, I believe for the first time in his life he was scared.'

'Why?'

'I think he found something in your mother he couldn't find in a lifetime of time exploration. He fell in love. He was scared of losing that. He wasn't prepared to risk the dangers of travelling anymore. It was several years after they were married before he started travelling again.'

'And why was that?' Becky asked.

A look of uncertainty crossed Uncle Percy's face. 'I'm not sure.'

'Was it to do with the Fleece?'

'I really can't say.'

Becky nodded. 'Was it you who first told him about time travel?'

'Actually, no,' Uncle Percy said. 'Bernard Preston did. That's why you may have heard his name before. Bernard was your father's tutor at University, you see, and your father his most gifted student. Your father, like Bernard, was also a keen archaeologist. So, inevitably, when Bernard introduced him to travelling, he took to it like a duck to water. Personally, I wasn't sure he was ready for it.'

'Why not?'

Uncle Percy smiled fondly. 'I just felt he possessed certain qualities that, shall we say, are not conducive to safe time travel.'

'Like what?'

'Your father was somewhat hotheaded. I suppose I just wanted to keep him out of harm's way, for a few more years at least.'

Becky nodded. Then another question suggested itself. 'How does someone else know I've got the pendant?'

Uncle Percy took a heavy breath and drummed his chin. 'That is the most intriguing question of all, isn't it? My honest answer is that I don't know. I suppose if this traveller found out what the pendant was and realised your father had it, then it's possible he could have travelled to the moment when he gave it to you. But that is just speculation.'

A wave of alarm swept through Becky. 'But that - that would mean I might have seen him.'

'It's possible. But there could be a thousand other ways for him to find out.'

Becky took a moment to process the information. 'Just one more question.'

'Go ahead.'

'What kind of time machine did dad have?'

Before Uncle Percy could answer, there was a breathless voice from behind. 'What are you two gassing about?' Joe's face shone with sweat. 'Becks, come and hang off Edgar's horns while he exercises. It's great fun.'

Becky grinned. Joe always seemed to pick the most inappropriate times to interrupt. 'I'm coming,' she said, walking over to Edgar. As she did, she glanced back at Uncle Percy. A spark had returned to his face as his lips silently mouthed three words. 'An ice-cream van.'

Becky's heart did a flip. Her dad's time machine had been an ice-cream van. She could remember it. It was her first memory: she'd been sitting on the front lawn, pulling the legs off her least favourite doll when he drove a ramshackle pink ice cream van up the drive. To her mum's embarrassment, he spent months renovating it. Then, as quickly as it had appeared, it disappeared … the same ice-cream van that to this day, remained Becky's favourite vehicle in the whole world.

*

Becky and Joe played with Edgar for the next twenty minutes, dangling from his horns as he whizzed round like a bizarre spinning top. All the while, Uncle Percy remained at the prow, preoccupied with the sky. He had a pair of what he called Amnoculars and trained them above.

Becky looked up but could see nothing but a tiny, moving speck, which she assumed was a gull. She watched curiously as Uncle Percy lowered the Amnoculars and whispered in Will's ear.

'What's going on?' Becky asked, walking over.

'I'm not sure,' Uncle Percy replied. 'But do you see that bird?'

She looked up at the sky and squinted. 'Just about.'

'It's been following us for quite some time …'

'So?'

'So I think I've seen it before,' Uncle Percy added.

'What do you mean?' Becky asked, confused.

'I think it was at Bowen Hall on the night Bernard was murdered.' He nodded at Will.

Baffled, Becky reeled with horror as Will loaded an arrow into his bow and pointed it into the air. 'What are you doing?' she yelled at him.

'Do it, Will,' Uncle Percy said coolly.

'NO!' Becky cried. But it was too late. The arrow had been fired.

Becky watched with dismay as it pierced the bird's neck and plummeted down, crashing into the water with a gigantic splash. Uncle Percy jumped in after it.

Becky was hysterical and glared at Will. 'You murderer!'

Uncle Percy swam over, but the bird had vanished. Taking a gulp of air, he plunged underwater and seized its ankles, appearing on the surface seconds later.

Becky watched as he swam towards them, dragging the bird's carcass behind him. Will grabbed a length of rope and tossed it into the sea. Uncle Percy caught it and heaved himself aboard.

'Now, Becky, Joe,' Uncle Percy said, smoothing back his soaking hair. 'That might've looked like a dreadful thing to do, but it only looked that way.' He tossed the bird on the deck. It landed with a particularly heavy clank.

'Dreadful?' Becky screamed. 'You just committed murder! I should fire an arrow into your throat.'

Uncle Percy grinned. 'Please don't. And to murder something it had to be alive in the first place.'

Becky wasn't listening. 'You've just killed an innocent bird for no reason.'

Uncle Percy ignored her, picked up the bird and, in one swift action, twisted its head off.

Becky yelped. However, instead of blood, she saw a thick gust of smoke and thin, wispy sparks of electricity.

'This is a very advanced piece of technology,' Uncle Percy said. 'Joe, would you pass me a knife, please?'

Joe raced to the hull. He snatched a large knife from an open sack of oranges and handed it over. 'What is it?'

'It's a Cyrobot,' Uncle Percy replied. Dropping to his knees, he plunged the blade into the bird's breastbone; it splintered to reveal a series of torn flesh, blood, cabling and electronic circuits. 'Look at the craftsmanship.' He sounded impressed. 'I believe, what we have here is an Enthium exo-skeleton, a voice relay tracking system, lycro-skin and solar-induced battery capacitors.'

'I-it's a robot?' Becky felt a sudden urge to be sick.

'Of sorts. A cyborg.'

'Huh?' Becky grunted.

'It's half-organic, half-mechanical,' Uncle Percy continued. 'It was a bird, now it's a tool. A very sophisticated tool.'

'And it was following us?' Joe said.

'Indeed.'

'Why?' Joe said.

'Because of this.' Uncle Percy pulled out a small metal cube.

'What is it?' Joe asked.

Uncle Percy stood up, raised the box into the light and examined it. 'It's a recording device and, unless I'm mistaken, a cellular broadcaster. Someone, somewhere, is watching and listening to our every move.' He dropped the cube onto the deck, raised his foot and smashed his heel down on it. 'At least they were.'

'So you can make a Cyrobot out of any dead animal?' Joe asked.

'Yes.'

'And you can maneuver it like a remote control plane?'

'That's the idea.'

Joe turned slowly to Becky, his face white as marble. 'The psycho budgie!'

Becky's stomach tumbled. 'Oh my God,' she panted.

'What is it, Becky?' Uncle Percy asked quickly.

Becky couldn't speak, so Joe did it for her.

'Becks was attacked by this mad budgie in our front garden a few hours before we came to Bowen Hall.'

'And it kept aiming for my throat,' Becky added quietly. 'But it was after my pendant, not me.'

'Then that's something, isn't it?' Uncle Percy said, trying to make her feel better.

'I guess,' Becky replied. 'But I nearly let that same budgie into my room just an hour before that. I nearly let the traveller into my bedroom…'

*

In contrast with Becky, the discovery of the Cyrobot seemed to raise Uncle Percy's spirits. He spent the rest of the afternoon forcing Becky and Joe to play the dullest round of I-Spy imaginable ('I-Spy the sea' – 'I-Spy the sky') and taking Edgar's lead in doing some exercise.

'What's put you in such a good mood?' Becky asked finally, watching him collapse after his second press-up. 'We are being followed!'

'Correction. We were being followed. That's precisely why I'm happy. And so long as there isn't another Cyrobot disguised as a bottle-nosed dolphin, then this traveller has no idea where we are.'

Day melted into night and Becky found herself lying under a blanket, staring wistfully at the glittering stars above. The only sound was the lapping of the water against the ship and the sail flapping as it gathered every trace of wind. She had so many questions to ask Uncle Percy, but judging by the soft snores coming from his bed now was not the time to ask them. What she was most eager to know, however, was something she felt sure he wouldn't tell her: the topic of the argument between him and her dad. What on earth could be so serious they hadn't spoken for so many years? She had no idea what it could be. And so she just lay there, gazing at the heavens, as the ship glided through the ocean.

*

On the second day, Becky sensed a mild but tangible air of tension as Uncle Percy busied himself by performing safety checks on Bertha. Edgar spent most of the afternoon sketching a detailed map of Kera, offering hushed words of advice to Will and Uncle Percy which were received with nods and murmurs of agreement.

Becky awoke on the third morning to find Uncle Percy, Will and Edgar staring fixedly on the horizon. She kicked her brother awake and ran to join them. 'Is that it?'

'It is,' Edgar said in a low voice. 'The Island of Kera …'

'It's big,' Joe yawned, appearing behind them. 'Do we know where we're going when we get there?'

Uncle Percy held up the map. 'We know exactly where we're going.'

As the island extended before them, Edgar lowered the sails and took up the oars. Fighting the current, he steered the ship to the shoreline. Kera was more imposing than Becky had expected. There were sprawling golden beaches, exposed reefs of coral and emerald blankets of scrubland. A vast, rust-coloured mountain range was just about visible.

Edgar guided the ship into the shallow waters, towards a bay that clung to the shore like a giant horseshoe. Raising the oars, he dropped anchor. Will positioned two wooden planks between Bertha and the beach. After loading their belongings, Uncle Percy drove on to the sand, before returning to the ship.

Uncle Percy, Will, Becky and Joe lined up before Edgar, whose black eyes were misty and lifeless.

'It's time to say goodbye, Edgar,' Uncle Percy said. 'Thank you so much for everything.'

'It has been an honour and a pleasure,' Edgar said glumly. 'Please, be careful.'

'We will,' Uncle Percy replied, extending his hand.

'Goodbye, Edgar,' Becky and Joe flung their arms around his waistline.

Edgar hugged them tightly. 'I will miss you both, very much.' His voice quivered. 'You must take excellent care of each other.'

'We will,' Becky and Joe replied at the same time.

Will stepped forward and offered his hand. 'Our thanks, my friend, and our best to your brothers.'

Edgar pushed Will's hand aside and pulled him close in a back-crushing hug.

Releasing Will, Edgar turned to the group. 'I refuse to weep,' he sniffed, 'but there is one more thing...' He reached down and lifted up his sack. He pulled out a long object swathed in matted brown cloth. 'I want you to have this.'

He unraveled it to reveal an orange dagger, which glistened in the sunlight. The dagger appeared to be made from the same curious metal as the Theseus Disc. 'It was my grandfather's.'

'We can't, Edgar,' Uncle Percy said. 'You've given us quite enough.'

'You must,' Edgar insisted. 'If you are to face the great beast your mortal weapons will be of no use. This is made from the metal of my motherland. It may bring you the fortune you need. I beg you to take it.' He offered the dagger to Uncle Percy, who took it.

What was a dagger in Edgar's hands was nothing less than a magnificent sword in Uncle Percy's.

'Thank you, Edgar,' Uncle Percy said sincerely. 'We've taken so much from you and given you nothing.'

The Minotaur gave a deep bow. 'Your friendship has been the finest gift I could have ever wished for…'

Taking it in turns, they each gave Edgar a final hug. Then they climbed into the time machine and drove off.

Grief-stricken, Becky turned and watched as Edgar grew smaller and smaller, his plate-sized hands waving madly.

What she couldn't see were the streams of tears rolling down his snout.

Chapter 27

The Red Caves

As they pressed deeper into the island, Becky felt a profound sense of loss swell inside. She missed Edgar terribly, and judging from the glum faces around her she wasn't the only one.

'I hope Edgar will be safe,' Joe said.

'He's the size of a monster truck,' Becky said. 'Of course he will be.'

'I know, but -'

'He will,' Will reassured them.

'According to the alto-radar,' Uncle Percy said, 'his family's island is less than a mile away. It'll be good for him to see his brothers again.'

Becky twisted to face front. 'Uncle Percy, why don't we know about Minotaurs? I mean, we know about dinosaurs and other extinct things. Surely, someone would have found Minotaur fossils? They're big enough.'

'That's an excellent question, Becky,' Uncle Percy said. 'And I was the biggest doubting Thomas about their existence, wasn't I? I suppose, the reality is that there are many creatures that we have no idea existed. If there was only a small population to begin with, the chances of finding remains are actually very remote. Alternatively, hundreds of new species of fish are discovered each year.'

'But that's just boring fish,' Joe quipped, 'not massive Bull-men.'

'The same principles apply, Joe,' Uncle Percy replied. 'There are many species that have managed to remain hidden from human eyes, some living in such hostile climes it's virtually impossible for humans to explore.'

'Like Yetis,' Joe said excitedly. 'Do they exist?'

Becky snorted. 'Of course they don't.'

'Actually, Becky, they do,' Uncle Percy said. 'I've met one.'

'You have?' Joe gasped.

'I have,' Uncle Percy confirmed. 'A community of them, in actual fact.'

'Where did you meet them?'

'I was in the Himalayas exploring the south-western slopes of the Menlung Glacier in 1950, and I got separated from my party, a British geological expedition. Anyway, I was at an altitude of about 15,000 feet, when I discovered some large footprints covered in blood. I followed the trail and found an injured Yeti. It had been attacked by a number of snow leopards. Fortunately, I had food and an extensive medical kit, and spent two days nursing him back to health. He told me his name was Gimbledok and -'

'Yeti's can talk?' Becky interrupted, sounding very skeptical.

'Not particularly well, I'm afraid,' Uncle Percy said. 'However, he was speaking in an ancient Nepalese dialect, and I, of course, was wearing my transvocalisor. Anyway, by way of thanks, he took me to his cave village, high in the mountains. There were about twenty Yetis in total. Gimbledok was their chieftain.'

'What were they like?' Joe asked.

'Very noble,' Uncle Percy said. 'Very loyal, peaceful unless provoked, and they love collecting things. Some things I found dated back hundreds, if not thousands of years. That reminds me, I really should visit them soon.'

'Would you take me?' Joe said immediately.

Uncle Percy chuckled. 'We'll see.'

'What other creatures exist?' Joe said eagerly. 'Ones I might've heard of.'

'Err, Unicorns,' Uncle Percy said, glancing at Becky in the rear-view mirror.

Becky's ears pricked up. 'Really?' Unicorns had always been her favourite mythical creature.

'Indeed, they do. As a matter of fact, they still exist on an unchartered island in the South China Seas. There are hundreds of them. Staggeringly beautiful creatures.'

'What about werewolves?' Joe asked enthusiastically.

'Not to my knowledge.'

'Vampires?'

'There were rumours during the seventeenth century, but I honestly can't say.'

'Dragons?'

'Again, plenty of rumours, particularly from twelfth century Europe. You're from then, Will. Did you hear of any dragons?'

Will smiled. 'Tuck claimed he saw one once. But the friar's fondness for mead clouded his vision on more than one occasion.'

For a further five minutes, Joe asked about which other mythical beasts existed and which hadn't. He was particularly disappointed to discover the Loch Ness Monster was a mechanical cow planted by an Irish time traveller, Fergal Murphy, in the nineteen twenties, the result of a drunken dare.

After much laughter, it was Becky's words that changed the tone. 'And what about Hydras?'

The campervan fell silent.

'That, Becky, remains to be seen...'

*

Soon the conversation dwindled to little more than the odd murmur. The gravity of their situation had dawned - they were approaching the Red Caves, the supposed location of the Golden Fleece.

Becky stared at Edgar's dagger. And she wasn't the only one. Joe was looking, too. Hesitantly, he leant over and picked it up.

'Be careful with that, Joe,' Uncle Percy said. 'It's extraordinarily sharp.'

'And this is what we're going to kill the Hydra with, is it?' Joe said.

'If there is a Hydra, Joe, I'm sure it will be dealt with in whatever way is necessary,' Uncle Percy replied. 'However, whatever happens, we are not going to be killing anything. At least, you're not. You and Becky are not taking one step inside those caves.'

Becky was gobsmacked. After all they'd been through together. How could he even consider them not being together at the end?

'But -' Joe spurted.

'But nothing,' Uncle Percy replied firmly.

'We can fight,' Joe said resolutely.

'I'm sure you can,' Uncle Percy replied. 'But not today.'

Joe's voice was rising now. 'So what are we going to do?'

'You can wait outside and guard Bertha!'

Joe turned beetroot red. 'From what?' he barked. 'Monkeys?'

Uncle Percy didn't rise to the bait. 'I'll be setting Bertha's remote to Bowen Hall. If Will and I don't return, you will travel back to the Hall. It is not open to discussion.'

Joe looked to Will for support. 'But Will?'

'I would have it no other way,' Will replied honestly.

Finally, Becky broke her silence. 'But you need us …'

'What I need,' Uncle Percy said, 'is for you both to be safe.'

'But you can't go in there alone,' Becky said.

'I never said we were going in alone,' Uncle Percy replied mysteriously.

'But -'

Uncle Percy smiled at her. 'And that is my final word on the matter…'

Chapter 28

The Great Gate

Becky and Joe sulked as the campervan weaved its way through dense jungle into the heart of the island. Joe had thrown the dagger to the floor. He refused to speak to anyone and stared furiously out of the window.

Much to Becky's frustration, Uncle Percy was ignoring their silent protest and acted like he hadn't a care in the world. He hummed loudly, pointed out interesting wildlife, cracked jokes and conferred with Will as they pored over Edgar's map. Then it swelled on the horizon: a red mountain.

'What the - ' Uncle Percy said, his gaze fixed on the road ahead.

Becky peered through the windshield and let out a gasp of surprise. Before them stood the ruins of a decimated village; flecks of sand carried on the air like a yellow mist, landing on the scarred remains of burnt out buildings. Her surprise turned to horror as she saw dozens of human skeletons scattered everywhere, their flesh long since torn off by scavengers. She felt bile rise in her throat as she saw a snake loop the black, empty eye-socket of a human skull.

'What happened here?' Joe puffed.

'No idea,' Uncle Percy said gravely. 'But whatever it was happened a long time ago. It's none of our concern.'

From the sound of his voice, Becky wasn't convinced.

Uncle Percy steered Bertha towards the Red Mountain. They were now close enough to see something gigantic and silvery fashioned into the rock.

The Great Gate.

A few minutes later, Uncle Percy drew Bertha to a halt and they all clambered out. Soon, they were standing in a dumbstruck silence before the colossal grilled structure that gleamed brightly in the high sun.

Reverently, Uncle Percy's eyes moved left and right, up and down, as he absorbed every inch of the magnificent construction. 'So this is Minotaur craftsmanship … remarkable!' His hands moved across the thick panelling to find a circular space on the far left-hand side. 'The keyhole…'

Becky's pulse raced as she felt Joe's hand slip into hers.

They were so close.

At once, Uncle Percy swivelled on his heels and marched to the campervan. He climbed in, inputted something onto the time pad, and wound down the window. 'Now Becky, Joe, I won't be a second. Literally…'

Becky and Joe exchanged as, with a BOOM, Bertha had vanished.

'What's he doing?' Joe said.

'Worry not,' Will smiled. 'His plan is - ' Before he could finish, Bertha reappeared in exactly the same spot as before.

Uncle Percy was sitting there, a broad grin on his face. 'I told you we weren't going in alone.' He flung open the driver's door. 'I've brought the cavalry.'

Becky watched; her curiosity spiked. She noticed the campervan was swaying from side to side.

Uncle Percy slid open the side door and, with a majestic roar, Milly leapt out, into Becky's open arms

Beaming, Becky ruffled her head. Then she heard a high-pitched whine and she knew at once that Milly wasn't the only Bowen resident to have made the trip. 'Sabian?' she cried, lifting the cub out of the campervan and clasping him to her chest.

Uncle Percy tickled Sabian's chin. 'I thought you might appreciate some company while we're gone.'

'You've been back to Bowen Hall?' Becky asked.

'I have, indeed,' Uncle Percy said. 'Maria wants to know if you fancy chicken and chips for dinner? Oh, and she's making blueberry tart for pudding, which I assure you is a real treat.'

Becky couldn't believe it. The world of Bowen Hall, Maria, and blueberry tarts seemed such a distant memory.

Uncle Percy entered more coordinates onto the time-pad. 'Bertha is now set to return to Bowen Hall. When Will, Milly and I have entered the caves, I want you to wait one hour. No longer! If we haven't returned I want you to press this button here …' he pointed to a winking amber button, 'and return to the twenty first century.'

Becky's eyes moistened. 'But -?'

'No, buts,' Uncle Percy replied. 'You must do as I say. Now, if we don't return in an hour, it doesn't necessarily mean that anything bad has happened to us. However, I do need you to return to the Hall. Then, I'd like you to ask Jacob to take you to a pub in Addlebury called The Magpie Inn. I want you to explain everything to Reg Muckle, he's the landlord. Now Reg is a smashing chap and an ex traveller, he'll know exactly what to do. Do you understand?'

Becky and Joe nodded.

'Will you do that for me?'

'Yes,' Becky mumbled.

'You promise?'

'We promise,' Becky said.

Reluctantly, Joe nodded.

'Thank you,' Uncle Percy said. 'But I don't want either of you to worry. We'll all be tucking into blueberry tart before you know it. Won't we, Will?'

'Of that I am certain.'

'I'm scared,' Becky said quietly.

'There is nothing to be scared of,' Uncle Percy replied.

Sensing her upset, Milly curled her head against Becky's leg.

'See…' Uncle Percy added. 'Milly isn't worried, and neither should you be. Are you ready, Will?'

Will looped his bow over his shoulder. 'I am.'

Uncle Percy inserted Edgar's dagger into his belt. Taking out the Theseus Disc, he approached the gate and slotted it into the hole. Then he inserted the Suman Stone into the disc and waited. For a second nothing happened. Then the key exploded into life. Jets of emerald light spread from the Suman Stone and slithered all around like cracking glass.

Within seconds, the light had fed every inch of the gate, turning the dull silver metal misty green.

Becky felt her heart racing.

Joe's mouth dropped open so much he resembled a fish.

A loud, creaking sound fractured the silence. Slowly, the gate edged open, revealing a long tunnel behind, lit by thin beams of sunlight that filtered in from cracks in the tunnel walls.

Uncle Percy knelt before Becky and Joe. 'I promise you that we will come out of this alive,' he said, 'and with a Golden Fleece. Now, I bet you didn't expect to do that in your summer holidays, did you?'

'We would've been happy with a day trip to Rhyl.' It took all of Becky's resolve not to grab him and not let go. Instead, she placed Sabian on the ground and watched sadly as he and Milly rubbed noses.

Uncle Percy turned to Joe, who wore his bravest face. 'Joe, I need you to take care of your sister and Sabian for me. Will you do that?'

'Course I will.'

Kneeling, Will met Joe eye to eye. 'Do not fear, I swear we shall return. There is still much about archery you have to learn, and I would not miss teaching it you for the King Solomon's fortune.'

Joe forced a smile and said, 'Just come back.'

'Come, Milly,' Uncle Percy said. Milly obediently padded to his side. 'Now, remember. If we're not back in an hour you must leave for Bowen Hall. Get to the Magpie Inn. Tell Reg Muckle everything.'

Becky took hold of Joe's hand. She clasped it tightly. 'We will.'

'We'll be back in a jiffy.' Flashing them a parting smile, Uncle Percy entered the gateway. Will followed, Milly at his side.

'Be safe,' Becky shouted, as she watched them disappear into the shadows.

There was no reply.

*

Becky and Joe stood there, alone and helpless. Sabian tugged at Becky's sandals. She picked him up again and pressed her cheek against his. A single thought flooded her mind: What if she never saw Uncle Percy again? She couldn't begin to explain how much he and Will meant to her. They were her family now.

'We should follow them,' Joe said.

'No,' Becky replied. 'For once, let's do as we're told.'

'But they might need our help,' Joe said. 'What if they -' he hesitated, '- what if they don't come back?'

'They will,' Becky replied. 'I know they will.'

'But - '

'No, Joe, we wait. That's what Uncle Percy asked us to do, and we promised we would.'

A voice came out of nowhere; a hollow, jeering voice. 'How very principled of you, Rebecca … a quality usually lacking in the youth of today. Bravo.'

Becky and Joe spun sharply round.

Standing before them was a tall man with raven-black hair, a gaunt face and tapered blue eyes. Dressed formally in a navy blue suit and tie, it would be easy to mistake him for a bank manager or an accountant, except he was a pointing a gun at Becky's head.

'I like to see obedience in a child,' the man purred.

'Who are you?' Becky panted, although deep down she already knew the answer.

She was staring at the traveller.

'That is of no matter to you. Let's just say I'm an old friend of Uncle Percy's.'

'You're no friend of his,' Becky snapped back. 'You're a murderer!'

'Am I now?' The traveller replied with a sneer. 'How very naïve of you. And if I am, what of it? What is a murderer anyway?' He laughed darkly. 'Was Winston Churchill a murderer? Was George Washington? Of course they were. They had men killed, many men. Considerably more blood stains their hands than mine … thus far, anyway. No, it seems to me that killing is an essential part of greatness - killing with motivation and just cause. And my cause is certainly just. In fact, show me the truly great man who wasn't a murderer.'

'My uncle,' Becky replied at once.

'Your uncle is but an ignorant fool,' the traveller scoffed. 'Why, even as we speak he is doing my bidding. He's just too stupid to recognise it.'

'He's not stupid,' Becky cried, her blood boiling. 'He's the cleverest man alive.'

'Clever? Oh, I really don't think so.'

'He is,' Becky shouted, 'He's -'

'He's my puppet. Nothing more, nothing less.'

'HE'S NOT!' Joe roared.

The traveller turned to face Joe. 'Ah, the other one has a tongue.'

'Yes, I do,' Joe barked. 'And when my uncle comes out of there he'll kill you.'

The traveller snorted. 'I doubt that. That would take genuine courage and he's far too much of a coward. He also possesses an uncommon measure of decency, which would also prevent him doing anything so bold.'

'Then you should worry about Will,' Joe said 'He'd kill you in a heartbeat.'

'Ah, in that case I have no doubt you are correct. But will he get the opportunity?'

'He'll make the opportunity,' Joe said defiantly. 'You just see. Your one little gun will be no match for him.'

'That is the first vaguely intelligent thing you've said, boy …' Reaching into his pocket, the traveller pulled out a thin pen-like device. 'But do you really think I'd come here with just one little gun?' He pressed the gadget's tip.

A tremendous gust of cold, artificial wind blew back Becky's hair. Terrified, she watched as coils of red and black electrical charge filled the air, followed by a succession of very loud booms.

Four large, grey military trucks appeared. Inside, were row upon row of stone-faced men, each wearing a dark suit, tanned leather overcoat and mirrored sunglasses. Each carried a machine gun.

Becky scooped up Sabian and buried his head in her tunic.

The men leapt from their benches and filed into line, pointing their rifles at the cave. One of them, a huge blond-haired man took charge of the others. Taking powerful strides, he walked over to the traveller.

'Any problems, Kruger?' the traveller asked.

Becky's blood froze as she recalled the picture of Otto Kruger she'd found on the net.

'No,' Kruger replied in a deep, gravelly voice. 'The containment area is set up at the time and place you requested.'

'Excellent.' The traveller looked down at Joe. 'You see, boy, I'm not alone at all.' A mocking smile curved on his thin mouth. 'And my Associates have plenty of guns...'

And then Becky did something she never would've thought was in her. She took a single step towards the traveller, raised her hand and slapped him ferociously across the face.

Chapter 29

Nephele's Fleece

Uncle Percy and Will heard nothing of the activity outside. They were deep into the caves and moving fast. Milly jogged alongside as if taking an afternoon stroll.

'Becky knows, does she not?' Will said. 'About her father.'

'Yes,' Uncle Percy replied. 'She's a bright girl. I had to tell her.'

A strange expression crossed Will's face. 'How much does she know?'

'She knows he was a traveller, that's all.'

'And the boy, what does he know?'

'Not a thing. Not yet, anyway. I thought it best we wait until he's older. Becky agreed with me.'

'He has much to discover,' Will said. 'They both do...'

They trekked further into the winding chasm, neither of them saying a word. The further they advanced, the more they became cloaked in a thick, impenetrable darkness. They had been walking for five minutes when Milly came to a sudden halt and growled.

'What is it, girl?' Uncle Percy said; looking ahead he could just make out that the tunnel arched to the right.

Will fixed an arrow to his bowstring.

At that moment, the tar-black walls began to shake, the ground shivered.

Uncle Percy glanced anxiously at Will. 'Is that wind?'

Will had no answer.

And then they heard it: a low wailing sound.

Uncle Percy pulled out two squid grenades as Will took aim.

The sound was growing louder, heading in their direction … an ugly sound; shrill, harsh, like fingernails on a blackboard.

Uncle Percy recognised it at once. 'TO THE FLOOR!' he yelled. Using all of his strength, he heaved Milly to the ground, shielding her eyes. Will dropped beside him. A moment later, a dense fog of winged creatures turned the corner.

Bats. Thousands of bats.

Uncle Percy clamped his eyes shut and braced himself.

The maelstrom hit.

Flapping. Screeching. Flailing. Thrashing.

A few seconds later, it was over.

Gasping for air, Uncle Percy opened his eyes and pressed his face softly against Milly's forehead. 'It's over, girl. Everything's fine now.' He turned to Will and smiled half-heartedly. 'Well, something spooked them.'

Will didn't smile back.

They dusted themselves down and set off again, pushing on in almost complete darkness for a few minutes when, in the distance, they spotted light. Racing over to it, they emerged into a cavern the size of a football pitch with four tunnels leading out. A thick shaft of misty sunlight shone down from a wide fissure above.

Uncle Percy's gaze tracked a steam to a huge oak tree in the centre of the cavern. His eyes widened. Hanging from the tree's largest branch was a glittering object that cast a flickering golden reflection like a thousand fireflies on the far wall. The Golden Fleece.

'It's really here,' Uncle Percy breathed, as if he never believed in its existence in the first place.

'Then seize it.' Will's eyes darted from tunnel to tunnel. 'We must leave this place.'

Slowly, Uncle Percy edged closer to it, moving as though in a daze, his feet struggling to find their natural rhythm. Reaching the stream, he leapt it in a single bound and moved over to the oak tree, where he found himself rooted to the spot, entranced, hypnotized by the Fleece's beauty. Taking the greatest of care, he lifted the Fleece from its branch. It felt weightless, extraordinary, unlike anything he'd felt before.

Then a very strange thing happened.

The Fleece fizzled with energy. His back stiffened as a power surge slammed his body. At once, visions crashed through his head - abstract, random visions. But he understood them. It was knowledge. Millions of years of knowledge. The knowledge of the ages. His brain screamed, but he couldn't stop. He needed more. He could see everything - the past, the future. It was he, not the Fleece that had the power.

He dropped it at once.

'What's the matter? Will asked.

'I - I don't know,' Uncle Percy said, struggling to catch his breath. 'I just know I shouldn't touch it. No one should.' He slipped off his cloak, dropped it over the Fleece and gathered the bundle in his arms. 'We must go …'

Then they heard something. A deep, stirring sound. Their eyes flicked to the tunnels. Nothing. They heard it again, louder this time. Where was it coming from? Uncle Percy and Will looked at each other. Then, simultaneously, their heads tilted down. They had their answer. Below.

'Oh, crikey!' Uncle Percy exclaimed.

The ground exploded and huge chunks of limestone, soil and rock flew everywhere. Uncle Percy and Will covered their eyes from the blast, paralysed with shock. Gradually, a giant head rose from the ruptured earth. And then another head, then another.

Uncle Percy gasped with shock as a curved talon gripped the earth and pulled its gigantic scaled body into the light.

The Hydra's nine heads coiled the air like serpents; eighteen fiery red eyes glowered down at Uncle Percy.

Milly roared.

'DROP THE FLEECE!' Will shouted, raising his bow.

Uncle Percy let the Fleece tumble to the floor.

'Now, move away!' Will added, taking aim at the head closest to Uncle Percy.

The largest of the nine heads, the central head, stared at the Fleece, before looking back at Uncle Percy, its thin top lip curling angrily. Then, with a tremendous howl, it lunged.

'RUN!' Will fired, striking the Hydra above its right eye.

Uncle Percy sprinted towards a tunnel. Milly roared again. She sprang at the head closest to her, sinking her long fangs into its neck. The Hydra squealed, its head twisted violently from side to side. Milly held on. The Hydra whipped its massive tail and struck Milly hard, dislodging her grip, sending her crashing against the cavern wall.

Milly landed heavily, unconscious.

Will sent another flurry of arrows. Although each one hit its target, the Hydra ignored them.

Uncle Percy watched as another head lunged, teeth bared. Dodging it, he hurled himself upon the neck. As the head coiled upright, he pulled out a squid grenade, dropped it into the open mouth and leapt free. *BOOM*. The head exploded into pieces.

Uncle Percy looked triumphant. His expression turned to dismay as another head emerged from the bleeding stump.

The Hydra had regenerated itself.

Will was unleashing arrow after arrow, but each proved useless. Then the far left head spied him and attacked. As it pounced, he somersaulted over the head and landed perfectly. Aiming above, he fired an arrow into where the heart should have been. Once again, it proved ineffective.

The Hydra repositioned for another attack.

An idea formed in Uncle Percy's mind. 'Aim for the eyes, Will,' he yelled. 'Blind it!'

Will sent two arrows into the eyes of the nearest head. The Hydra screamed. He trained his sights on the remaining heads. Again and again, he fired each arrow hitting its target. Eye after eye was pierced, until six of the nine heads were blinded. He reached into his quiver again. Empty. He cast his bow aside and drew his sword.

The Hydra faced him, rearing onto its hind legs.

'Over here!' Uncle Percy tried to distract it. He threw a grenade at the Hydra's feet. BOOM! No damage. Uncle Percy pulled out another, when the tail whipped round and caught him off-guard. He crashed into the tree's trunk and landed badly, blood pouring from his arm. The Hydra refocused on Will. A head swooped down. In one powerful movement, Will severed it, only for it to be replaced almost immediately.

Two more heads attacked; one head knocked the sword from his hands, the next hit him full in the stomach. He fell, winded. A claw pinned him down. Then, slowly, the central head opened its huge jaws.

His vision blurred, Uncle Percy saw the Hydra ready its strike. No. Not Will! He clambered to his feet. Then it struck him: Edgar's Dagger. He tugged it from his belt and sprinted towards the Hydra. He jumped and landed on its back. For the briefest of moments, the Hydra was distracted.

With all his strength, Uncle Percy ploughed the dagger through the thick, armour-plated skin into its heart. Leaping to the ground, he watched as the Hydra twisted in agonising spasms. Then, with a mighty crash, it fell. One by one, each head became still.

For what seemed an age, Uncle Percy stared vacantly at the lifeless creature. Then, to his surprise, he heard the most unexpected sound. It was applause. Slow, mocking applause.

Chapter 30

The Traveller Revealed

'Bravo, Percy, Bravo.' The words echoed through the cavern. 'Quite the dragon-slayer. I would never have thought it possible.'

Uncle Percy wiped the blood from his eyes and looked at the left-hand tunnel. A figure emerged from the shadows. 'Who's that?' he shouted over.

'You don't remember an old friend?'

Something stirred in Uncle Percy's memory. He knew the voice. The man walked into the light, his pale features illuminated. Uncle Percy's face drained of colour. 'Emerson?' he gasped. 'Emerson Drake?'

'Ah, you do remember!' Drake said.

'B-but - you're -'

'Dead?' Drake tutted. 'You do like your little exaggerations, don't you?'

Uncle Percy watched as a stream of armed men followed him into the cavern. His eyes widened with horror. At the back, held by a powerfully built man, were Becky and Joe. His heart sank further when he recognised their captor: Otto Kruger.

'Uncle Percy?' Becky shouted, Sabian squirming in her arms. She broke free from Kruger. Hardly noticing the

Hydra, Becky raced into Uncle Percy's open arms. Joe sprinted over and embraced Will.

'They captured us,' Becky said. 'I'm so sorry. We let you down.' Then she glanced at the unconscious Milly. Her heart sank. 'Is Milly -'

Uncle Percy stared proudly at her. 'Milly will be fine. And, Becky, don't ever think you could possibly let me down.'

'How sweet,' Drake crooned. 'I do enjoy family reunions.'

'So how did you do it, Emerson?' Uncle Percy said flatly.

'Do what, old friend?'

'Fake your own death?' Uncle Percy said. 'I was at the airport. I saw you board the plane and I saw that plane explode on take off.'

Then Becky remembered what Uncle Percy had told her at Mammoth Gorge. Emerson Drake was a university friend of Uncle Percy's - a member of the Oxford Time Travellers Exploration and Research Society – and was supposed to have died in a plane accident.

Drake gave a mirthless laugh. 'You saw precisely what I wanted you to see. I boarded the plane with all of the other passengers. I wanted you there. I wanted all of those ridiculous Otters there. You see - what the eyes witness, the mind does not question. However, what you wouldn't have seen was the portravella, the portable travelling device, I carried in my hand luggage. Of course, the accident had to appear to be genuine - that was the tricky part. After all, I didn't want any unwelcome investigations. Anyway, I left the plane just before it exploded. I was already in the departure lounge watching you when the fireworks commenced.'

'FIREWORKS?' Uncle Percy roared. 'There were hundreds of people on that plane. Dozens of children. You killed them all just to fake your own death?'

A cruel smirk formed on Drake's mouth. 'It worked didn't it. I could never have taken my intended path if that absurd Institute knew I was alive. In the end, all they could offer me was Gerathnium, and, as I have perfected a way of generating my own, I didn't need them anymore. You see, I am on a journey you could not possibly comprehend and I certainly didn't want the rest of you getting in my way.'

'What journey?' Uncle Percy asked. 'I think you can tell me now, judging by your friends over there, I'm not going to live to tell a soul.'

'That is true,' Drake gloated. 'And you have assisted me a great deal, perhaps you do have a right to know. Anyway, in many ways the journey has only just begun … with that!' Drake pointed at the Golden Fleece.

'How so?' Uncle Percy said. 'If it's the Fleece you're after, you have it.'

'The Fleece is merely the beginning; the first step in something considerably more important.' Drake revelled in Uncle Percy's look of utter confusion. 'Why on earth do you think it was essential that I died? What do you think I've been doing for the last ten years? Well, let me tell you… I've been constructing an empire - a legion of scholars, experts in many fields.'

'Like Otto Kruger?' Uncle Percy spat out.

'Indeed. And Otto is an expert in mayhem. Are you not, Otto?'

'I hope so, sir.' Kruger replied. He pulled a handgun and aimed it at Will.

'Now, now, Otto,' Drake said. 'There'll be plenty of time for that.'

Will's face remained impassive; he stared Kruger down. Kruger cocked the pistol and smiled. Terrified, Joe launched at Will, to block him from sight, but was pushed away. Kruger grinned wildly. Then he fired.

'NO!' Joe shouted as Becky screamed.

Will didn't even flinch as the bullet scraped his ear and punctured the wall behind.

Otto Kruger laughed cruelly. 'I see you have no fear of death, groundsman.'

'That's enough, Otto,' Drake said, turning back to Uncle Percy. 'As you can see, Percy, I have many supporters, in many times. I call them my Associates.'

Struggling to compose himself after the shooting, Uncle Percy turned to Drake. 'What are you doing, Emerson? What don't I know?'

'As always, there are countless things you don't know. The question is … should I tell you?' He drew an excited breath. 'I don't think I will.'

'You'll fail, Emerson,' Uncle Percy said calmly. 'Whatever it is you're trying to do, you will fail. And I'll tell you for why, shall I?'

'Please do.'

It was Uncle Percy's turn to smile. 'Because you're not quite as clever as you think you are. Even at Oxford you were a poor excuse for a scientist. The rest of us knew it, but we let you survive on our coat tails. No, let's be honest, Emerson, you were never quite as brilliant as you liked to believe. You're quite thick, really.'

For the first time, Drake looked shaken. He marched over and struck Uncle Percy in the face.

Unfazed, Uncle Percy maintained eye contact and continued. 'You see, that's what sets you apart from a man like Bernard Preston. He was an intelligent man and an excellent scientist. And that's why you had him killed - jealousy, pure jealousy.'

'I didn't have him killed,' Drake spat. 'I did it myself. And I rather enjoyed it.'

'And I'm sure you'll enjoy killing us, too,' Uncle Percy said.

'Oh, I don't want all of you killed. Just you and this idiot friend of yours.' He stared pointedly at Will.

Uncle Percy's brow furrowed. 'And Becky and Joe?'

'They are more useful to me alive.'

'How?' Uncle Percy said urgently.

'I'm sure you'd love to know that, wouldn't you? Let's just say these charming brats are going to help me retrieve information.'

'How?' Uncle Percy asked. 'From where?'

'From someone who would rather die than give me what I want,' Drake said coldly. 'Someone I've tortured to within an inch of his life, and yet he still won't talk. Someone who will now tell me all I need to know …'

Uncle Percy looked dumbfounded. 'J-John?' he managed to reply. 'John's alive?'

Drake's beady eyes gleamed. 'I believe so…'

The words struck Becky with the force of a sledgehammer. She turned slowly to Joe, her lips forming an incredulous smile. It was clear from Joe's expression he couldn't believe it either.

Together, and for what seemed like an eternity, Becky and Joe stood there in silence as if time itself had stopped, tears of joy filling their eyes.

John Mellor was alive.

Their father was alive.

Chapter 31

Rumble in the Jungle

'Of course he's alive,' Drake sneered. 'He's been my guest for some time now. To be honest with you, I couldn't believe you fell for my little charade in the first place.'

Uncle Percy's fists clenched.

Becky saw he was about to do something foolish and said, 'Uncle Percy, please don't...' He calmed at once.

Drake watched his reaction with glee. 'Would you like to hear about it?' I'm sure the children would …'

Drop dead!' Joe shouted.

'Let me tell you anyway,' Drake continued ignoring the outburst. 'I was already hidden on his boat when Mellor set to sea, along with Otto, a short-range portravella and a life-like replica of him, a little creation of mine I call a Hyperclone - a perfect copy of him, even down to the teeth and hair. When we were into the open water, Otto overpowered him and I threw the Hyperclone overboard. Two days later, that's what the authorities found. My creation even had a lovely funeral, from what I hear.'

'Where is he?' Uncle Percy said.

'He's quite safe, I assure you,' Drake said. 'Rather uncomfortable, I imagine, but it's his fault. He simply refuses to talk, and the sad thing is he does have a vast amount of knowledge that I desperately need. He's a courageous man, no question about it. He's proven resistant to truth serums, to all manner of torture, but he still won't talk. Of course, with the assistance of these two - ' he waved his hand at Becky and Joe, '- I believe matters will be very different.'

'WE'D NEVER HELP YOU!' Becky yelled.

'Believe me, your presence is all that's necessary. I doubt he'll want to see his own flesh and blood executed before his very eyes.'

'Where is he?' Uncle Percy repeated.

'Let's just say, he's a part of history,' Drake replied.

'Then I'll find him.'

'Find him?' Drake snorted. 'Find a man hidden in time and space? Now, that is like finding a very small needle in a rather large haystack.'

'Nevertheless, I will find him.'

'Really?' Drake said. 'That may be somewhat difficult, as I intend to leave your dead carcass outside for the vultures to pick at.'

Otto Kruger smiled.

'One more question,' Uncle Percy said, ignoring the threat. 'How did you know Becky had the Suman Stone?'

'Actually, that was the most remarkable piece of fortune. For many years I had known of the Great Gate, and of the two pieces of the key. And I knew Mellor was obsessed with legends related to Stonehenge. He even started his own investigations into the whereabouts of the Fleece. However, although he knew of the Great Gate's existence, and of the Disc, he had yet to learn of the Suman Stone. Anyway, when I captured him I discovered he had unwittingly found it in the course of his research. Needless to say, he wasn't about to tell me where it was. It was only recently, when I revisited his belongings, that I found a photograph in his wallet - a photograph of you, my dear.' His steely gaze fixed on Becky. 'You were wearing the stone.' He turned back to Uncle Percy. 'Now, agreeable though this has been, I think it's time we proceeded with the small matter of your execution, don't you?

Drake gave a curt nod and four Associates rushed over and stood behind Uncle Percy and Will. Becky made to cry out in protest. With a sharp shake of his head, Uncle Percy gestured her to stay silent.

Drake approached the Golden Fleece. Anticipation coursed through him, He knelt as if in prayer and unfurled the bundle. He threw the discarded cloak at Uncle Percy, who caught it and slipped it on. He stared down at the Golden Fleece; its reflection cast a golden shadow on his colourless face. 'It's beautiful.' His eager fingers stroked its bristly exterior. 'It's magnificent.' Suddenly his back jerked straight. His chest swelled as the awesome power of the Fleece flooded him. His eyes rolled back, whirling in ecstasy. 'I CAN FINALLY SEE!'

Otto Kruger tilted his head to one side, a hungry glint in his eyes.

Reluctantly tearing himself away from the Fleece, Drake wheeled round to the nearby Associate. 'Bring the bag.'

The Associate ran over, clutching a black leather kitbag. Drake raised the Fleece and placed it carefully into the bag.

Then he turned to the mob, his arms outstretched. 'WE HAVE WHAT IS RIGHTFULLY OURS!' The Associates cheered.

Becky's heart sank. Then she spied a curious thing. In the midst of the jubilant faces, one Associate wasn't smiling.

Drake had noticed it too and walked over to him. The young red-haired man looked strangely disheveled as though woken from a deep sleep. 'YOU!' Drake hollered. 'What's the matter?'

'N-nothing, sir,' the Associate mumbled, swaying slightly.

'Are you not delighted?' Drake snapped.

'Y-yes, sir,' the Associate said. 'But I - I don't think I'm well, sir.'

Uncle Percy watched, suddenly fascinated.

'Pull yourself together or I'll have you shot.' He snatched the Associate's rifle and moved to the far wall. Then he turned abruptly to Uncle Percy. He was standing over Milly.

'I take it this is your pet, Percy?'

Will made to move, but felt the barrel of a gun against his temple.

'No, Emerson,' Uncle Percy shouted over. 'I beg you. Please don't.'

'Begging?' Drake smirked. 'The great Percy Halifax begging?' He fired three shots into Milly's chest.

Becky screamed, smothering Sabian's head. Joe turned white. Even Will turned away.

Pushing his guard aside, Uncle Percy raced to Milly. Falling to his knees, his hand edged through her fur until his fingers traced the holes. For a moment his face became impossible to read, until it cracked with grief. 'Sleep well, girl,' he whispered, as an Associate dragged him away.

Becky couldn't breathe. She stared at Milly, tears flowing down her cheeks. Then she glowered at Drake. She felt something she had never felt before. It was hatred. Pure hatred! This was the man who had kidnapped her father - had murdered hundreds of people in a sabotaged plane - had executed Milly.

She wanted revenge.

Drake's taunting voice stabbed the air. 'Now, Percy, what say we relocate outside? Surely you would relish the sun on your face one last time?'

Uncle Percy and Will exchanged helpless looks. Two Associates cuffed them before leading them at gunpoint out of the cavern.

*

Some time later, the group emerged from the Red Caves. Becky watched as the Associates who had remained to guard the time machines joined their comrades to celebrate. Loud, ugly cheers echoed all around. Then she saw something that completely bewildered her. Uncle Percy was smiling again. She didn't get it. Even Will looked confused.

Drake was baffled, too. Glaring at Uncle Percy, he spat, 'Why do you smile?'

'What's not to smile about?' Uncle Percy replied. 'The sun is shining, the birds are - '

Viciously, Kruger grabbed Will's neck and forced his gun barrel into his mouth. 'Are you smiling now?'

Uncle Percy's expression turned sober. 'No.'

Drake smirked. 'Now, Otto, let's not rush it. I cannot begin to tell you how long I have waited for this special moment.'

Reluctantly, Kruger lowered the gun.

'We have had a long and complex history together, haven't we, Percy? I'm glad Jason failed to kill you. For now the moment belongs to me.' He whispered in Uncle Percy's ear, 'And when I have no need for them, I will make sure your niece and nephew share your fate.' Drake gestured to four Associates. 'Chain them to the trees.'

Becky watched horrified as Uncle Percy and Will were dragged away.

'I have failed you, Percy,' Will said, his hands bound to a tree trunk. 'I never did repay my debt.'

'If there ever was a debt, Will,' Uncle Percy said, 'you have repaid it a thousand times. Besides, we're not dead yet …'

Becky felt powerless. Six Associates had filed into line before Uncle Percy and Will. She wheeled round to Drake. 'Please don't,' she begged. 'I'll make dad give you anything you want, just don't kill them.'

Drake grinned wildly. 'Your father will already tell me what I need to know. Now, be quiet, before I lash your brother to a tree and do the same to him. After all, I only need one of you.' He approached Uncle Percy. 'Your time is up, Percy Halifax.' Whirling round, he stepped away from the trees. 'Firing squad! Ready.'

Becky heard the clack of raised rifles.

'Take aim …' Drake shouted. 'Ready!'

Becky locked her eyes shut.

Just then, a booming voice came out of the jungle. 'Deary, dear me…what do we have here?'

Instead of gunshots, Becky heard loud gasps of shock and astonishment.

Edgar stood there, smiling. 'Hello, Becky, Joe,' he said cheerily. He gave them a little wave. 'Surprise…'

'Edgar?' Becky panted.

'At your service, little lady.'

Hesitantly, Drake stepped forward. He sounded alarmed. 'Beast. We have no quarrel with you. Be on your way.'

With a huff, Edgar folded his arms. 'Beast? How very rude. I don't think I like you too much. No, I don't think I like you at all.'

'What are you doing here, Edgar?' Uncle Percy asked.

'Hello, Perce, my most excellent friend… How are you?'

'I've been better,' Uncle Percy said. 'Edgar, you really must go. These men will kill you.'

Edgar gave a hearty chortle. 'I doubt that. They can't kill me. I told you. Not with these weapons, whatever they are. These are mortal weapons. And I'm a Minotaur. I told you, only a weapon forged by the Gods can - '

Drake bloated with fury. 'SHOOT IT!'

'NO, EMERSON!' Uncle Percy shouted back.

Drake ignored him. 'NOWWW!'

Immediately, the thunder of machine gun fire rang out. Hundreds of bullets pierced Edgar's skin. Dust filled the air, shell casings clattered to the ground. Seconds later, the onslaught was over.

Chapter 32

Brothers in Arms

Becky inhaled sharply, terrified of what she would see when the thick dust cloud settled. Her panic was soon replaced with shock. Edgar was unscathed. There wasn't a mark on him.

The Associates were stunned, too.

'Ooh, that tickled,' Edgar chuckled. 'Now, I believe I have made my point. Anyway, my friends, William and Perce, look uncomfortable. And I don't like that. So if you would kindly - '

'LEAVE MINOTAUR,' Drake screamed. 'THIS IS NOT YOUR FIGHT.'

'Fight?' Edgar replied calmly. 'I don't fight. In fact, I despise violence of any kind.' A twinkle formed in his eye. 'My brothers, on the other hand – well, they do so enjoy a good tussle.' Clapping his hands twice, Edgar rotated towards the jungle as if introducing a stage act. 'Lady and gentlemen, I give you my brothers, Gergo and Gergan.'

At once, the treetops rustled wildly as if a powerful wind raged through them. Edgar winked mischievously at Becky. 'I never mentioned this, but I'm actually the runt of the family.'

Becky's mouth fell open. Emerging from the undergrowth were two colossal Minotaurs, each about six feet taller than Edgar, and considerably wider. Unlike Edgar, however, they wore very fierce expressions and carried enormous clubs, the size of lamp posts.

Edgar turned back to the Associates. Now, I am going to release my friends, whilst my brothers keep you entertained. So, Gergo, Gergan … enjoy yourselves...'

Gergo, the slightly taller of the two, smiled at Edgar and grunted his accord. Then he slammed his club into the two closest Associates, who were hurled into the air as if struck by a giant flyswatter. The other Associates opened fire, but, once again, the bullets proved useless.

A breathless Becky watched as Gergo and Gergan ripped into them like a terrible whirlwind. Before long, Associates were flying everywhere.

Walking over to Uncle Percy and Will, Edgar tore off their cuffs like ripping paper. 'Lovely to see you both again,' he said. 'Did you find what you came for?' An Associate flew past them and hurtled headfirst into a tree.

'We did,' Uncle Percy said.

'Goody,' Edgar replied. 'Then I beg you leave this dreadful place.'

Will gulped a lungful of air. 'Soon.' Then, to Edgar's astonishment, he raced into the fray - kicking, punching, butting and pounding everything in a suit and coat.

Through the bedlam, Becky noticed two dark shapes, one of them carrying a large leather kitbag, racing to a limousine parked nearby. 'Uncle Percy, Drake's got the Fleece,' she said frantically. 'He's getting away.'

'Oh, no,' Uncle Percy breathed.

Joe didn't hesitate. 'I'll get it.' He launched himself forward, fists clenched, when Uncle Percy's arm held him back.

'No, Joe,' Uncle Percy insisted. 'It's too dangerous. Let him have the Fleece for now. We'll track it down again. I promise.'

Becky watched Drake scramble into the limousine and hurl the kitbag onto the back seat, Kruger following close behind. Hope deserted her. It was over.

Drake had the Golden Fleece.

But then it happened again. The top of her head felt like it had been doused with water. The same strange feeling she'd had in the throne room at King Minos' Palace, a moment before she saw the mysterious stranger. But stronger this time. Much stronger. The watery sensation spread from the top of her head and oozed into her eyes. She lost her grip on Sabian and he tumbled to the floor.

Confused, Joe scooped up the tiger cub and looked at Becky. He gasped with dismay at what he saw.

Becky's eyes had rolled white; her face seemed older, paler, devoid of emotion. She looked frightening, inhuman.

'Becky, what's the matter?' Joe asked, distressed. He turned to his left. 'Uncle Percy, it's Becky. Something's wrong!'

Uncle Percy looked at Becky. Speechless, he watched as Becky extended her arms before her.

Drake peered back at the chaos behind and smirked. He punched six digits onto the time-pad. 'Time to depart, Otto,' he said, when - CRASHHHH –the back window shattered. Shards of glass sliced the air. He shielded his face. Kruger did the same.

Recovering, Drake wheeled round to check on the Fleece. It wasn't there. Bewildered, his gaze shifted upwards through the glassless window.

The Fleece was hurtling through the air as if suspended on an invisible wire. It bobbed, ducked and twisted past everything and everyone, before soaring into Becky's open arms.

Drake glared at Becky. 'NOOO!' he shrieked, reaching for the door-handle, but it was too late. The limousine was wrapped in a cyclone of dark red light, and, with a thunderous BOOM, it disappeared.

Becky stared at the bag. Her eyes had returned to normal, her face its usual color. She glanced over at Joe to see he was staring at her wide-eyed, confused and frightened.

Even Edgar's massive jaws had fallen wide open.

'H-how did you do that?' Joe said, alarmed.

Becky looked down at the Fleece again. She had no answer. 'I – I didn't do anything,' she stammered.

'The Fleece has chosen its new guardian,' Edgar said softly.

Joe ignored him and rounded on Becky. 'You did. Your face went weird and -'

Becky turned to Uncle Percy. 'I didn't do anything. I was just standing there when...' She paused for a moment, and then repeated in a weak voice, 'I didn't do anything.'

'Of course, you didn't, my dear' Uncle Percy replied hesitantly. 'I'd better have that.' He took the bag.

'It would be best if you left now,' Edgar said to Uncle Percy.

Uncle Percy nodded. 'I couldn't agree more…'

Will floored two Associates with a single punch as Uncle Percy tapped him on the shoulder. 'I'm afraid I have to stop your fun, William. We have to go…'

Moments later, they were negotiating the mounting heap of unconscious Associates as they advanced to the campervan.

Becky remained at the rear, head bowed. She felt confused, confounded. What had just happened? And why did Joe look at her as though she were guilty of something? She hadn't done a thing. For some reason, the Fleece had broken free from Drake and come to her. She couldn't explain it. She couldn't even remember it happening. She'd blacked out and came round to find it there, in her arms. Perhaps Edgar was right - perhaps the Fleece had chosen its guardian. Besides, what did it matter? They had the Golden Fleece.

At once, she felt considerably better. They could return to Bowen Hall and concentrate on what was really important: finding her dad. However, as she approached Bertha, she couldn't resist one last look at the mayhem behind.

Glancing round, she saw Gergan hoist a squirming Associate by his ankles. Then the giant Minotaur turned on his back foot and threw the man over the trees like a hammer throw. She gave a satisfied grin.

As everyone clambered into the van, Uncle Percy rolled down the driver's window and called to Edgar. 'Would you thank your brothers for me, please, Edgar? They're jolly good sports.'

Edgar beamed. 'Of course, I will.'

'Oh, and one more thing,' Uncle Percy said. 'When you have the time, could you take the Theseus Disc back and throw it in your lagoon on Crete. A gentleman named Arthur Evans has to discover it in a few thousand years.'

'It would be my pleasure,' Edgar said.

'Thank you,' Uncle Percy said. 'And goodbye.'

'Farewell,' Edgar replied. 'May good fortune track your every path.'

'Bye, Edgar,' Becky and Joe shouted.

Will waved. 'Farewell, my friend.'

'Stay safe and sheltered,' Edgar said, his voice quivering.

'Oh, and Edgar,' Uncle Percy said. 'I hope you don't mind but we'd love to pop back sometime for a visit.'

A wide grin curled onto Edgar's snout. 'Please do. I miss you all already.'

'Until next time then,' Uncle Percy said.

'Absolutely! Oh, and Miss Becky…'

'Yes, Edgar?' Becky said.

'You are a very special human child,' Edgar said sincerely. 'You are at one with the Gods.'

Chapter 33

Harold's Lair

A moment later, Bertha appeared on the front lawn of Bowen Hall. For a moment, relief flooded Becky and made her forget all the amazing things she'd seen, the good and the bad. Even Joe seemed to have stopped looking at her as though she'd grown a second head.

Nevertheless, she couldn't help wonder what happened outside the Red Caves. She'd never blacked out before. And besides, it wasn't as simple as that – the more she thought about it, the more fragmented but distinct images entered her head. She remembered seeing the limousine's window smash; the Fleece flying towards her; the kitbag landing in her arms. In fact, she hadn't blacked out at all.

She could remember everything.

Her gaze fell onto the Golden Fleece. So this was what the fuss was all about? She wanted to tear the bag open - to touch it - to feel what sent Drake into such a wild frenzy. Just then, she was distracted by a quiet, playful growl. Sabian was curled on Joe's lap, clawing at his tunic. A harsh reality struck her and she felt a raw, burning ache inside. Sabian would never see his mother again.

He was an orphan.

'I can't believe Milly's dead,' Becky said quietly, ruffling Sabian's ears. Joe nodded gloomily. Then an idea sprang into her mind. 'Uncle Percy - about Milly - couldn't we - '

'Let's worry about Milly later, shall we?' Uncle Percy said, rather too abruptly for Becky's liking. 'We have more pressing matters to deal with.' He leapt purposefully onto the grass.

More pressing matters? Becky could have thumped him. She knew very well what had to be done. But she also knew what it was like to grow up without a parent. Before she had a chance to dwell on this, however, Joe slid open the door and leapt out.

Becky followed him. For the briefest of moments, she forgot about Sabian and took a deep, satisfying breath. They were home. What an adventure! They had found the Golden Fleece, befriended a vegetarian Minotaur, met the legendary Argonauts, defeated a Hydra and discovered the identity of the traveller. And even more incredible than that: her dad was alive.

As Becky stood there, an earsplitting shriek echoed from the Hall. She jumped, startled. Turning quickly, she feared the worst. Instead, she saw a beaming Maria waddle towards them, apron flapping, her chubby hands waving madly. 'Angels! Angels! You are back.' Jacob followed close behind, an equally broad smile on his face.

'My little darlings, you are back and you are safe,' Maria blubbered. 'I told him.' She wagged her finger at Uncle Percy. 'I told him you should be coming back when he came for that cat. Oh, I have been so worried.'

'We're fine, Maria,' Becky said, forcing a smile.

Maria released her and faced Joe. 'And the young master?' She grabbed his head forcefully and pulled him to her chest. 'Ooh, I missed you so much.'

'Hi, Maria,' Joe said, turning bubblegum-pink as she squeezed the life out of him.

Finally, Maria let go. She marched past Uncle Percy, cast him a very nasty scowl, and embraced Will tenderly.

'Our dad's alive,' Joe said excitedly.

'What?' Maria took a moment to absorb the information. 'Alive?'

Joe nodded.

'He's alive?' Maria repeated. Then her face exploded with delight. 'D-did you hear that Jacob?' Her eyes started to water. 'Master John is alive. B-but how?'

'That, Maria, is a very long story,' Uncle Percy said.

'Is he here?' Maria glanced at Bertha expecting him to jump out at any moment.

'No,' Becky said. 'But he is alive … somewhere.'

'Uncle Percy's going to find him,' Joe said.

'Of course he is,' Maria replied, her voice quivering. 'Oh, it is a wonderful day. I am so happy for you. Now, where is that big cat? I have fresh sirloin for her.'

'She's dead,' Becky stared at the ground.

Maria's head jolted up. 'She's what?'

'A man called Drake shot her,' Becky replied. 'The traveller. The man who sent Otto Kruger here.'

Maria glowered at Uncle Percy. 'Is this true?'

'We haven't time to think about that now,' Uncle Percy said urgently. 'Will, might I ask you to get me the Molivator and the Bio-rifle, please, we haven't much time.'

Will ran off in the direction of the Time Room.

Maria noticed Uncle Percy's injured arm. 'And you - you are bleeding,'

'It's nothing,' Uncle Percy said, entering a new set of coordinates on the time-pad.

'What are you doing?' Becky asked.

'I have to get the Fleece as far away from here as possible.'

'We're leaving again?' Becky said.

'We're not,' Uncle Percy said. 'I am.'

'I want to come,' Joe said quickly.

'And me,' Becky added.

'Absolutely not!' Maria said sharply. 'Come inside, I have made crumpets.'

'Not this time,' Uncle Percy replied.

'We want to come,' Becky pressed, ignoring Maria's scowl.

'It's not safe,' Uncle Percy said.

'Neither was Ancient Greece, but we're still in one piece.'

'You have to take us,' Joe pleaded.

Becky flashed her sweetest smile. 'Besides, the Fleece came to me. I'm its guardian. Apparently, I'm at one with the Gods.'

Uncle Percy couldn't help but laugh. 'Okay then, but you're to do exactly what I say. No questions asked.'

'We will,' Becky said eagerly.

Will appeared pulling a shiny contraption that resembled an old fashioned vacuum cleaner; a gigantic silver rifle hung from his shoulder.

'Thanks, Will,' Uncle Percy said, lifting the Molivator into the campervan.

'That's a gun!' Joe said, his eyes wide with surprise.

'A bio-rifle,' Uncle Percy replied, wedging the rifle onto the passenger seat. 'A tranquillizer gun.'

Becky stared at it with disbelief. It was the biggest gun she had ever seen. 'What're you going to tranquillize: King Kong?'

'Something like that,' Uncle Percy muttered.

'Where are we going?' Joe asked. 'The North Pole? The Himalayas?'

'Somewhere far more tropical,' Uncle Percy said. 'London …'

Becky and Joe exchanged disappointed looks.

'London's about as tropical as Joe's feet,' Becky said.

'You'd be surprised,' Uncle Percy replied. 'Now, there's just one more thing I need to do.' He bounded onto the driver's seat, started the engine and drove Bertha into the Time Room.

Becky and Joe followed, intrigued. They watched as Uncle Percy hopped out and sat at a workstation. There was a loud click and a steel partition dropped from the ceiling. With a faint buzz, it launched a broad shaft of sapphire light onto the van. The light probed and prodded and skimmed every inch of Bertha's bodywork.

'What's happening?' Joe whispered.

Becky shrugged. 'Dunno.'

Uncle Percy watched the monitor closely; his face flickered white as a stream of data crossed the screen. Then the words 'Unknown device detected' appeared.

'Very clever, Emerson,' Uncle Percy muttered to himself. 'Very clever, indeed.' His hand rummaged beneath the front wheel trim. When he withdrew it, he was holding a shiny metal disc that resembled a milk bottle top.

Becky approached him. 'What is it?'

'It's a chrono-tracer,' Uncle Percy replied. 'And an old one, to boot.'

Becky looked puzzled.

'A device for tracking time machines through time and space,' Uncle Percy explained. 'I was wondering how Emerson was always one step ahead of us, how he knew precisely when to send Otto Kruger to Bowen Hall. This is how he's been able to do it.' He crushed it in his fingers.

'But when did he put it there in the first place?' Becky asked.

'Well it was Emerson and some others who helped me construct her fourteen years ago. He could've installed it then.'

A shiver ran down Becky's spine. Emerson Drake had been tracking Uncle Percy all that time. 'Is it true what you said in the caves… is he thick?'

Uncle Percy gave a heavy sigh. 'Unfortunately not, I only said that because I know how arrogant he can be, attacking his intellectual vanity was the only weapon I had at the time. Make no mistakes about it … Emerson Drake is a brilliant man, a genius. And if he possesses his own Gerathnium, the world as we know it is in great danger.'

He hit another key and two enormous blocks of Gerathnium landed with a flump in the slot beside the terminal.

'And what about dad?' Becky asked. 'How will we ever find him?'

Uncle Percy gave her a kindly smile. 'The wonderful thing is he's alive, and, from the sounds of it, Emerson will make sure he stays alive, at all costs. He needs him. I don't know why … I don't know what your father knows … but I know this, if Emerson has kept him alive for all this time, then it must be something significant. Now, I swear to you, that I will do everything in my power to find him. I will devote the rest of my life to finding him, if need be.' He inserted the Gerathnium into the rear slot. 'Fancy sitting up front with me?'

Becky and Joe jumped eagerly into Bertha and settled themselves on the front seat. Uncle Percy joined them.

'So how far back are we going?' Joe said.

The campervan shuddered as a power surge swelled from below. Uncle Percy winked at Joe. 'One hundred and sixty two million years…'

*

A moment later, they materialised on a beach.

However, Becky had never seen an English beach quite like it. Stretching plains of white sand faded into a shallow crystal blue sea and soaring palm trees lined the coastline. It looked like a desert island. 'Exactly what part of London are we in?'

'Piccadilly Circus, I believe,' Uncle Percy replied, opening the door and climbing out.

'Will we see a T Rex?' Joe asked hopefully.

'I'm afraid not, Joe. They won't exist for millions of years.' He hoisted the Bio-rifle onto his shoulder.

Becky suddenly felt nervous. 'What will we see?'

Uncle Percy grinned. 'Who knows? Joe, would you carry the Fleece for me, please?' Uncle Percy wheeled the Molivator onto the sand.

'Course.' Joe heaved the kitbag over his shoulder.

'What exactly does it do?' Becky said, nodding at the Molivator.

'It's a digging tool.' Uncle Percy disappeared into the palm trees. 'Follow me.'

Becky and Joe trailed close behind. As the soft sand merged into hard topsoil, they found themselves in a dense forest surrounded by ferns and conifer trees. After a few minutes of walking, Joe spoke, 'Where we going?'

'We're visiting an old friend of mine, Uncle Percy replied. 'I call him Harold.'

'A time traveller?' Becky asked, although somehow she knew she wasn't going to be that lucky.

'A Megalosaurus.'

Becky's stomach sank. She had no idea what a Megalosaurus was, but judging by the size of the gun in Uncle Percy's hands, she knew it wouldn't be small and fluffy. Then she saw something that made her feel sick. Propped between two trees, like the leftovers of a gigantic Christmas dinner, were the bloody remains of a dinosaur; small remnants of flesh hung from its bones and hundreds of flies buzzed around it.

Becky stifled a wretch.

Joe, on the other hand, was fascinated. 'That was a Stegosaurus, right?'

'Excellent, Joe,' Uncle Percy said. 'Harold's breakfast, I imagine.'

'That's gross,' Becky slurred, covering her nose with her hand.

Uncle Percy came to a sudden halt. He raised his hand, gesturing them to stop. 'We're here…'

Becky froze. Glancing back at the Stegosaurus, she thought the Bio-rifle wasn't anywhere near big enough.

Uncle Percy buried the butt of the rifle into his shoulder. His eyes glanced from side to side, and he waited. Seconds passed.

Just then, Becky heard movement from the undergrowth. Her stomach lurched with terror as a giant head appeared. Steadily, the Megalosaurus rose to its full height, arched its neck and roared deafeningly.

'Hi, Harold,' Uncle Percy took aim. 'Bye, Harold.' He fired. A huge dart pierced the dinosaur's neck. The Megalosaurus froze with shock. Then it staggered to the left and fell backwards, crashing into the ferns behind.

'A-awesome,' Joe stammered, half-impressed, half-petrified.

Becky's face had turned the colour of porridge.

'Right,' Uncle Percy said calmly, throwing the rifle to the ground. 'We have precisely twenty minutes. I suggest we get busy.'

'That sure looks like a T Rex?' Joe blustered.

'Well, they are very much alike, Joe,' Uncle Percy said, swinging the Molivator into position. 'Tyrannosaurus Rex was slightly bigger, of course, and relatively more intelligent, but there are similarities. In point of fact, the

Megalosaurus was the very first recorded fossil ever discovered in 1676… Are you okay, Becky?'

Becky let out a muffled squeak. Now was not the time for a history lesson.

'She's fine,' Joe said.

Uncle Percy entered two digits onto the Molivator's keypad. 'Three hundred feet down should do the trick. Now, stand well back, please.'

Becky watched as eight paddles emerged from the Molivator's outer shell, until it resembled a spider wearing flippers. Then with a clack, the paddles rotated at incredible speed. Faster and faster they spun. They attacked the earth and started to dig.

In no time at all, it had disappeared beneath the ground, scattering heavy chunks of soil at Becky's feet. Within minutes, a mound of earth the size of a small haystack had formed. The Molivator crawled out and fell still.

'There we go,' Uncle Percy said. 'Joe, Becky, would you do the honours?' And he passed over the kitbag.

Hesitantly, Joe took it. 'May we have a peek first?' he asked tentatively.

'Of course, but be quick. Harold will be waking up soon.'

Becky's eyes flitted from the unconscious Megalosaurus to the bag. Then she knelt down next to Joe, who slowly unzipped it. Becky and Joe looked down at the Fleece, their features bathed in a golden hue.

Becky's heart fluttered. She had never seen anything like it. It was magnificent. Stunning. The prettiest thing she had ever seen. However, she also knew what it represented. It was the reason her dad had been taken from her, the reason Bernard Preston and Milly had been murdered. For something so perfect, so exquisite, a great deal of evil trailed in its wake.

'Wow!' Joe breathed.

'It's beautiful,' Becky said flatly.

'You're quite right, Becky. It is beautiful,' Uncle Percy said, 'beautiful and exceptionally dangerous. Come on, let's get rid of it and get back to the Hall for those crumpets.' He draped his long arms around their shoulders.

Becky and Joe nodded. Zipping up the bag, they lifted it together and dropped it down the hole, watching as the bag plunged into a seemingly endless darkness.

They didn't hear it land.

'Right, let's clean this mess up,' Uncle Percy said quickly. He recalibrated the Molivator and in a matter of minutes the hole had been refilled. Soon, they were back at the beach, standing before the campervan. As Uncle Percy loaded the equipment, they heard an angry growl drift over the trees.

'Harold's awake,' Uncle Percy said.

'Can we go now, please?' Becky asked urgently.

'Best had,' Uncle Percy said. 'He can run at over thirty five miles an hour.'

Becky knocked Joe out of the way as she hurtled into the campervan.

Moments later, Uncle Percy was resetting Bertha's time-pad. 'Do you want to see where the Fleece is buried?' he asked. 'In our time, I mean.'

'Yes, please,' Joe said.

'Whatever. Just do it quick…' Becky said, casting an anxious eye at the jungle.

'Okey dokey,' Uncle Percy said. 'I think you're going to like this...'

Chapter 34

London Calling

Bertha materialised on a long street in Central London. The immediate area was deserted and a dull sun framed a large and very impressive building. It was the building that caught Becky's eye. A building she had seen many times before. 'You-are-kidding-me?' she said, flabbergasted.

'Not at all,' Uncle Percy said with a grin. '162 million years ago this was Harold's lair, and this is where the Golden Fleece is buried to this very day.'

Joe's expression turned from surprise to wild delight. 'U-n-b-e-l-i-e-v-a-b-l-e!'

They were staring at Buckingham Palace.

'Unbelievable, but true,' Uncle Percy replied. 'I'd like to see Emerson Drake go digging under that.' Becky and Joe laughed. 'Now, if you don't mind there are a couple of things I have to do, and I can only do them alone. But if you would just stand over there.' He pointed at the curb. 'I'll be back in two ticks and half a jiffy.'

'What things?' Becky asked curiously.

'Just a couple of mercy missions,' Uncle Percy replied, fumbling through the glove compartment. He pulled out an assortment of small metallic objects and a small bottle filled with amber liquid. 'Out you go, quick as you can.'

Becky and Joe followed his instructions. They had just enough time to cast each other a puzzled look, before Bertha vanished.

Joe turned to his sister. 'What's he doing?'

Becky shrugged. 'I have no idea.'

Before either of them had time to wonder why they were standing alone in the middle of London, the campervan reappeared.

'All done,' Uncle Percy said, his face slightly redder than before. Leaping out of the van, he skipped over to Becky and gave her an unexpected and somewhat jubilant hug.

'Where've you been? Becky asked, puzzled. 'And what's done?' Then she noticed he was sporting a quarter inch of stubble on his chin. 'And how long have you been gone?' Before Uncle Percy could reply, she spied movement in the back of the campervan. She looked inside to see a huge pair of auburn eyes staring back at her. 'MILLY!' she cried.

Joe's mouth fell open.

Uncle Percy slid the door slightly ajar. Becky raced over, heart pounding, and started patting Milly's silky-soft forehead. Milly purred loudly and forced her head out further.

Uncle Percy struggled to push her back inside. 'Now, Milly, you're not getting out,' he said. 'You're not wearing an Invisiblator, and I don't think the Metropolitan police, the Royal Family, or the Corgis, for that matter, would take kindly to a Sabre-tooth tiger charging down the Mall.'

'B-b-but how?' Becky stammered. 'S-she was dead. I saw her die.'

'Not exactly - well, yes, in one timeline, I suppose she may have been dead, but not really… I could change it.' Uncle Percy sounded almost as confused as Becky. 'The Omega Effect never occurred, you see...'

Becky and Joe glanced at each other, more bewildered than ever.

Uncle Percy sighed. 'Er, let's just say that fate allowed me to save her. When I rushed to her in the caves I believed, as you did, that Drake had killed her. But when I stroked her she was breathing. I also felt tiny blood-packs and remnants of micro-squibs. She had been rigged to look like she'd been shot, but was, in actual fact, alive. Still unconscious from the Hydra battle, but very much alive. Therefore, I deduced that in the future I must have been able to go back and make it look like Drake had shot her. That's why I was so happy when we went outside. I would've only been able to go back if we'd survived in the first place.' He scanned Becky and Joe's blank faces.

Eventually Becky thought she'd better say something. 'Err, how?'

'I travelled back to the Red Caves just after Drake first appeared. Remember when he was pointing a gun at the two of you and boasting he was not alone - how he'd got so many guns? Just before you socked him one around the chops.' He smiled proudly at Becky. 'Do you remember?'

'Yeah,' Becky and Joe said in unison.

'Well soon after that I abducted the young man Drake took the rifle from, and injected him with Sodium

Mentantathol, so he would forget everything. Then I loaded his gun with blanks. That's why when you saw him in the caves he looked so disheveled. Are you with me?'

Becky and Joe nodded.

'Then I went back to Bowen Hall, to Milly, and fitted her with the micro-squibs. After that I travelled back to the Red Caves and triggered them to explode at the precise moment he shot her. Do you understand?' He smiled weakly.

Becky shook her head. 'No. D'you, Joe?'

'Haven't a clue.'

Uncle Percy was about to explain again when Becky interrupted, 'But it really doesn't matter … Milly's alive, that's all that counts.'

'Yes, it is.' Uncle Percy said, looking relieved he didn't have to tell the whole story again.

Then, just behind Milly's left shoulder, Becky saw something else move. There was another animal in the van. 'Is there -'

'Oh, yes,' Uncle Percy said. 'I think Bowen Hall has a new resident. A rather special resident.'

Becky peered over Milly's shoulder. She saw a small white creature looking nervously back at her. 'Pegasus…' she exhaled.

'I thought she might prefer a new home, and a new owner, for that matter,' Uncle Percy said. 'Please don't tell Annabel.'

'It was you I saw at the Palace?' Becky said, astounded. 'You were rescuing her?'

'Something like that,' Uncle Percy said.

Then something occurred to Joe. 'The fire in King Minos' Palace, was that you?'

Uncle Percy nodded. 'Yes, Joe, I needed a diversion. But there was no fire, just a smoke pellet.'

Pegasus edged forward and allowed Becky to stroke her. Becky shivered as her fingers caressed the horse's soft fur. 'And she can live at Bowen Hall?'

'Of course. And you can visit her whenever you want,' Uncle Percy replied. 'In fact, I'd like you to do me a small favour if you would, Becky. I'd like you to be her keeper. Certainly until you have to return to Manchester. If you don't mind, that is.'

'I don't mind,' Becky said softly. 'I don't mind at all.'

'Good,' Uncle Percy said. 'That's settled then. And when she's older, I'll attach an Invisiblator to her so she can take to the skies whenever she wants, and no one will be any the wiser.'

Becky turned sideways so Joe couldn't see the tear that rolled down her cheek.

'Now, I think it's time we went home, don't you?' Uncle Percy said. 'I think we've earned a nice, quiet summer holiday, don't you?'

'Yes,' Becky agreed.

'Absolutely,' Joe said.

Becky and Joe clambered through the side doors, squeezing onto the back seats, next to an overexcited Milly and a rather nervy Pegasus. Becky reached over and gently cupped the tiny horse in her arms. 'Uncle Percy?'

'Yes, Becky?'

'Can we drive home?' she said. 'You know, the normal way.'

'Of course we can. It will take slightly longer but - '

'- But time isn't really an issue,' Becky grinned.

Uncle Percy chuckled. 'It certainly isn't.' He started Bertha's engine. 'Oh, and Joe… remember I once told you there was a traveller who kept returning to 1966 to watch England win the World Cup.'

'Yes,' Joe said.

'That was John.'

A broad smile crossed Joe's face. 'Cool…'

'And one more thing, Becky…' Uncle Percy searched through his cloak pocket. 'I think this belongs to you.' He reached over and held out his hand.

A delicious shiver shot up Becky's back. In his palm, coiled like a thin snake, lay her lucky pendant. It looked as good as new - the Suman Stone was securely fixed again and gleamed like an emerald star. She looped it over her neck. 'Thank you. Thank you so much.'

'My pleasure,' Uncle Percy replied, facing forward. Pressing his foot on the accelerator, he steered Bertha away from the curb. She gathered speed and rambled into the distance.

Becky allowed the gentle silence to wash over her. Taking lingering looks at Joe, Milly, Pegasus and finally Uncle Percy, her heart swelled with pride and contentment. She couldn't remember the last time she'd felt this happy. Her father was alive; Milly was alive; and she would be the keeper to the most beautiful animal to have ever walked the earth. And, for the first time in her life, she found herself thinking about her own future. She didn't know what it held. She didn't want to know. But there was one thing about which she felt certain.

Her adventure had only just begun.

Becky, Joe, Will and Uncle Percy will return in 'The Time Hunters and the Box of Eternity'

CARL ASHMORE

Carl is a children's writer from Cheshire, England. He has written four books for children - 'The Time Hunters,' 'The Time Hunters and the Box of Eternity,' 'The Night They Nicked Saint Nick,' and 'Bernard and the Bibble.'

He is currently working on the third book in the Time Hunters series: 'The Time Hunters and the Spear of Fate.'

He can be contacted at carlashmore@mailcity.com